Enjoy the journey!

Laureen Giulian

MOON OF CHANGE

LAUREEN GIULIAN

BALBOA.PRESS
A DIVISION OF HAY HOUSE

Balboa Press books may be ordered through booksellers or by contacting:

Balboa Press
A Division of Hay House
1663 Liberty Drive
Bloomington, IN 47403
www.balboapress.com
844-682-1282

Original Cover Art by Laureen Giulian. Mixed media, natural elements and acrylic on canvas
Author's Photo Credit: Dawn Greco, FGPhotography Port Franks

Print information available on the last page.

ISBN: 978-1-9822-7575-4 (sc)
ISBN: 978-1-9822-7577-8 (hc)
ISBN: 978-1-9822-7576-1 (e)

Balboa Press rev. date: 11/30/2021

If all that is seen and unseen is a manifestation of a Holy Creator, how do we honour our sacred relationship with creation and with one another?

This book is dedicated to all of those starseed souls who committed to a third dimensional Earth experience, in order that they could assist the Ascension transformation for the good of All. I Am so incredibly grateful for your efforts!

Namasté

CONTENTS

SPECIAL THANKS...

Rivers of gratitude flow from the core of my heart to so many people who listened while I mused and got excited when I expressed my overwhelming passion throughout the years that brought this book into being.

I'm especially grateful for my parents' unwavering support of my own journey throughout my lifetime – my Mom who taught me to read and my Dad who made reading empowering. They have unfailingly supported my connection with the mystical and magical realms throughout this life experience. Without my dear husband's support, this work would never have seen the light of day! Thank you for making it happen!

I would be remiss if I didn't include my closest friends who have cheered me along the way – Angela (God Bless the Oxford Comma!), Anne ("I didn't know you could write like this!"), Gabby ("You've got this, Lo!"); my Energy Healer – Arlene ("Do you realize how important it is to get this work out?"); Sr. Jean – a scholar, teacher and trusted friend; and my Editor, Paloma Vita ("No, the gerund works here.") I've learned so much from all of you! The list of people who have championed this courageous endeavour exceeds this space, but would be incomplete without the mention of my friend Ruth and an amazing author, Marianne Maguire. Ruth shared her own magical story of growing up on a reservation. Marianne provided her own magic, a list of scheduled writing tasks and constantly saying "You can't edit the book if you have no book – WRITE the book!") I'm so grateful to all the rest of my cheerleaders who count too many to name and are on the list to buy 'the very first copy'. Thank you!

May all of your lives be filled with the Light and Love of our Creator and the knowledge that you Co-Create your own magical experiences. I am so grateful and humbled by your love and friendship.

Many Blessings to each of you and your families.

FOREWORD

We humans encounter many sacred expressions and religious customs along our way to discovering our soul purpose. Some of us have life experiences in families rich with recognizable roots of our heritage, while others have their history hidden from their knowing. Regardless of where our journey of self discovery begins, with or without ancestral knowledge, our journey always leads us to our source - Great Spirit, Creator God.

Laureen Giulian has authored a colourfully descriptive journey of self discovery and the relationship we have with Creator and creation. This book is a masterfully penned work of surrender to divinity, a work of majestic honour to creation, a work that acknowledges a sacred circle of eternal connection to all things. Our Creator Source has a bountiful experience for us to embrace on this planet we call Mother Earth. This work has moved my heart along the paths taken by the characters Kiera and Joshua, into a gleeful and harmonious place of awe. The vibrant description of adventures with spirit and self, flow gracefully through-out the reading experience. I am grateful to have held these pages in my hand and I am grateful to have journeyed with the characters of this book.

I resonate with and wish to share the words of the prayers offered by Kiera and Joshua. Truth is found in their journey of self discovery and gratefulness. It leads them. Shall you journey with them?

"I believe I'm finding my way, and I'm grateful..." *(Kiera)*

"I'm so grateful for the ways in which the land has spoken and called me to my destiny". *(Joshua)*

Connie MacDonald

CHAPTER 1

INITIATION

Kiera Clark could not focus. She wanted to unpack one more box before quitting for the night. A stack of art history and drawing books littered the floor around the still half-full box, one of several stacked against the wall.

"I have no idea where to put these now. I'll need to put up more shelves first, I think," she stated aloud.

Deciding she had done enough for today, Kiera opted to answer the stirring need to get outside. Grabbing a sweater from the back of the chair and a mag-lite from the kitchen counter, she headed through the screen door, letting it slap behind her. The noise startled half a dozen crows in the trees along the driveway.

Having grown up in the mountains, Kiera felt a kinship to nature and the ruggedness of the land. As an artist, she took in each minute detail that culminates as a whole into magnificent vistas. Dusk cast a soft glow as she crossed the road in front of the small house she'd purchased upon returning from the big city. There was no other soul around.

Following a deer trail from the edge of the woods, she marvelled at the thick mosses and wildflowers filling out the forest floor between large boulders and the tall pines – graceful sentinels of the boreal forest. Birds nestled down for the night. A wary fox slipped back into the thick foliage. Flying squirrels and chipmunks chattered and scampered away as she moved quietly among them. A sudden hush fell and as other creatures quieted, the peepers and tree fogs woke to sing the night into being.

At the rounding of a bend, the trail opened into a small glen, and revealed the first glint of stars in the sky above. A hot spring bubbled between the rocks; a secret oasis hidden from the world.

Most people would not be so foolish as to walk in the mountain woods as darkness fell, yet Kiera felt an overwhelming sense of peacefulness surround her, drawing her toward the water.

"Why not?" She thought to herself. "It's just what I need."

Kiera sighed as she sank into the steaming pool under the light of the supermoon. It peaked through the branches of a centuries-old jack pine, beaming with mystic energy. Immersed in the soothing waters, Kiera thought that the forest was so alive.

A great horned owl called out as moonlight glinted

from the water's surface. Kiera tipped her head back to say a prayer of thanks, whispered through her mind.

"Moon Goddess of the night so bright
I give thanks to you for your light.
I offer thanks to the Great Spirit Apistotoke
for bringing me to this spring tonight.
I open my heart to the moon and the stars
to fill me with the knowledge
of that which I seek to see."

Kiera felt the beauty of the sentiments deep in her heart and wondered what made them come to her consciousness. It seemed ancient – yet faintly familiar. She was sure it must have Indigenous roots but there were so many unknowns in her lineage, that she couldn't be certain.

Her chest lifted as she drew the night air into her lungs and held it there. She was fully aware of all that surrounded her in the widening circle of the moon's bright light. She exhaled as her lids lowered to close and she breathed deeply once more to silence the chatter of her mind.

Kiera slowly drifted into a state of deep relaxation, as a vision rose in her mind's eye. The vision felt near but she remained apart from the scene before her – a witness to the experience. Within the heart of the inner sanctum of a long-gone temple, stood a maiden not unlike herself. She was draped in a gown of thin, silvery-white gauze appearing to have no seams and belted with a golden cord. She saw her kneel before a woman of commanding presence who wore a similar gown. On this woman's head was an ornate circlet of gold bearing a unique golden disc framed by delicate cow horns. Her hair fell in thick waves of deepest black over her shoulders and down her back.

A thought flickered in Kiera's mind that she was observing a ritual of immense significance. "This must be a High Priestess and her novice."

Realization dawned that this was Aset, Egypt's Queen of the Throne.

The vision continued. Arms raised, palms up to the heavens, Aset commanded more light from the temple columns of iridescent Lemurian crystals, illuminating the distant recesses of the temple. Until now, Kiera had not been aware of the vastness of the space. She saw an altar, raised upon a dais and placed beneath an opening to the dark night sky, several hundred feet above. The altar was very impressive, comprised of layers of phenacite[1], rose quartz, amethyst, and selenite. A lithium quartz slab sat directly under the phenacite altar. The floor of the temple was made of rosophia[2] stone (rose of Sophia) – the Earth Stone, and the ceiling of azeztulite[3] – the Heaven Stone.

---

[1] Phenacite are potent high vibration crystals, a crystal of the Light that will generate pure, clear white light.

[2] Rosophia – Rose of Sophia is a newly discovered crystal found in New Mexico and the Rocky Mountains of Colorado in the United States of America.

[3] Azeztulite is a special type of quartz. Its colour is clear to white, and it shares the same physical characteristics with the quartz. Azeztulite is said to have originated from star beings called The *Azez*, which means *"Nameless Light"*.

The altar table was positioned in such a way that the head was aligned with the rising sun in the East and the foot with the sunset in the West. Above the table in the East were two sunstone crystals, one on either side, above and slightly behind a citrine cluster. In the West were moonstones and a celestite cluster in a similar formation, above and slightly behind the moonstones. Jade crystal blocks stood as sentinels at each corner of the altar.[4]

Spreading a great distance beyond the dais, more towering luminescent pillars of Lemurian quartz could be seen. These were hemmed by a perimeter wall of the same luminosity as the pillars, although slightly more rose in colour. A gallery walkway, suspended above these columns of light, was filled with honoured guests. It appeared as though the temple had no entrance or exit, since no doors could be seen.

The Priestess commanded the novice rise and led her to the dais in the centre of the sanctuary. Her head facing East, the Novice lay down upon the altar. Kiera sensed her full trust in what was about to occur and felt the commitment of the novice's heart to her destiny.

Aset intoned a sacred prayer of guidance and protection for the ritual of Novitiate Devotion, gathering more power and strength with each syllable. The temple walls, infused with a rich glow,-vibrated in tune with the intonations.

---

[4] Description of the Temple of Aset is based upon a temple created in the etheric realm by Light Worker and Litios Priestess Arlene M. Dewdney, while conducting an energy healing for a close friend and client.

A voice spoke through the silence:

"I Am the Light of the Violet Fire
Lit with a pure heart's desire.
I Am the Light of the Violet Fire
Fuelled by the Divine I Am."

Abruptly, an immense violet flame erupted from beneath the altar and enveloped the novice and Aset in a shimmering light of deepest amethyst through gold fingers of fire. Unconcerned that any danger was present, the witnesses breathed as one. A heartbeat pulsed through the temple in time with the dancing flame, which though it could be seen and heard, would not burn the flesh. It only burned impurities and energy blockages held within the body, soul and spirit.

A temple server approached the altar from a far corner bearing a golden platter. Upon it lay a variety of objects, assembled to facilitate the ritual of cleansing. Water, the second element, was poured liberally from a pure golden decanter over the novice's feet, hands, and her crown – symbolically "washing" her soul.

Aset lifted her hands to the heavens once more, and commanded the air to breathe over the novice. The third element dried her body.

A small bowl contained fine red river clay, desert sand, and Dead Sea salt. The ornate bowl was reverently retrieved from the server's platter. Next, the grains of earth – the fourth element – were distributed to form a complete circle around the body of the novice upon the altar.

A prayer of thanks, purity, and grace rose like music and floated toward the sky seen far above. Aset's body began to sway into a dance of gratitude, tracing arabesques around the dais and the still-burning violet flame. Three times she circled the altar, lifting her voice to the Great Cosmic Creator, the Divine. Her thanks complete, the Priestess rose again to stand at the side of the novitiate and lowered her head in homage.

A silent server approached once more, platter extended. A small bag of cloth, woven of the finest linen bleached the purest of whites was untied. Aset withdrew several precious gemstones from its contents, which she placed with deliberate precision, softly intoning corresponding sacred sounds with each stone. The obsidian she placed at a point several inches below the feet on the altar, inside the circle of clay and sand. A brilliant ruby, the size of Kiera's fist was settled between the novice's knees. Carnelian was then placed slightly below the navel. Next, she placed a pure citrine just below the rib cage, on the solar plexus. An emerald followed above the heart. Aquamarine was then nestled at the base of the novice's throat. Lapis was positioned above and between the brows at the third eye and a large amethyst crystal pyramid was set on the altar's surface, several inches above the crown of the novice, as a counterpart to the obsidian. Finally, four double-terminated clear crystal wands were positioned around the body on the surface of the altar. These represented the four directions within the circle.

Channelling the energies of the Cosmos through her hands, Aset drew a thread of pure silver light over the clay and sand perimeter of the altar, effectively sealing the circle. Returning to the feet of the novice, the High Priestess traced the corresponding sacred geometric symbol over each of the gemstones that had been placed on the chakras – the energy centres of the physical form – one symbol at a time.

The symbols delivered, Aset lifted her arms, palms to the heavens. Her hands traced one more symbol over the novice, marking her as One of the Light. Calling down a column of pure white light from above the temple, she intoned the final activation of Light Coding.

> "I Am the Light of the purest Fire
> I Am the purity of the Divine's Desire.
> I Am the Divine white Light.
> I Am the Great I Am."

Her voice filled the space as the column of Light united both Priestess and novice as one. The Light continued to move through them, far into the core of the earth below the dais. Its purity radiated throughout the temple in waves of crystalline Divine Presence.

Kiera, no longer a witness to the vision, was immersed in the energy of the Light. She realized how deeply its ecstasy completed the novice. She felt it ebb and flow throughout her body, while nerves thrummed and vibrated in tune with the dancing light in the centre of the dais. The tinkling of bells, the strum of harp strings and a general hum of joy could be heard floating over the air. Kiera felt at One with the Creator and High Priestess Aset, as she realized she *was* the novice. Her awareness expanded to include all of her surroundings. All the colours she saw seemed to vibrate and dance around the sanctuary. The sounds took on a visual and etheric quality. The scent of frankincense permeated the air while limitless joy and unconditional love became tangible essences. Overtaken with emotion, Kiera was unaware that tears were pouring down her cheeks.

The melodic chants of Aset broke through to Kiera's consciousness once more, as prayers of intercession were made to the Great Creator. Aset asked for guidance and protection through the service of the novice – now an acolyte of the High Priestess herself.

The acolyte rose from the altar and was presented on the steps of the dais to the witnesses gathered in the temple. Aset placed a glistening, thick, white hooded mantle over her shoulders, the weight of which almost forced the acolyte to her knees. Regaining her balance, she straightened up and began a dance of dedication, the mantle appearing to become lighter with each step of the dance.

Aset continued her melodic chant, calling upon the forces of the Universe to bestow their gifts upon the initiate and accompany her on her journey of discovery and mastery. As the power of the energies increased, the sanctuary became electric. Sights and sounds grew brighter, clearer, and richer still.

The acolyte moved like a whirling dervish. Extending her arms heavenward, she lifted with them the mantle from her shoulders, and welcomed the powerful energies into her being. The mantle shifted and transformed until it was no longer made of cloth and gilded thread but a sacred white serpent twisting and dancing in step with her, wrapped around her shoulders. Its delicately featured head rose like a crown over her, rocking to and fro in harmony with the music and her rhythmic undulations. A simple flute accompanied the pair as they danced, enthralled as they were with each other, moving as one.

Mesmerized by the spectacle, Kiera recalled a bit of tribal lore about the power of snakes shared by her Indigenous grandmother. "A white snake has more significance for us. White is the symbol of purity, good feelings, good intentions, and a clean heart. The snake represents healing and transformation.[5] Dreaming of a white snake means rebirth for you and your spirit. Snake energy helps us open and embrace sacred sensuality in body and in spirit." A deeper awareness and greater understanding of the purpose of this ritual bloomed in Kiera's mind.

High above the acolyte's head, the serpent turned to

---

[5] Spirit animals have different meanings and are thought to bring their own kind of medicine (knowledge). To learn more about their meanings, check out these websites: whatismyspiritanimal.com/animal-spirit-guides/white-and-albino-animal-symbolism-meaning/ and www.spiritanimal.info/snake-spirit-animal/

engage Kiera's gaze, bowed its head in greeting and then looked skyward. At that precise moment, the full and magnificent orb of the moon was centred exactly above them, still dancing to the music of the mystery realms. It loomed close enough to touch, it seemed, pulsing with energies in tune with the dance.

Kiera felt the energy of this supermoon surge throughout her being, drawing her up and into the dance. At once she was viewer and participant with the acolyte and the serpent, dancing as one with them both.

***

With a sharp intake of breath, Kiera suddenly became aware that she was still soaking in the hot spring in the middle of the forest. Looking up, she was not surprised to see the same moon near perigee – its closest proximity to earth – vibrating with the power she'd just witnessed in the temple of the Goddess!

Feeling its energy coursing through her, Kiera brought her hands together under the water. In her gently cupped hands, she felt like she was holding the moon itself. When she drew her hands up to the water surface, the moon's reflection broke into twinned orbs in her palms. Like a flame that separates into two separate flames, each a unique colour, and then become one again – two halves of a whole, one unified colour.

The great horned owl abruptly called out in the night. Kiera felt moved to chant to the moon, the words she heard welling up from the midst of her soul.

"Full moon rises in the night
Fills the sky with light.
A breeze waves the pine branches gently,
A sentinel of the night.
Owl greets the night.
Owl greets the night.

Stars twinkling in the indigo sky
While wisps of fog flit and dance between
them,
Calling colours of the moon.
Owl questions the night.
Owl questions the night.

A maiden bathes in a spring-water pool
By the light of a full moon bright
Cupped within her hands a pool of light
Until the moon splits and two appear –
Sun's reflection and Moon's light dancing
upon the night
Until one again they become.

Light upon the night.
Light upon the night.
While owl guards the night.
Owl guards the night."

Thus was revealed the duality of life, the Sun and the Moon; the Yin and the Yang; the masculine and the feminine; the positive and the negative that create balance in the world and all of life. The Divine energetic twin pairing of the soul – two halves of the whole – the twin flames came to be.

The moon in the sky above completed the Triad, representing the Universal Creative force, the Divinity from whom all life force springs. Together, these three elements form the Sacred Trinity.

Intuitively Kiera knew that this vision would hold great meaning for her and that her life would be forever changed. She had a new reality. She had been endowed with a new and greater awareness of the Universal Mind and was now aware of the vital role she was meant to play. Kiera sensed all this earnestly within her but could not begin to realize the extent of what she had yet to learn!

She relished the way the energies playing upon her body caused her to feel, and allowed the light of the moon and the water to wash over her. Kiera continued to bathe in their power and strength for some time, ever watchful of the position of the moon, cognizant of its reflection on the water and the path it traced in the night sky. As it moved across the heavens, the moon slid in front of the furthest end of the Milky Way, appearing as a comet leaving a tail of light to brighten the night, then flickered and faded, never to shine that way again.

Kiera mused, "I wonder at the number of stars and nebulae that comprise the Milky Way, each star burns as a bright sun, supplying life to the planets that might be orbiting it, each with its own moon or moons. Each star burns brighter as it dies, then flickers away, taking all life in that system with it, for all time. Am I as a flash upon the Universe of Life, here to burn brightly and then fade without a trace, all the while an integral part of the Cosmos? Are we all connected to Source?"

A twig snapped. The owl hooted again into the dark. Kiera jumped and turned to look all the way around her, peering deep into the darkness of the trees around the spring. She sat in the water, completely still, waiting for the sound of movement again. There was no other sound – not even the nocturnal forest denizens. Hearing nothing and seeing even less in the shadows on the forest floor, she passed it off as small animal scurrying through the underbrush. Taking a few deep breaths to slow her heart again, she shivered and realized the time had come to leave the hot spring. Still pondering the secrets of life, Kiera rose from the water to return home.

Walking barefoot was arduous but the way was well lit by the full moon shining through the trees overhead. As she neared the roadway, Kiera stopped to witness the moon's brilliancy. An open field lay across the road and she only had a short distance to travel to her cabin on the far side of the field.

There was a light on in the window, a sign that someone was waiting for her. Reaching the log cabin, Kiera drew another deep breath before turning the knob to enter by the kitchen door. Hair still dripping, she stepped briskly into the kitchen to stand on the mat in front of the sink. Her grandmother was sitting at the table waiting for her with a steaming cup of tea and a small plate of ginger snaps. The aroma of cedar was pungent and thick. Grandmother had smudged before setting the tea. This was to be a significant visit.

"Hello Grandmother. I followed the deer trail and found a hot spring in the heart of the forest. The moon is fantastic tonight."

Grandmother replied: "I thought as much. And what did you see?"

"*So* much. And I have so many questions."

***

"Sit down and tell me all about it." Grandmother settled more comfortably in her chair and Kiera was pleased with her visit as she had so much to tell her.

The tea was strong and warm and Kiera drank deeply, as she thoughtfully retold the experience of her vision.

"It felt so *real*!" she explained. "I don't understand how I could have been *watching* and *experiencing* at the same time. And yet, I *know* I did. I can still feel the eyes of the serpent, as if he could see right into my head – like he was reading my mind!

"I thought of when I was little and we found the garter snake in the garden. You told me about what snakes mean to our people and about rebirth. This is very different from our legend of the Horned Snake, Omahksoyisksiksina, for it was not a dark water snake, but rather creamy white and seemed very spiritual. I remembered you talking about how Snake energy helps us embrace our sacred sensuality in body and in spirit. But I don't understand what this means for me."

Grandmother took another sip of her tea and released the breath she had been holding. "Well," she said. "You know that I didn't grow up knowing much of our culture. I had to learn it later in my life. I can't know for sure, but it sounds like you have been initiated into a new chapter of your life. It sounds like what the Elders called a vision quest."

"A vision quest? But wasn't that for young men to determine the direction of their life? How can I know the meaning of my life when it seems all I do is spin in circles, fighting to go nowhere?"

"You will know where you are going... and when to go... when the time is right. For now, you have to feed your soul. You are searching for answers to the questions you have about your past. You must heal your own grief so that you can move forward with your life's journey. You must learn to look inward and seek the silence there. You have all the answers you need."

Grandmother pointed to Kiera's heart. "You keep our family history within you. You have only to look to the past to see your future. Without repeating the mistakes of our ancestors, by moving forward without carrying the weight of our sorrows and pain, we learn and heal the past. Then you will be what you are meant to be. You hold great power and will command great respect among our people. You are a great leader and always were."

"What do you mean that I always *was*?" asked Kiera, perplexed. "How do you know?"

"Do you think this is your first time here on Turtle Island?"

"I don't know. I don't remember anything but being who I am now."

"This is why the serpent has come to you. It is time you wake up to your truth and remember who you are. You are not just a lonely child. You are all people, from all places and all times. Mother Earth has fed you for thousands of years and your spirit has grown and evolved with her. The moon has broken a spell that was cast on your memory and turned the key to unlock your gifts. It is up to you to discover those gifts and to share them in ways that respect the gift and the giver, Apistotoke - God."

As Kiera nibbled pensively on a ginger snap, she pondered her Grandmother's words. "So who, or what, is the Sacred Serpent? And why do I feel such a deep connection with him and no fear?"

"He embodies energy and spirit, and is showing up as a guide to you. He is your teacher... for now. He will reveal his name if you ask him the next time you meet."

"But a snake? Why?"

"Who are we to question the form of our teachers? Our Elders say that we choose a spirit animal long before we take life form. It is not until we are ready for the lesson though, that our spirit animals and guides come to us. You have been ready for some time, but have not accepted your readiness until now. The full moon has brought about a shift in your awareness of your spiritual path. For that I am grateful because I was hoping you would not wait until it was too late.

"You have enough of the blood of our people within you, to cause you to do certain things and act a certain way. You cannot know what it will be or how it will take shape, just that it will be. This is who we are. We act from instinct. We are guided to be and act by forces we cannot see. We are connected by an invisible thread to all things, not just to Turtle Island, our home.

"The time has come for you to take your place among us, to become who you are meant to be, to listen to the voice of the universe around us, to act your part in its healing."

"That's a lot of responsibility Grandmother! How will I know I am doing the right things?"

"You will know by listening to your inner voice, the one that's connected. And you will know by paying attention to the things around you. You must practice listening to what isn't heard. The wisdom of the Creator is known to us all and will be shared whenever you ask. Then you must be open to receive the answers that come. We are all a part of Creator. You will understand as you begin to work with the energies of our island home.

"You know, when I went away to school, we were taught about God and the Bible – about how he sent his only son to earth – the man called Jesus. He told the people that they were all connected and responsible for the earth and the animals and to care for one another. He taught about Love.

"It is unfortunate that not all of our teachers and the people who cared for us followed the words of Jesus in the Bible they preached. But I saw that there was some good in their book. I saw the similarities between their teachings and our Indigenous ways."

CHAPTER 2

NIGHTSONG

The horses snorted and stamped restlessly in the barn. Standing in the doorway, Joshua Marshall searched the distant treeline for signs of intruders that may have set them on edge. Horses have such a keen sense of smell. Dusk had long passed and, edging ever higher above the treeline in the night sky, the moon was full and radiant, making the night as bright as day.

A great horned owl greeted the night.

Joshua swore to himself. "Damn horses! It's just the moon that has you spooked. What do you think is going to happen? There's no wolf or coyote out there."

He made the rounds of stalls, replenishing feed bins and checking that water troughs were clean and filled. Snagging a carrot from a tack room bin, he stuffed it into a back pocket and opened the stall closest to the open barn door. Nightsong nudged his head into the palm of Joshua's hand.

The horse's fur around his muzzle felt soft as velvet. The mustang twitched one ear, then the other and uttered an audible sigh, feeling more secure in Joshua's presence. He would do or go anywhere for his human.

Joshua had found the feral horse, newly birthed, in a meadow not far from home six years earlier. The sight had been heart-wrenching. A mare lay dead beside her colt, having hemorrhaged after giving birth. Her body was not quite stiff yet. No other horse could be seen anywhere around. Something must have spooked them. Clearly frightened by his situation, the fragile colt had stayed beside his mare.

Joshua had spoken slowly and softly, hoping to gain the confidence of the skittish colt. After several minutes of unsuccessfully alternating between smooth talking and lunging after it, Joshua had sunk unceremoniously on the ground with his back to the young mustang. He had been patient and remained very still, for what seemed like hours, before the colt nudged him from behind. The force of the nudge had almost pushed him face-first into the long grass. "Now you want to be friends! You're a smart little fella, aren't you?" Joshua had exclaimed.

Turning his head, he had found himself staring directly into the softest, big brown eye framed with long black lashes. The look had spoken of grief and lifetimes of loss. Joshua had lifted his hand to stroke the velvet muzzle in awe and said, "Well, I guess I'll have to be your family now. I'll call you *Nightsong,* since your story sounds like a bad country & western song." He had allowed the colt to become familiar with him, sitting for some time like that, stroking and talking softly.

He had then slowly removed the belt from his jeans, fastened it into a loop and slid it around the colt's long neck – this had made it easier to lead Nightsong home to give him food and shelter.

Once back at the barn, Joshua couldn't have been sure that his mare would accept the colt into her "herd". She had lost a gelding just the day before and was mourning the loss. Joshua hadn't quite known how to help her cope. This had prompted him to leave her in her stall to go for a long walk over the gentle hills around his property, and had led to finding the new colt.

The mare hadn't even acknowledged his return to the barn that day with a twitch of an ear, she had been so desolate. Not certain he should go ahead with his plan, Joshua had opened the stall gate and walked right in with Nightsong in tow.

Animals are so intuitive! Once the mare had caught a whiff of the new colt, she rose to her feet, and faced him with wide-open eyes. Joshua had wondered if she maybe thought this was her gelding come back from the dead but figured she would have known the scent of her own offspring. Nightsong would certainly smell different, being feral. She had danced around full of disbelief, taking in all she could of what she was seeing, smelling and hearing.

Joshua had backed out of the stall, leaving the colt with the mare and, after a few short minutes, he had seen her nibbling at the colt's withers and settling into the role of surrogate mother. Nightsong had turned to look at Joshua on the other side of the gate with such a deep sense of gratitude in his eyes.

As the days, weeks and months flew past, Joshua and Nightsong had become inseparable. They began and ended their days together, understanding each other with a single look, a quick prompt, a nudge, or a twitch of the tail. An outsider would almost wonder if they didn't share a mind – the two acted as one in everything they did together.

Nightsong grew to imitate Joshua's calm yet strong manner, especially as other horses were added to the herd. He was a born leader, proud and virile.

Moving to the barn's open sliding door, Joshua leaned against the door jamb. Nightsong approached to stand at his side.

This night, they stared together at the moon, marvelling at its nearness to the earth. Having finished the carrot he'd taken from Joshua's pocket, Nightsong pawed the soft ground just inside the barn door. Wanting to run free and unbridled in the light of the full moon, he flared his nostrils. He blew and snorted what sounded like an urgent call to Joshua.

Knowing his mustang as well as he did, Joshua understood the call. He mounted bareback and they rode off at breakneck speed across the yard toward the fields beyond the fenced paddock.

Joshua allowed Nightsong to run without exerting any control over their direction. Their mutual trust was explicit. Joshua had no desire to know where they were headed, but knew the horse would run himself out eventually and slow to a walk when he was ready. Digging his fingers deep into Nightsong's mane, he tightened his grip and enjoyed the freedom of the ride in the light of the giant full moon.

They slowed to a canter as they neared a dense wood. Joshua spotted a narrow path through the tall trees and Nightsong entered without hesitation. The trees blocked the sight of the moon, yet the silvery light drifted through the branches overhead, illuminating the path.

The way wound around and seemed to bend back upon itself. After about fifteen minutes, the path presented more twisted roots and the edges filled in with thick, lush underbrush which blocked the light of the full moon even more. The air bore the tang of spring water and steam hung in the air ahead. Hooves settling firmly on layers of loamy soil and rock was the only sounds to be heard. The birds had settled for the night and nocturnal creatures were eerily silent.

Joshua encouraged the mustang to move deeper into the forest, drawn by an opening in the canopy ahead and a steaming spring reflecting the light of the moon. Nightsong's ears perked up as he stepped on a twig, snapping it sharply – piercing the stillness of the forest.

An owl hooted among the shadows.

Movement broke the moon's reflection on the water's surface. Nightsong stopped mid-step and Joshua didn't dare breathe, lest they were seen by the vision in the water. Blue-black wings of hair fanned out around shoulders all but immersed in the steaming spring. Straining to see more clearly from the distance, Joshua was afraid of moving any closer. Not expecting to meet anyone this deep in the forest and not wanting to intrude on their privacy, he commanded Nightsong to stay.

Still as statues, they watched, mesmerized by the sight. Moments later, the vision rose and moved to the other side of the spring. A golden moonbeam caressed a long and graceful back as she climbed onto a flat rock at the water's edge. Waist-length, thick black hair steamed in the cool night air, hiding the features of the woman's face; her shapely figure draped in soft folds of fabric and belted all too soon. Even from this distance, Joshua's heart felt drawn as a moth to the flame. Surely, he must be dreaming!

A cold, wet muzzle at his ear drew him from a dreamlike state. Not wanting the scene before him to fade from his memory, Joshua catalogued every detail of this moment. He noted the position of the moon; the way the light played on her hair as she wrung the water from its length; the sound the water made as it splashed onto the rocks at her feet; the silence of the forest around them. She moved swiftly and soon disappeared down the path leading away from him and the spring.

Realizing he'd not breathed since sighting her, Joshua inhaled several deep breaths as he led Nightsong through the forest on foot. Joshua was lost in thought as they moved like the wind in the night, the moon enveloping them all the way to the house.

CHAPTER 3

REFLECTIONS

Kiera's grandmother had stayed to visit for a little while after she shared her moonlight experience at the spring. Then Kiera drove her home to a little cottage a mile away. She talked about how important it was to listen to what the moon goddess, Ko'komiki'somma, and the Mother Earth had to say.

The next morning, Kiera considered the advice given by her grandmother. "The path of the ancestors continues to live through us all and we must heed the whispers of our souls."

Mavis Deerfoot's people, the Siksika, were direct descendants of the original Blackfoot tribe who migrated north into Alberta many generations ago as a nomadic people. Her people had suffered greatly at the hands of other warring tribes and the settlers.

Although not full blood, Kiera cherished and respected

her Indigenous heritage. She returned from Calgary after finishing college to be closer to her grandmother and assist when the need arose.

Mavis had raised Kiera following the death of her parents, only three years apart. As a result, Kiera held a great respect for her grandmother and felt the need to repay her somehow. Her grandmother had scrimped and saved to put away money for Kiera's education. Kiera had won a residential scholarship to study art and only worked part time to pay for the supplies. In her final year, a gallery that supported the college artists had held a show, displaying a number of the pieces created during that year. Three of Kiera's paintings had been sold to private collectors, providing enough money for the down-payment on the cabin.

Kiera reminisced about her parents as she ruminated over coffee on the veranda. A small ground squirrel seemed interested in sharing her thoughts. She handed over a peanut from a jar on the window sill, kept for occasions such as this.

Kiera felt drawn to her mother's Indigenous culture but also felt the pull of her father's heritage. He was descended from British settlers who came to Canada before the first World War. They had travelled west on the promise of the gold rush. Those promises unfulfilled, the family had sought employment in one the larger settlements on the Great Plains.

Her parents love for one another was the stuff of fairy tales. Their courtship had been a whirlwind. Following their marriage, they settled into a rental house on the outskirts of Calgary and it wasn't long before they were blessed with a joyful little bundle.

The blessings ended though, when Kiera's father died in an accident at the oil field site where he had been employed as a labourer when she was only four years old. Her mother never recovered without the love of her life. Unable to manage financially, they had been forced to seek social assistance. One day, Kiera found her mother lying cold on the couch of the dismal apartment they called home, having found death at the bottom of a bottle.

Kiera had spent thirty-six hours alone in the tiny apartment, at the tender age of only seven. With no telephone service at home, the police and Children's Aid Services arrived when she failed to show up at school.

Mavis Deerfoot saw to it that Kiera was loved and had a home where she felt wanted and loved.

"It always hurts to think of my parents, and their absence in my life. I used to feel so angry all the time," Kiera remarked to the squirrel. "Gran tries to make up for them and I will always be grateful. But I will always wonder what kind of life I would have had if they were still here with me – both of them. I guess it doesn't help to continue to wonder and relive the grief I feel.

"The grief gets worse some days, though. It seems like the weight of the world lies on my shoulders. I recall stories Grandmother told me about her life as a child and realize that mine could have been so much worse. But some days the grief can be very overwhelming.

"I think Grandmother knows this. She seems to

know everything that goes on in my mind and in my life. Sometimes she says something very simple and soothing. At other times she allows me to wallow in it. I have to wonder if she doesn't *talk* to God, the ancient spirits and her sky people to find out what to say, her responses are always so carefully measured when she speaks. Grandmother's words last night make me think that there is more to life than what we see."

Kiera recalled something her grandmother had said, "You have the knowledge of our ancestors behind you."

Kiera pondered the meaning of Mavis' words. "I know that I have often 'sensed' things before they happened and know, without being told, how people feel. When I paint, it's as if I am giving voice to thoughts and images that need to be released or acknowledged. More often lately, I find the images I paint have more depth than I had intended, as if a hidden meaning reveals itself through me. It's not like I plan it that way. I start to put the paint on the brush and then suddenly realize I've finished and hardly any time has passed. If I look closely at the images on the canvas, they hold great meaning – not just to me – but to people or situations that are relevant to my life or the world today. It's as if someone is relaying a story through the canvas. I wonder if there is any connection to what happened last night at the spring?

"I saw so many images in my vision last night. Perhaps I should try to paint the scene I saw. At the very least, maybe I need to take more time to listen to the mountains, the forest and the animals around here. I could look for something at the library in town that would help me deepen my connection, like Grandmother suggested."

Kiera noted the absence of canvasses large enough for the exhibit project and made a shopping list as she finished the last dregs of her coffee. She cleaned up her breakfast dishes and donned a pair of light blue denim capris and a sunny yellow floral t-shirt before heading out the door.

It would take the better part of the day to make the trip to town, given that she needed to purchase groceries, gas, and art supplies, as well as visit the library. The drive was a good forty minutes from home along a narrow mountain back road and then a short trip along the main highway. A trip to town almost always included a stop to see a friend at Mountain Gallery on the south side of the Yellowhead Highway just outside of town. She had to be certain of the number of paintings expected for the exhibition at the end of summer. Of course, it would take more time if her shopping coincided with the daily visit from the local herd of elks.

Windows open and the sun shining, Kiera pointed the nose of her battered old Jeep south on Highway 16. Popping her favourite CD into the player, she sang along with the summer tunes. A few cars passed in the opposite direction, heading for the hiking trails at Snake Indian River, but otherwise there was little traffic. She supposed it would be a good day to be heading to town and away from the sight-seers.

***

Mavis Deerfoot rose with the sun. As she lay in bed, she stretched each of her joints to be sure they would all do what they were supposed to do. As she took a deep breath of the mountain morning into her lungs, she let her thoughts wander. "The mighty Creator is not finished with me yet, though I know not what he has in mind for me to do. But I am grateful, ever so grateful to be able to be his hands." So many of her generation had already passed on ahead of her.

The sky was that soft hue of rose that appears just as dawn breaks. It promised to be another glorious summer day.

Her bones creaked and groaned miserably as she rose from her bed but Mavis could only be grateful. It meant she vibrated with life's energy.

Donning an old chenille robe and a pair of slippers, Mavis padded down the hall. Though the house was quiet, birds were chirping loudly in the trees outside. She had been named for the song thrushes that sang outside the window of a small wood shack on the reservation when she came into this world. A smile brightened the lined features of the face that stared back at her in the bathroom mirror.

She loved her little house. It amounted to not much more than a cabin in the woods, but it was all she desired. It had stood her well when she needed it. The roof was strong and the old wood stove kept her warm in winter. She hadn't always been so comfortable and at peace though. As an Indigenous woman, life was something you fought to keep.

Her parents had lived on the Rez outside Calgary when the priests and nuns had taken the children, with the promise they would be educated. It may have been an education, but it was not what people think of today.

The many horrors of the residential schools took the lives of hundreds of children and forever changed those who survived. Mavis was a survivor and she was grateful for the lessons learned while living at the residential school, even though she had lost the culture and language that had been her birthright.

On some days, she grieved for all the children who had died of the foreign diseases brought by the white man. There were no hospitals for Indigenous children. They could not be ministered to in the white man's hospitals. Many of her friends had been abused, molested, raped or worse… had disappeared. She had cried herself to sleep many nights, lost so far from her family and friends.

Many children went to work in the big cities, after they finished being schooled. A few returned to their families but didn't feel welcome among their own people. They had been stripped of their culture, their hair had been cut short and they had been forbidden to speak the language of their tribe.

Mavis had been more fortunate than most. Her parents were still living on the reservation when she returned, though time had not been kind to them. They were delighted to have her home again, though she lacked any knowledge of her culture. She insisted on doing things the way she had been taught at school. She had no taste for traditional Siksika foods and didn't respect the old ways, since they were no longer natural to her. Mavis felt like a child lost on the vastness of the Plains by herself.

It would take a very long time and a great deal of patience to fill that void. When she did, she recognized similarities between Indigenous cultural beliefs and those she had learned at the residential school and church.

Time and love heal many things.

Daniel Deerfoot was a handsome man. They had fallen in love after meeting at a pow-wow when she was eighteen. His father came from the Blood Reserve and his mother was the daughter of a white fur trader who had lain with a young woman from the same tribe. By the following spring, Daniel and Mavis had married and soon began their own family.

Life was not without its challenges! There weren't many jobs for a young Indigenous man in the white man's world and their traditional ways were restricted to life on the reservation. They did what they could though, to raise their three children. Mavis always counted her blessings and despite the difficulties in her life, she found ways to feel complete.

It was her deep faith that kept her going when tragedy struck so many times throughout her life. Blessings were counted again and again, reminders that life was for living. Then she became a grandmother! This was the greatest blessing of all. Kiera instantly became everyone's darling. She was a bright and cheerful child, always inquisitive and well-behaved.

Tragedy continued to reign over them though. Still,

Mavis counted her blessings. She thanked the Lord for the fortitude and ability to take in her granddaughter, teaching her to be a patient and loving person, despite the grief they had both endured.

Together, Mavis and Kiera did more than survive. Their experience of the woods taught Mavis the value of spirituality. The more she cared for her granddaughter, the more she remembered things she'd learned at a very young age, and she continued to learn after Kiera left to pursue fine arts at college.

Deeply grateful for the peace of her surroundings, Mavis walked in the woods and foraged for native herbs she used in the kitchen and the medicine chest. She knew what grew where and when to seek it out for harvesting.

When she visited friends at a nearby reservation, Mavis sought out the Elders who taught her more of the medicinal herbs and how to use them.

Throughout her life, Mavis had learned the value of breath – how to breathe deeply of the energies of the earth and the forest. Mavis learned to listen for the voice of Creator and felt Divine energy all around her. Even the most subtle energy shifts were noticed.

Something about this Buck Moon had alerted Mavis Deerfoot to a major energy shift. She knew that there would be a change in her granddaughter, Kiera, that night. She also knew that Kiera would have questions and would need to talk about her experience.

She couldn't have been more right!

As Mavis nursed her first coffee of the morning, she reflected on the conversation of the previous evening.

The book *The Broken Way* sat on the table, open to a passage she'd read yesterday.

In it, Ann Voskamp took up the challenge to find God in everything, every day. How was this different from finding a Great Cosmic Creator who formed the world and her Turtle Island home? There was no difference! The message remained the same. *Give Thanks.* In all we do, see and feel … give thanks to the one who Created us. In giving thanks we shall see the face of the Creator – God, Apistotoke, or whatever name you call the great force of Creation. *Give Thanks* was the message.

Kiera was coming to know the face of Creator. Her time had come to learn to work with the energy that is Apistotoke or God; to bring the message forth; to build respect for Turtle Island and our home; to know it is we who create disharmony here.

It was time to pass on the sacred knowledge of her people to Kiera, along with the knowledge that we are responsible for our thoughts. *Thoughts are things, and things, once thought, become manifest in our lives.*

If Kiera was to find focus and fulfill her destiny, she would need to believe that her destiny is achievable. She would need to guard her thoughts, think positively, and give thanks for the grace present in her life. She would need to learn how to ask for what she needed – for the wisdom of the Sky People, the sovereignty of the eagle, the courage of the hawk, and trust in the Creator as Jesus did.

Mavis had been giving thanks for many years. She wrote daily in a gratefulness journal, similar to the one used by Ann Voskamp. She would have to share it with Kiera.

CHAPTER 4

GATHERING

Getting to all the places she needed required some careful planning, given the town planner's one directional street design. Kiera's habit of mapping out her route saved valuable time and fuel. Her first stop was to fill up with fuel at the Esso station, before finding a central place to park in the busy tourist area of the centre of town. She parked across the street from a small shop that held a laundromat, copy shop, and art supplies.

Isobel was folding laundry for a client when the door's tinkling announced Kiera's entrance. She looked up and smiled a greeting. "Sonja's in the stock room but I don't think she'll be long. How are you?"

"I'm good thanks. You?"

"Grateful for a quiet morning. I expect it will pick up

just before lunch time though. I swear that full moon last night has everyone and their uncle out this week!"

Laughing, Kiera nodded. "It was special last night, wasn't it? I didn't really just come to visit with Sonja this time. I need to pick up some paint supplies. That moon seems to have stirred some creativity in me and the girls at the gallery are bugging me to put some pieces together for a show. I'll come back another day to visit."

Quickly sifting through a rack of coloured tubes of acrylic paint for five specific colours and a jar of gesso, Kiera placed them on the counter and returned to the art corner to fetch three large canvases. On the way back to the cashier, she spied a tin of brush cleaner to add to her purchases. "All set, I think. Would you please tell Sonja I said hello?"

Isobel rang up the total and assured that Sonja would be informed of the impending "visit" with a laugh as the door signalled another customer was coming in. Kiera gathered her purchases and, placing the smaller items in a cloth bag she pulled from her pocket, tucked the canvases under one arm. Turning to leave, she bumped into a broad-shouldered man, almost knocking the canvases out from her arms.

"Hey, watch where you're going!" he gruffed.

"I'm so sorry," Kiera stammered.

Put off by the indignant reprimand, Kiera stepped out the door and exhaled. She took a deep, restorative breath as she gazed lovingly at the sun-lit sky. "Well, that was interesting. I wonder how anyone could be so crabby on such a beautiful day."

After depositing her new art supplies in the back of the jeep, Kiera headed a block west on foot, to a little deli for a take-out lunch. As it was nearing noon, most of the tables were occupied when she joined the line at the deli order counter.

A brightly coloured chalk menu board on the wall behind the counter drew attention to the daily features. Kiera ordered a Japanese salad with almonds and teriyaki chicken strips, along with a mango smoothie, the thought of which started her taste-buds salivating while she waited in line.

Having decided she had time to sit and enjoy her lunch, she settled at the last available small table by the window where she could watch the tourists as they passed. A cheerful face plunked itself unceremoniously in the opposite seat as she began to eat.

"Kiera! I'm so glad you're here! We need to talk about the show for the end of August. Tracy and I want 15 pieces of your best work. We'll have a number of dealers from the city and a couple of private collectors that we know will be in the area at the end of summer. I've already talked you up with them and they are keen to see what you have for sale. I told them about the last one we sold of yours and they are really stoked to meet you. Please tell me you've already got lots ready!"

"Slow down Meadoe! How do you know they'll like what I do? I mean, okay, I did sell a couple of pieces but . . ."

"Kiera, your art is so different from other artists around here. You make it come *alive*! Your images speak to people. I don't know how you do it but you manage to tell a whole story with a simple, yet elegantly complex image."

"I don't know if I'll have quite enough pieces done that soon. I have five done and I just picked up some more supplies. That's why I came into town. I was running low on some colours and canvases. I have a couple of things in mind that I'd like to work on when I get home."

"I know you won't let us down. Tracy has a feeling that this show will be your best yet. You know how intuitive she is with things. She is rarely wrong!"

"Sometimes I wonder how she knows the things she knows. I keep telling myself that I will have to ask her about that one of these days."

The conversation switched to gossip about who was back in town, who was dating whom and why there weren't any decent men around for the long-haul relationships they all sought. Before long Meadoe raced back to work at the gallery.

Kiera felt introspective as she headed to the grocery store a half a block away. She covered the short distance quickly.

A middle-aged woman with a plume of purple in her hair waved hello from the customer service desk as Kiera retrieved a cart from the storage area a few feet inside the door. Smiling, she asked "Hi Marjorie, how's Mark doing?"

"Great, thanks Kiera! His cast comes off next week." Marjorie's grandson had broken his wrist climbing one of the many hiking trails a few weeks earlier when he lost his footing and slipped down a rocky slope. The boisterous teen had been on a class trip, studying the geological formations of the Rockies.

Pushing the cart through the aisles of the store, Kiera gathered all the items on her shopping list and added a couple of ready-to-eat meals to save time while she was in "paint mode".

The dashboard clock read 1:34 pm when she loaded her bags into the jeep. She had plenty of time to stop at the library before leaving town since she no longer needed to stop at the gallery to see Tracy and Meadoe. Kiera hoped she could even get home early enough to go for a short walk before dinner.

The County Library was silent and decidedly empty this afternoon. Making her way past several rows of book-laden shelving on both side of the wide-open room, Kiera noted that the big desk in the centre of the room was vacant.

"Doris must be shelving books somewhere," she thought to herself. She knew where to find what she was looking for and so, continued two more rows past the desk and turned right toward the Indigenous Arts section of the library. There were four shelves of titles on the subjects of Indigenous Crafts, Indigenous History of Alberta, Stories of the Rockies, Healing the Indigenous Way and a couple of new books including, *The Reformation - A Journey of Forgiveness.*

A small paperback book fell from the shelf just inches from her hand. Kiera bent to pick it up, ready to place it back on the shelf, when she noticed the cover. The title consisted of two simple words over a background image of smoke, *Spirit Talk*.

"Hmmm. Is this meant for me, I wonder?" It slipped from her fingers and fell to the floor again, opening to well-worn page to a chapter heading, *Spirit Snake*. "Okay. I guess that's a yes." Excited, but with a bit of reservation, she picked the book up and looking around, noticed Doris watching from the far side of the room.

"I see you found what you needed. Are you looking for anything else?"

Holding the book up for Doris to see, she said, "I'm not really sure what I was looking for – this just sort of fell off the shelf and it seems it may have some answers for me. Grandmother was talking about something last night and I thought I might find more information here, if I looked. I actually thought I was looking for something more along the lines of meditation techniques but I'm also curious about some of the stories of my grandmother's Siksika heritage."

"Looks like it found you. I'll sign it out for you. I've got some CDs over here that have some guided meditations for beginners. You might try a couple of these. You'll need to return them within two weeks. Say hello to your grandmother for me."

"Oh. That's a great idea! I will check those out. And thank you, I will pass the message on."

The town's resident herd of elk was just beginning their daily saunter onto its main street, reducing traffic to a near crawl as Kiera started on her drive home. Three majestic elk stood, filled with strength and grace, on the passenger's side of the jeep. Rolling the side window further down, she greeted the one nearest her. "Hello Beautiful! I hope you've had a wonderful day. Grandmother would have me thank you for blessing us with your presence today, so I'll say Thanks for the blessings."

Thinking to herself that she didn't really understand the blessings that came to her most of the time, and more often didn't even recognize them as such, Kiera felt hopeful that this would soon change.

As recognition of some deep revelation warmed within her chest, Kiera slipped one of the meditation CDs into the jeep's player and headed toward home. The sounds of nature surrounded her as a clear voice began to explain the benefits of meditating and working with the energies abundantly present in the Universe to build and maintain peace and harmony in life. The Narrator also advised against actively meditating while driving.

The soothing voice went on to describe how to invoke these energies through meditation, build a greater connection with them, and awareness of the subtleties in our environment, other people, and ourselves. It continued to explain that these same energies come from two sources – Mother Earth and the Universal Source or Creator God. They have many names and yet are recognized together as the One Great Source of All that Was, Is and Ever Will Be.

By consciously connecting to the energies available to oneself, we can use these energies to build, heal, and sustain life and creativity, and effect changes in our world. The possibilities are limitless.

The voice then explained that there are two basic keys to working in harmony with the Universal Energies: Giving thanks to the Creator and asking for what we require. It seemed to Kiera that it was just too simple to accept as even remotely possible.

CHAPTER 5

ANCESTORS

The sun breached high overhead as Joshua finished mucking out the stalls in the barn. Heaping the last load from the wheelbarrow onto the compost pile, he mopped the sweat from his brow with the back of his forearm. The horses stood at the far side of the paddock, in the shade of the trees.

Nightsong lifted his head at that precise moment and from clear across the field, nodded and neighed. He began to paw the ground and cantered toward Joshua. He made a beeline across the pasture to stop and snort directly into Joshua's face.

"You want to go for a run, don't you? You know I have a lot to do today. I told you that earlier."

The mustang threw back his head in reply and pushed at the pitchfork, knocking it from Joshua's grasp. Swinging his head toward the mountains above the tree line and returning his gaze to Joshua, Nightsong lowered his head to push at Joshua's shoulder. Joshua's heart filled with a sudden intuition that for some reason he needed to go up the mountain. Nightsong, while generally pushy and opinionated, was not usually this demanding.

"Okay, okay, you win! Just let me put the tools away, grab some water and my pack from the house." A small leather bag hung by its strap on the fence post a few feet away. Joshua lifted it over his head and one shoulder and then moved toward the barn with his tools. Setting them inside the barn door, he shook his head at his best friend and headed to the house.

Returning a few minutes later, he found Nightsong dancing around, pawing the earth impatiently. A small backpack over his shoulder, Joshua leapt onto the back of the mustang and they cantered toward a low spot of fence on the far side of the paddock closest to the barn.

Jumping easily over the fence, Nightsong continued at an easy pace on the even ground toward the treeline and the rocky face of the mountain. Holding lightly onto the mustang's neck, Joshua trusted his ever-growing hunch that there was a purpose to this ride; something important was afoot.

The ground soon shifted from the rich loam of the valley to the loose mulch of the forest floor and before long, fine stone chips littered the way before them. The treeline was sparse here, not as dense as on the other side of the low ridge. Silver-grey lichens crawled over rocks and decaying trees, felled by time. Stone chips made way for larger rock and granite outcrops by the time they reached the top of the ridge. From here, they could see for miles around – to the low lands beyond the eastern foothills and the mountainous range to the west, north and south; a truly magnificent view filled with the colours of summer in the Rockies.

Loose stone would have made finding a foot purchase challenging for most but for Joshua and Nightsong, this was sure ground, having explored the ridge countless times over the years. Still, caution was taken to make sure the mustang did not slip on uneven ground as they continued on their way.

An eagle soared on the wind high above and called out a greeting to the familiar pair of travellers. Nightsong nickered back without missing a step on the barely visible trail before them. Continuing along the crest of a ridge, the two enjoyed the rays of the sun that beat upon their backs and the fresh mountain air. Far below, water sprang from between the rocks and spilled further down the mountain slope to form a river through the valley floor below.

Joshua loved these unexpected rides up into the mountains with Nightsong. They brought him a sense of peace and rightness to being. Centering his awareness on his breathing, Joshua filled his lungs with fresh air until he felt its energy feeding each cell of his body, the blood coursing with a steady pace, in tune with his heart beat. After holding it for several seconds in his lungs, he exhaled very slowly, allowing the air to slip through pursed lips and following it with an emphatic "ha-a".

Nightsong snorted, tuning his breathing with that of his riding partner.

A sun dog glistened in the sky, forming a perfectly circular rainbow that embraced the sun at its core. The air brightened above the ground directly in front of Joshua and Nightsong. Heat waves appeared over ground baked in the heat of a noon sun. The scenery seemed to split, revealing an alternate view. The light often played tricks up here on warm days. The air tingled, filled with the electric charge that commonly follows a lightening strike.

The hair on Joshua's arms and the back of his neck bristled to match that of the mustang's mane. Nightsong began to prance and dance on the spot, flaring his nostrils, rather than moving ahead on the path before them. Joshua leaned forward to soothe the beast and whispered into his ear "Shush. It's okay. You're okay. We'll stop for a minute to see what's here." He then dismounted, landing softly on a large flat rock beside the horse.

The ground wavered and settled. Joshua noted that the foliage was greener and lusher than it had been before, and though the landscape was the same, it felt dynamically different. It seemed more alive, if that was even remotely possible.

Taking stock of the surroundings, he noted the same waterfall emptying into the valley below. But what was this? There were tepees around the widest point of the river which flowed from the falls – more than a dozen of them, marked with the colours of their clan. Children played and ran along the water's edge while a handful of women sat cross-legged around a fire in the centre of the camp. Another woman carried a pot in one hand and a roll of what looked to be an animal hide toward them. At the far end of the camp, several painted ponies were corralled among saplings behind one of the tents.

It was as if he and Nightsong had travelled through a vortex into another time in this very same place.

Just then, a man opened the flap of the larger tepee nearer to the campfire and stood tall. Calling over to the women, they rose to gather supplies, some of them moved to light a fire farther away, others placed large flat stones onto the fire, and they began to prepare a meal. Seeing this done, he raised his gaze to the ridge upon which Joshua and Nightsong watched and nodded. Turning to the water, he motioned with his arm that they should descend the ridge to the camp. After washing his face and hands in the water, the man looked back toward Joshua and saw that he had not moved. Again, he waved, indicating impatiently that Joshua should come down to the camp.

A sense of curiosity filled Joshua and the man's impatience broke the spell that had held both he and Nightsong in its thrall. He mounted the mustang once more and began a careful descent to the camp below. So many questions filled his head. Joshua allowed Nightsong to lead the way down to the treeline, all the while staying aware of their direction, and made sure they joined up with the stream some hundred feet above the camp.

The rest of the way down was a bit trickier, there being more boulders, broken rock and scrub trees along the way. Twenty feet from where the spring made its last fall from the rocks to the valley below, the tall, muscular, young Indigenous man stood in the middle of the path leading to the camp. He wore a pair of pants made of animal hide, a small beaded leather bag hung from his neck, and a feather was braided into his hair. The young man unfolded his crossed arms and indicated that they should follow him. He led them to the area where the ponies were tied and stopped beside a sapling a short distance from the remainder of the horses. It was far enough for Nightsong to feel less threatened by the presence of the wild horses, though Joshua knew that his companion would have felt at home among this herd.

After tying Nightsong loosely to the sapling, he turned to face the man who had beckoned for him to come down to the camp, and offered his hand in friendship. The young indigenous man took the offered hand and said, "Brother, we've been expecting you. What took you so long?"

Concealing his surprise at these words and the fact he understood him, Joshua followed as they walked toward the fire in the camp's centre, joined by others who appeared from the woods and other tents.

The young man introduced himself as Red Feather, son of Chief Rain Dancer. As the two approached the central campfire, the chief intercepted their path. "Walks Through Time, welcome to the clan of the Nakota people." A number of the Elders were already gathered in a circle around the campfire and introductions continued. Curious children drew nearer to the circle of Elders, as their mothers hushed them to be quiet and listen. They knew that this stranger's visit was a story they would share with their great-grandchildren many, many years from now.

Joshua thanked Chief Rain Dancer for making him feel so welcome and wondered how they could have possibly known he was coming? And why did they call him "Walks Through Time"? It seemed a complete impossibility.

It was then, that Red Feather nodded to one of the Elders of the clan, a willowy man with snow white hair hanging down to his waist. On his shirt, the man wore brightly coloured beads made from seeds and pieces of stone of various hues. The patterns were very ornate, fashioned in wide bands from his shoulders to the wrist. Several equally ornate decorated pouches hung from thongs around his neck. His clothing also bore long leather fringes extending from wrist to wrist, much like the shirt worn by Chief Rain Dancer. In his one hand, the Elder held a clutch of eagle feathers and in the other, a clay bowl with a mixture of leaves in it.

Eagle Man set his feathers on the ground beside him and reached forward to take a small piece of wood from the fire with which to light the smudge pot. Rising nimbly to his feet, he gave thanks to the Great Creator and offered smoke from the bowl which he fanned with the feathers held in his other hand. He gave thanks and appreciation for Mother Earth and to each of the four directions of the Medicine Wheel for the wisdom and gifts they offer each day. Then he directed the smoke over his hands and his body, saying:

"I wash my hands in the sweet smoke so that they may be constructive and reach out to others in a good way. I bring the smoke over my head and down my back to lighten my troubles and bring clarity of purpose. I smudge my eyes so that I will see good things in people and learn from them. I smudge my mouth so that I will speak good things to people and learn to choose my words carefully. I smudge my ears so that I will listen carefully to others, learn from what they say and become someone they want to talk to. I bring the smoke towards me to surround my heart so that what has been damaged can heal and what pain is to come will help me be strong and grow in a good way. I wash my feet in the smoke so that I may walk a path of purpose, compassion, balance, and kindness. May the smoke wash over me, collect my messages of gratitude and gather my worries. Let them rise up to the Sky World. May my ancestors see that I live with good intentions.[6]"

Standing in front of Joshua, Eagle Man held the bowl up in front of Joshua and waved smoke through the feathers, up and over him. The chief was next and then the bowl was passed around the circle as Eagle Man made his way to his blanket to sit down.

Gently swaying, he closed his eyes and began to hum, first softly to himself and then louder. As he broke into song, time seemed to slip from existence and Joshua felt a deep sense of belonging, that they were all one or

---

[6] There are many references and instructions for smudging available online. The author has been honoured to have participated in many different smudgings.

at one with one another. As the song grew in intensity and volume, the ceremonial drum joined, adding the heartbeat of the earth to the song of time immemorial.

Many voices joined in the medicine man's song and the drum. Joshua got caught up in the experience and closed his eyes. His heart beat quickened with that of the drum. His soul revealed the words of the song to his heart and he rejoiced, adding his voice to the others.

When the drum beat slowed and the voices hushed, Eagle Man accepted the talking stick from Chief Rain Dancer, indicating that he was ready to speak.

"I had a vision when the sun began to rise and the land awoke from its sleep just a handful of moons ago. I looked up to the ridge and saw Walks Through Time looking over the land. The sun danced on his head and the Eagle greeted our brother as he has done today. The Eagle spoke with him and then came to me to say that he would come to us at the time of the Buck Moon at our harvest camp at a time of spiritual significance.

"We brought a small group of our clan to this place to wait for you. The rest of the Nakota Nation are at our summer camp at Lake Wakamne and will arrive in time for the harvest. It was important for us to be here to greet you, my brother.

"The Eagle told me that you would travel a great distance by the moon and that our people have suffered greatly and been stripped of their ways. Eagle says our land, Turtle Island, is not well. Many of our people cannot hear her call for help. They don't know our language and have forgotten how to heal our home. They have lost their connection to the Mother and cannot feel the sacred energy she so freely gives us, when we care for her. They have forgotten how to ask for Spirit to guide them in their daily life and in times of trouble.

"He said there are three who will know what to do and that they must lead our people back to their sacred ways. Eagle said you are one of those people. You are our brother by blood. You can trace your ancestors to our chief. His blood runs in you, though it is thin and will require you to build its strength in ways you will be shown when the time is right."

Feeling stunned and honoured at the same time, Joshua was not sure if there was anything he could say in response. So, he bowed his head in deference to the shaman and then to the chief.

Eagle Man continued by saying: "It is necessary to create a place within your soul where may dwell peace, harmony and oneness with the Source of all life. Eagle told me it would be very difficult to do in the world in which you live as you have such a fast-paced life, it is almost impossible to sit to listen to your inner voice. This must be made a practice of daily doing if you are to continue to live at this pace and function as a man doing what is expected of you. In order to maintain peace and order, one must become aware of his own uniqueness and the Source of his life.

"The natural, physical world is one in which our people move and live our daily lives. It is also a world of spirits, those of the trees and animals, accessible through our dance and song, our rituals. We are connected by the energy of Creator, which flows in and through each of us and the trees and creatures who share life on this land. To access it, you must listen to your breath, to the wind and to your inner knowing. To quicken the energy flow in us, from Spirit, we sing and dance in a circle, moving in the direction of the sun from the east to the south, then the west and the north. You need only ask for clear thought when you are in doubt. The answers to our questions often find us before we ask.

"Any time you return to this place, you will find the tools you need as you search for greater awareness. Know that the wisdom of the ancestors walks with you each step of your journey. That is all I can tell you for now."

The Talking Stick was returned to Chief Rain Dancer, who had made signs to the women among the group that it was time to feed their guest. The small band shared a meal of tender new greens, roots and seasoned meat, listening to the children's chatter and recalled clan stories.

Some time later, feeling full and appreciative, Joshua headed back to the top of the ridge by the same path he had travelled down to the autumn gathering camp. He thought to himself "No one will believe me when I tell them that I have met a three hundred and fifty-plus-year old medicine man! Wish I had a camera with me!"

CHAPTER 6

SASHA SPEAKS

Clouds shifted over the moon, deepening the night, as Kiera trod softly along the forest path to the spring where she planned to soak after a long day. A doe stopped munching on new growth of an Elderberry bush to gauge Kiera's intent. Deciding she was no threat, the doe turned and continued grazing at another bush a few steps away.

Thinking about the vision she had seen the previous night under the full moon, Kiera wondered if it might have been influenced by the combined effects of the warm water, the fullness of the moon, and her vivid imagination. Grandmother had been very sure though, that Kiera had participated in some sort of initiation. Still, she couldn't help but wonder. It just seemed so fantastic and a bit hard to believe.

Upon reaching the large flat rock at the side of the hot

spring, she carefully folded her clothes as she removed them and placed a large towel on top, before stepping into the steaming water.

It wasn't long before an owl's wing beat sounded like a drum in the night, thrumming through the darkening sky overhead. One call pierced the silence. "Hoo-ooot!"

Instinct awakened in Kiera as she heard a voice say: "Owl calls to harken you to the heart of the Mother, who nurtures and supports us. Listen…"

"I hear the earth sigh.
I feel her breath catch and tremble.
She is weak and weary,
I feel her tears well within me.

Hear my cry, make me whole.
My waters are turned to acid,
My land no longer feeds my children,
The buffalo are all long gone,
My depths have been raped of my bounty.
I cannot go on."

Overcome with emotion, Kiera started to sob, not knowing how to comfort what she knew to be the voice of Mother Earth. A great sense of compassion welled within her breast, straining with a desire to comfort her.

"What can I do?" asked Kiera.

Mother Earth sighed once more. "The damage that has been done can be reversed with focused energy and intention. I wish to shine like a star. It is through ascension, acknowledging grace and universal enlightenment, that this will be possible. But a leader is needed, to awaken and teach my children to work together. The Sky People and others can help. They will come to you when the time is right."

As the words still rang in her mind, all became quiet again. The clouds above shifted to reveal the light of the moon, barely a sliver less full than on the previous night. The artist in Kiera studied the moon's cratered face and the play of light shining down upon the tree limbs, casting shadows on the forest floor. The moon's reflection drifted over the water, interrupted by the ripples of her hands moving to and fro. She studied the colours, or lack thereof, and the shapes made by moonlight on water, all the while feeling an immense empathy with the Mother's words.

Leaning her head back to the stones on the edge of the spring, Kiera closed her eyes to "feel" the light from a starlit sky filled with the after glow of the full moon. She drifted on emotions and steadied her breath, matching it to her heart beat just as Grandmother had suggested on the previous night.

Kiera inhaled deeply into her chest, counting to four as she held the air in her lungs before exhaling for another count of four. She exhaled through pursed lips, as slowly as she could, as if she were the breeze herself.

Her breathing deepened to a slow and steady beat that seemed to echo the pulse of the forest, the water, and the stars. Kiera's hearing became super-sensitive. She could hear the leaves gently swaying high above her head. She heard the water reaching the opposite side of the spring and begin its return toward her. She felt the energy of the water seeping into her being. Her body tingled with the awareness of the flow of energy welling up from the earth, coursing through her spine and filling her up like an empty vessel. Like liquid gold, the energy sloshed around inside Kiera's body flowing like a fountain from the crown of her head back to the earth again. It felt warm and invigorating, like a good towel rub, waking up every one of her cells until her whole body was vibrating.

Kiera wondered if this was what nirvana felt like. She was experiencing a deep and boundless connection to the trees, the water and the sky – all at once. It was as if she was a part of them all, or they were a part of her.

She almost missed the softest of sounds from the underbrush twenty feet away. It was like the sound of a little summer rain falling on dry grass. Lazily shifting her head toward the sound, a long low glow appeared to shimmer through her closed lids. The glow brightened to a golden hue and seemed to sway a bit as it pulled itself into a conical shape.

Remembering the luminescence of the temple she'd seen the previous evening, Kiera allowed the light to wash over her and breathed it into her being. As she took a deep breath and held it in her lungs, she saw a thin silver chord extending from the light and into her body and centering itself at the core of her heart. The thread grew stronger as she took another breath, forging a deeper connection with the light's very essence.

The sensation of floating in the light came over her and Kiera gave herself to the feeling of Oneness as her whole being filled with love – a free-flowing, all-consuming, and unconditional love. Bliss!

Forever the inquisitive child, Kiera wondered to herself "What is this? What is causing this feeling?"

"I am a ssservant of the Light, the Great Cosssmic Creator, God. You are ready to take your placsse among the Light Workersss and I will be your guide for thisss part of your ssspiritual journey."

"Grandmother said something similar. I have always felt that I am part of something more than just myself, but I'm not sure what that is."

"Your Elder isss a very wissse woman. She hasss travelled far and learned much in her exssperiencsse of thisss life in thisss time. Dessspite many attemptsss by othersss to sssteer her from her truth, she hasss remembered her path and remainsss connected to the Sssource of All, the one she callsss God or Apissstotoke, in her native tongue. Her wisssdom will alssso guide you from time to time, when you require clarification of the messsagesss that we bring to you."

"I have always wondered if her wisdom came from outside herself. I know that she has lived a long and difficult life. She has learned a great deal about people from living in the Residential School as a child. I cannot imagine the horrors she saw."

"Her wisssdom comesss from within – asss doesss yoursss. However, it isss becaussse of the nature of man towardsss hisss fellow man and more ssspecssifically, racsse againssst racsse, that we have come to you. It isss time to unite all of human kind together again asss Children of the Light. You have all decssended from one Creator and have forgotten your connection to that Sssourcsse of all life and therefore to one another. It isss time to reclaim that connection, that heritage.

"Your sssoulsss are all connected, in a sssimilar way asss the sssilver thread you have drawn between you and I, to the Sssource. Lying deep within your heart isss the Light of the Creator that isss your heritage, the tiny flame you call 'Sssoul'. It isss that part of your DNA, if you like, that sssignsss you asss a child of the Creator. By that right, you are alssso a co-creator of the Light. Humanity hasss been taught to look outsssside itssself for Divinity and hasss forgotten the connection within that removesss the illusssion of ssseparation from Sssourcsse.

"Thisss isss why we are called to work with you now, to fan the flamesss of that Light, to ssstrengthen the bond – the connection – to the Sssourcsse, God. You will sssoon reconnect with another sssoul whom you have known in the passst. Together, you will dissscover waysss to enlighten othersss who will be brought to you. Your life choicssesss and examplesss will ssserve to remind humankind of their resssponssibility asss co-creatorsss to thisss planet earth. You will hold the Light high asss Warriorsss and lead to their exssperiencsse of At-one-ment."

"This sounds like a lot of responsibility. I don't know that I am ready for this. How do you know that I am even worthy?"

"Your humility isss sssign enough. In fact, it isss your purity of thought and ssselflesssnesss that makesss you worthy. Thoughtsss are thingsss. Pure thought, without malicsse, is the basssisss of love. It isss thisss unconditional love that isss necssesssary in your world at thisss time. By holding a light to thisss type of love, you can help heal the earth of the damage done by millennia of hateful deedsss. By building on thisss love and holding the Light of the Creator high, ssstrengthening the grid of light around the earth, you will create a new and brighter world for humankind and all of Creation – the way it wasss intended to be from the beginning of time."

Kiera pondered the possibility of a beautiful world, full of peace and unconditional love. Instinctively, or perhaps a bit wistfully, she could imagine it to be possible and an image grew in her heart.

"Thisss isss how creation beginsss - asss thought. All thoughtsss are made manifessst. Thusss, guard your thoughtsss wisssely, to ensssure that only the highessst and the bessst of the power of Divine Light will be made manifessst. Believe with all your being that it will be. Indeed, it isss already manifesssted in a future timeline. Ssso it isss."

These words brought an increasing sense of peace to her heart. It was no more of a stretch to imagine a peaceful world than it was to imagine a scene in her mind before sketching it and bringing it to life on a canvas.

"Thisss isss correct. You learn very quickly and asss a result, will remember more of your giftsss asss you practicsse intentional thinking. For now, though, you require ressst. Until we meet again."

Opening her eyes, Kiera was not surprised to see the sacred white serpent from the temple, curled up on a large stone several feet away. "What do I call you?" she asked.

"I am called by many namesss but you may call me Sssasssha." With that said, Sasha nodded and vanished into thin air. As he did so, the colours of the trees and small plants around her seemed to come to life. They shimmered vividly with a soft glow around their edges, more brilliant than before.

CHAPTER 7

AWAKENING TO SPIRIT

Sunday morning, Kiera donned a sleeveless floral print dress, sandals; put on some mascara and a sheer lip tint before heading out the door to pick up her Grandmother. She was not a regular attendee but had promised that she would accompany her Elder to Church that day. For a reason unknown to Kiera, the woman had felt it was going to be very important to have her granddaughter attend.

As the sun rose early in the eastern sky, it took some time for it to climb above the tree tops of the foothills. As Kiera reached her Grandmother's cabin just a mile away, the brilliant rose light that kissed the morning sky was fading into a golden glow.

The Elder woman was already on the doorstep, waiting for Kiera to pull in the dirt driveway off the range road. Kiera reached over to unlatch the door and waited for her Grandmother to settle into the seat and fasten the belt before kissing her on the cheek. "Did you sleep well?"

Grandmother nodded and exclaimed, "I did, thank you. What a glorious sunrise! It is a sign that today is going to be very special."

Twenty minutes later, they pulled into the parking lot of the little town Church, a white clapboard building, proudly boasting a bell tower above the large red double doors. One of the doors was propped open and a small woman, all smiles, was standing just inside, ready to greet all who entered therein.

The parking lot was almost full and several cars were parked on the street. Kiera spotted more than a few vehicles she recognized. As they stepped through the big outer doors, it took a minute for her eyes to adjust.

"Good Morning Mrs. Deerfoot. You look lovely today. Is this Kiera home from college? It's so nice to have you with us this morning, dear. I hope you'll stay for coffee and fellowship after the service. I know Rev. Steve will want to meet you."

Grandmother replied "Kiera has been searching her soul this week, seeking answers to difficult questions. I reminded her that throughout my life, I have turned to the giver of all life for answers to my daily needs. No matter what has happened in my life, God has never let me down. And you know those prayers right in the beginning of the *Book of Common Prayer*? I read them every day to ask for guidance and He listens."

"Of course you do!" said Mrs. Pruitt. "I don't know

anyone whose faith is as deep or as easily observed in everyday circumstances. You truly do live as an example to all of us; how easily we can follow Christ's footsteps, all the while being faithful to our own traditions. I think your faith runs as deep as the heart of these mountains!"

Kiera had to laugh at the truth of that statement. Despite all her Grandmother's life experiences – the trauma of isolation, and segregation – Mrs. Deerfoot doubted not the Will and Work of the Creator in her life. She had found a way to balance the gifts of her native ways and her faith in the white man's God to find a peace and comfort with which she could live a life of fulfillment.

"Thank you, Mrs. Pruitt. I'm happy to be here."

Her Grandmother then steered her toward the second pew from the front and to the left of the centre aisle. It took more than a couple of minutes to get there though, for all the greetings and conversations that had to made along the way. The Elder was not the only person passing greetings. Kiera spotted Marjorie from the grocery store with her grandson Mark and had to sign his cast before being seated.

"You go in first so I can get up to do the reading, okay?"

"Sure Gran." Kiera moved along the row to give her grandmother ample room to sit and place her purse on the bench beside her. When the sun beamed through the stained glass window at the end of the pew bench, it created a jewelled rainbow that lit the sanctuary.

A slight movement drew her attention, setting her senses on high alert. It made her aware that she was being watched from the row directly behind her. The man, with striking features and dark hair, had a look of shock in his eyes for an instant before noticing that she was returning his gaze. He brazenly winked at her and turned his attention to the choir being seated in the loft.

Feeling a bit unsettled and flattered at the same time, Kiera faced forward again as the service began with a hymn. Her friend Sonja would say her "spidey sense" was working overtime as the hairs on the back of her neck stood on end and she felt shivers run up her spine.

Not sure what all this could possibly mean, she shoved it to the back of her mind and focused on the service now unfolding.

Grandmother read a selection from Genesis that speaks of Creation and how the power of God rests in humanity to care for this world and its inhabitants. Being made in the image of God, each human also has the ability to create.

"Is the Universe conspiring to tell me something?" Kiera wondered.

The second reading was out of Hebrews and talked of humans as co-creators.

"What are human beings that you are mindful of them, or mortals, that you care for them? You have made them for a little while lower than the angels; you have crowned them with glory and honour, subjecting all things under their feet.[7]"

---

7 Heb. 2:6–8, quoting Ps. 8, from New Revised Standard Version Bible: Anglicized Edition, copyright © 1989, 1995 National Council of the Churches of Christ in the United States of America. Used by permission. All rights reserved.

The reading continued to say: "Jesus is not ashamed to call them brothers and sisters.[8]" The point made was that Jesus said that only by working together, as One, are we restored to fellowship with God.

The messages in the readings resonated with Kiera. She wondered if this was what Sasha meant when he told her that she would be working with someone else to "create a new world". She would have to ask her Grandmother later.

***

As the service commenced, Joshua's thoughts were distracted by the sight of the young woman from the forest. Shocked was more like it! He would know that hair and beautiful face anywhere. As the initial realization of her identity gave way to excitement, Joshua knew he would make every effort after the service to learn her name.

He didn't come to church often, but his sister, Janet, had needed a ride because her car was in the shop. The local mechanic, Dan, had called on Saturday to say that her car wouldn't be ready until the following day.

Shaking his head, he could barely contain a chuckle, thinking that he had actually winked at the raven-haired beauty! A sharp elbow in the ribs brought Joshua's attention back to the service just as the older woman

[8] Heb. 2:11, from New Revised Standard Version Bible: Anglicized Edition, copyright © 1989, 1995 National Council of the Churches of Christ in the United States of America. Used by permission. All rights reserved.

beside the object of his attention rose and moved toward the lectern.

The readings reminded Joshua of the conversation he'd had with Eagle Man. The idea of being a co-creator with God was not new to him, as he had participated in the creation of many good things in his lifetime, his farm being one of them. He was beginning to wonder though, if the woman from the hot spring was one of the people he was meant to work with to heal the earth and the relationship that his native people had established with the land.

So many ideas began to reconcile themselves to his mind as he listened to the words of the Bible and the hymns throughout the remainder of the service. It struck him that humanity had not understood what dominion over the animals and plants really meant. Rather, humans had taken it literally as giving them licence to abuse the land and animals for purposes other than intended. They had upset the natural balance of eco-structures, becoming self-centered and entitled, causing the land to grieve. In essence, humans had removed themselves from the vital fellowship with their Creator God.

While Jesus impressed through his teachings that all humans are equal and imbued with the same gifts as himself, humanity walks yet in a wilderness of its own making, having forgotten its connection to the Source of all Things and Creation. Of this, Joshua had been reminded by Eagle Man. Now he only needed to find a way to discover the manner of his Truth and how to bring it forward for the good of his people. First, he had to find the two people who could help. Then he would need to find and build a connection with the people who shared his Nakota heritage.

At the sharing of a sign of peace[9], Janet hugged him and then reached across him to greet the two women in the pew ahead of them. Hands were extended and when he reached for hers, Joshua was entranced by her shy demeanour and hair that resembled the inky night sky. As her hand briefly joined his in an introductory handshake, an electric spark moved through his palm and flew up his arm straight to his heart. Startled, he searched her eyes for any sign that she had felt it too. A brief dilation of her pupils, quickly shuttered, confirmed his suspicion. Too quickly, or so it felt to him, she withdrew her hand and turned as Mrs. Pruitt greeted her and her grandmother from over the front kneeling rail.

"Who is she?" he whispered to Janet.

"Who is who?" she replied, returning to her seat.

"Her! The one beside the lady who read the lessons." he hissed.

"With Mrs. Deerfoot? That's her granddaughter. She has been away at college for a few years. I heard she bought a place not far from her grandmother's cabin. Why?"

"I don't remember ever seeing her before. There is something about her that I can't put my finger on – something familiar."

Casting a sideways glance at Joshua, Janet said "You

---

[9] In many cultures, members of a faith community may offer a sign of peace, either a handshake or hug, as a gesture of goodwill toward others.

mind your manners! She's had enough grief in her life without the likes of a wild cowboy like you."

"Who, me? Wild? I just prefer the company of animals to people."

***

The Sunday service ended with the hymn *All Things Bright and Beautiful.* Afterward, people filed out into the lobby and either bid Rev. Steve good-bye or headed for the stairs leading to the community hall a few steps down and to the right of the worship space.

The aroma of rich coffee greeted Kiera as she stepped into the hall with her Grandmother. "Why don't you sit down and I'll get us a cup of coffee? If they have some cookies, would you like one or two?"

"I won't turn down any cookie that shows up on my plate, so I will leave that up to you. Would you put a bit of milk in my coffee please? It's likely pretty hot."

Kiera grinned at the response and made her way over to the table spread with plates of goodies and coffee supplies. A sign on the table read "Nut and Calorie Free". The generous selection of various church lady treats made choosing just one difficult. Kiera settled on a lemon square that she added to the plate she intended to share.

"You don't have to be shy. Take another one! Your Grandmother loves these" said Mrs. Pruitt. "Now that you've finished school, I hope we'll see you more often."

"Oh, Gran will make sure I'm here more regularly than when I was at school! I know it means a lot to her to be here. I'm actually grateful that she has so many friends that have kept a close eye on her while I was away. I know I shouldn't, but I do worry about her living alone sometimes. The weather can be pretty cruel out here in the winter. She mentioned to me that more than a few people make sure she has supplies from town and pick her up for church. It means more than you can imagine."

"She's a very special lady to us. We all understand what it is to want to age as gracefully as possible and know we may need a helping hand once in a while. I get so much more out of helping her than she realizes. Your Grandmother's faith has been a rock for me too. If I'm looking even a bit frazzled when I go see her, I know that she will say just the right words to lift my heart and make me see that I don't carry all my troubles alone. And you know, she gives the best hugs in the county!" Mrs. Pruitt giggled as she poured two cups of coffee, placing just the right amount of milk into one of the cups.

"Thank you, Mrs. Pruitt."

"Angela. Just call me Angela," she replied as she reached forward to give Kiera a one-armed hug, balancing the teapot in her other hand.

Kiera stacked the plate she carried on top of one of the cups and headed back to where her Grandmother was waiting, talking with the young woman who had sat behind them earlier.

"Oh, thank you dear. Do you know Janet Daniels? She lives on the other side of Ridge Road, south of the Gallery and works over at the Health Centre."

"I've heard a lot about you, Kiera. Meadoe told me

you will be showing some of your art at the end of the summer" exclaimed Janet.

"Nice to officially meet you. The girls are really putting on the pressure. I just spoke with Meadoe yesterday about the show again. I have a lot of work to do to complete everything in such a short time," answered Kiera.

"Oh, you'll manage to get it all done and it will be the best you've ever done, honey!" assured Kiera's grandmother. "I have a feeling that what you paint this summer will be a reflection of your heart, your soul, and all the inspiration that these mountains provide for you, presented in a way that will inspire us to think and act as God intended us to – filled with His love and a joy for living."

A look of shock came across Kiera's face as she looked from her Grandmother to Janet and back again before asking "How can you possibly know this Gran?"

"God has big plans for you Sweetie, you know that. Are you going to eat that lemon square? You know they're my favourite."

"You are prejudiced Gran, but that's very sweet."

"Janet, I got you some date squares. The lemon's mine though. Hi, I'm Joshua." Extending his hand toward Kiera, Joshua braced himself for the heat and excitement he expected to wash up his arm as he grasped Kiera's hand once again. His eyes locked on hers and drew him into liquid pools of dark chocolate.

Still reeling from her grandmother's prophecy about her art, the shock of the electric spark generated by their joined hands for the second time caused her to stammer out a weak greeting. "Kiera. Hello."

She noted that he was quite tall, but it was his eyes that held her captive. They sparkled like sunlight on cold, clear water, almost grey and not quite blue. Kiera couldn't understand why he should have such an unsettling effect on her.

Janet filled in the blanks for a visibly quizzical Kiera. "This is my brother, Kiera. He drove me to church this morning because my car is still in the shop. Joshua doesn't get here very often. He tries to find other things to keep him busy on Sundays" she offered, laughing.

"It's not that I don't like being here, it's just that there is a lot of work to keep me busy on the farm and I just don't think they want to hear my caterwauling through all the hymns" Joshua chuckled. "Do you come here often?"

Kiera pulled her hand from where Joshua still held it loosely in his own, having rubbed his thumb across the back of it. More than a bit self-conscious and unsettled, she replied "I've just returned a few weeks ago from the city. I finished my art degree and am back here working and trying to help my grandmother when I can."

Janet piped in "Kiera is one of the artists that Tracy and Meadoe will be featuring in a show at the Gallery the end of August." Facing Kiera, she said, "I can't wait to see your work! The girls have said that you paint like no one else they've seen. And Mrs. Deerfoot says that it's pretty special too."

"I see," replied Joshua. "I guess I'll have to make sure I get to see you at work. Where do you find your inspiration?"

"Well, I guess I just do what comes to mind when I sit to paint. I can't say it's any one thing or another. Mostly, it's about what I feel at the time." Turning to her grandmother, Kiera sighed. "Well, I guess we should get going since there are so many people with such high expectations for my showing!"

"If you need a break from painting and want to just get together with some of the girls and have fun, give me a call, Kiera. Here's my number." Janet hastily scribbled a phone number on a napkin that had appeared out of nowhere and placed it in Kiera's hand.

"Thank you, Janet. It was nice to meet you." Kiera smiled and turned to Joshua, nodding curtly. "Joshua."

"Enjoy your day," he replied. Joshua nodded toward Mrs. Deerfoot. "Ma'am. A pleasure to meet you."

Kiera couldn't usher her grandmother away quickly enough, feeling as if a million butterflies were fluttering in her stomach.

***

"What was that all about?" Mavis inquired when they were settled in the car and pulling onto the roadway. "You were almost rude to that nice young man!"

"Nice young man – my foot!" Kiera muttered not quietly enough. "He winked at me! In Church! Who does that? I just have a weird feeling he isn't quite who he seems to be."

"Oh honey, I think you're overreacting. What are you afraid of? Would it hurt to make new friends? You haven't been out much at all since you got home, you've been so busy painting. Why, I know you haven't even finished unpacking!"

"I just don't think I need all the stuff I used in the city. That's why it's not unpacked."

As they neared her cabin, Mavis Deerfoot decided that there was no better time than the present to have a little talk with her granddaughter about destiny's call.

"Come inside and I'll make us some lunch. I boiled some of Mr. Naylor's fresh eggs this morning. There might still be some raspberries out in the garden, if the birds and the deer haven't got to them first."

Kiera hesitated, thinking about the pressure she was under to produce enough paintings for the show. "Thanks Gran, that would be nice."

Once back at the cabin, they worked together to prepare lunch and sat by the window to eat. Mavis offered Grace, giving thanks for time to sit with her granddaughter and for the joy that always brought to her heart.

"You're right. I have been working hard and haven't taken much time to socialize."

"It was nice of Janet to invite you to go out with her and the other girls. You should take her up on her offer."

"I think I will. I'll call her later this week. I need to get another painting done though. If I can produce two a week, I should have enough for the show."

"I have every bit of faith in you Kiera. You can do this and do it well. You just need to keep yourself open to the energy around you. Listen to Mother Earth and she will guide you and your hands."

Kiera took a long considerate look at her grandmother and slowly exhaled. "I went back to the spring last night and saw another vision. I think that Mother Earth spoke to me. The snake was there too. He said I should call him Sasha."

Mavis listened intently as Kiera unravelled the feelings brought on by her encounters. She was not surprised that Kiera had experienced two such episodes so close together. The girl had always been more conscious of the effects of humankind on Turtle Island. Her openness to her own creativity meant she would be more aware of the subtle energies of what the Elders called "the little people", the shy native spirits.

It was no small wonder that Kiera would be questioning herself right now. Most people were not as "tuned-in" to their surroundings, much less open to hear the voice of God through nature.

Mavis' eyes narrowed as she remembered Kiera's reaction to the young man introduced to them at church that morning. She grinned knowingly as Kiera finished speaking. "He's part of this!" she thought to herself.

CHAPTER 8

HIDDEN MESSAGES

Monday morning Kiera worked in the shade of the overhang on the front verandah of her little cabin, hips moving to the beat of her favourite indigenous band on the CD player blaring through the open window.

Beside the house, wild flowers reached toward the sun as it crested the tree tops behind them. The view was as vibrant as any she had seen. The play of light and shadows intrigued her and as inspiration took hold, Kiera found images hidden in the shapes of the light patterns reflected on flower petals, re-creating them on canvas. As paint layered over paint and images took form and shape, the painting came alive in unexpected ways.

Mixing a few grains of sand to burnt umber paint on an old saucer, she added texture and dimension to a field stone in the garden bed. Then some wadding mixed with a bit of gesso brought depth to what would become a bed of daisies.

The process of manipulating texture and paint always proved soothing to Kiera; she slipped easily into the emotion exuded by the image on the canvas. Kiera felt bright joy soaring through the sky as an eagle appeared to drift on the breeze high above the upturned faces of the daisies. The sharp sound of its call brought her a feeling of the awesome wonder of nature and its spirit, alive and breathing through each living thing.

The appearance of the eagle brought the book that Kiera had found at the library a couple of days prior to her mind. It was apparent that spirit animals, guides to life's lessons, were to be observed carefully. Their presence often held deep meanings and provided insight to indigenous people around the world. It was thought that the tribe's spiritual leader, called a Medicine Man, had the greatest understanding and ability to interpret the meaning of the presence of spirit animals, each with their own message.

Kiera didn't know any Medicine Men, nor was she particularly well versed in her own indigenous culture. Her grandmother was really the only link to that world. Oh, she had friends who had lived on the Rez at some point or another in their lives, but their culture was not part of the friendships she shared with them.

In a way she couldn't have explained, Kiera felt she'd lost something that was as vital as breath itself, yet right now, in this moment, she felt hope spring fresh and new. The sun was warm and its light shimmered on flecks of minerals in the rocks between the flowers in the bed at the base of the tall trees that stood as sentinels along the lane way and wrapped half-way around the cabin.

Between the shimmering colours appearing on the canvas, Kiera was drawn to a sense of movement among the dense foliage extending from the base of a massive white pine she had started to paint on the canvas. The low and rhythmic movement eased into the foreground and revealed itself to be a magnificent pure white serpent – her Spirit Guide, Sasha.

It was no surprise that Sasha had chosen this way to appear. After all, Kiera was coming to expect to see the serpent in the least expected places.

"Aaaahhh, it feelsss ssso good to have the sssun shining itsss warmth on my body. It feedsss and nourishesss the sssoul."

"It does Sasha."

"I like what you're creating here Kiera. Itsss esssencsse isss that of pure light and exudesss a love and ressspect for nature and our Prime Creator. Asss you lossse yourssself in your work more and more, you will find great fulfillment. The work you do will impart a messsage to thossse who view it and insspire them to care more greatly for our Mother."

"I don't understand Sasha. How will my art move people to discover what we've lost and begin to repair the damage we've done?"

"Forcssesss are at work to guide your handsss. Sssubliminal messsagesss are being hidden in your imagessss that insspire and ignite their desssire to work with the Creator themssselvesss. A piecsse of your esssencsse isss imparted with each painting you producsse. You do more than you know.

"You have reached for new awarenesss and committed yourssself to working with the universssal energiesss to build a greater level of awarenesss among othersss. You made this promissse many hundredsss of moonsss ago, when the earth wasss young. Your consciousssnesss hasss now awakened to that commitment.

"You have been shown the duality of life and have met a partner with whom you will share the dissscovery of the nuancssesss of that duality. Together, you will awaken energiesss forgotten, that will add a vital dimensssion to your communicationsss with othersss and to one another'sss ssspiritual development. You mussst lisssten to your intuition and trussst what you learn. Thisss isss how your Elder knowsss jussst what to sssay and when."

"What partner? Do you mean Grandmother?"

"No. The one who completesss your desssstiny hasss returned to asssissst in your own Creation ssstory. There exissstsss a cord of memory that connectsss you with one another. Thisss is how you recognizsse each other.

"Be obssservant. Breathe. Lisssten to the whisssspersss around you and ressspond with heart-felt love for life."

As Kiera pondered Sasha's words, she heard the cry of the eagle above, heralding another message. Someone was coming.

The light shifted and Kiera found her gaze focused on the spot in her painting where a brilliant flower was blossoming on the canvas before her. In its multitude of petals were gemstone colours reflecting the sun's rays back out of the painting. It appeared as though a second bloom was bursting forth from the centre of the first blossom, just moments before the petals would unfold – a beautiful twin flower nestled within the original flower bud!

***

Joshua had been struggling to get any work done on the farm for the last couple of days. Every time he set his mind to the design of a new shelter he wanted to build in the far pasture, or the list of supplies he'd need for it, he just couldn't concentrate and ended up staring off into space. Of course, that space was filled with the image of a woman with hair like black silk floating on a pool of water under a full buck moon in July.

It startled him that he could remember so clearly the way she looked or the feeling of smouldering heat as their hands met in an exchange of the peace at church on Sunday morning.

Spookier, was how he felt when, after riding Nightsong for a couple of hours, he ended up following the flight of an eagle that led him over to the other side of the range and through thick woods, bringing him to see her on the verandah of a small wooden cabin applying paint to canvas.

She was wearing a bandana around her head to capture droplets of sweat from her brow. The length of her hair had been captured into one long braid that hung down to her hip, casually slung over the front of her shoulder. It reached the bottom edge of shorts that rode up the back of her thighs, revealing just a suggestion of a well-shaped rump beneath the denim fabric. A summery tank top covered the rest of a shapely torso.

Bringing Nightsong to a halt, he watched as she breathed life into the canvas with textures and colours, vibrant and full. She seemed to *listen* to the canvas as she worked, applying layers upon layers of paint, first building what appeared to be the garden between the trees and the cabin and then covering it with images that seemed to take on a life of their own. It told a story, one of creation and *being* and the need to feel the sun nourish the soul. Life bloomed from the canvas – surreal, yet with a deep truth emanating through it.

She pulled back from the easel and put the brush down on the small table beside it. Stepping back from the painting, she turned to reach for a cloth with which to wipe paint from her hand and was startled to find herself being watched from the edge of the woods about twenty yards away.

"You! What are you doing here? How did you find me? And how long have you been sitting there watching?"

A slow grin appeared on Joshua's face; it lifted one corner of a mouth that was at once compelling and full of challenge. "Is that how you greet everyone who visits you? I thought your grandmother would have taught you better manners," he said with a laugh.

Ashamed and not just a bit resentful at being watched

while she worked, Kiera raised a jug of lemonade and offered to get another glass.

Joshua urged Nightsong around the flower beds to the front of the house, dismounted easily, and tossed the reins loosely over the railing of the verandah. He took the steps two at a time and had just reached the place where she had stood in front of her painting when the screen door slammed shut behind Kiera. He spun around and offered "It's incredible! I don't know how you make it appear to draw the viewer right inside the image on the canvas."

"It just happens sometimes. I'm not quite sure how."

She filled the iced glass with lemonade and refilled her own, then directed him to one of the two chairs at the other end of the verandah.

"In answer to your question, I'm not really stalking you. I didn't know you lived here. Nightsong and I were riding the ridge as we often do and an eagle called out to us. He led us here, where you seemed to be both aware of your environment and yet, deeply immersed in creating this amazing piece."

"You followed an eagle? You know, people might think you're a bit wacky if you tell them that you follow birds and talk to animals." Kiera wasn't about to tell him that she thought the eagle had been a figment of her very own active imagination!

"Is it that hard to believe? I thought you, of all people, would understand and appreciate such abilities, as they are the birthright of our people. I was sure you would have noticed him, or heard his call, heralding my arrival."

"I thought he was only in the painting. It sounds kind of crazy and hard to believe, but I did think I heard him say that someone was coming. That's when I realized that the image of the twinned flower finished the painting. I turned around and there you were. I really didn't have time to think about it."

"I'll admit I've always been able to connect with animals, but lately I've had some pretty weird experiences. In the past few days, I've received the message that I have to listen more closely; pay more attention to my surroundings; and get closer to my roots. Something tells me you've been feeling similar intuitions."

Kiera's heart skipped a beat while she considered what Joshua had just said. She tried to sip her lemonade and gaze nonchalantly toward the trees, wondering if this could really be happening. It seemed a bit far-fetched, and yet, here was this incredibly handsome man on her verandah with a shock of thick, dark hair and ruggedly chiselled features. The air seemed to sizzle around them.

Nightsong chose that moment to shove his head over the railing toward Kiera, nod his head in agreement with Joshua and knicker softly.

"Oh! Okay, that's weird! Who are you two?"

"Nightsong is his name. His mother was wild and died as she foaled. He followed me home. That was six years ago. He'd probably appreciate a drink of water. I saw an old well and pump out back. Does it work?"

"Most days, yes. But there's a tap and pail out by the back door. I'll get it for you."

Joshua rose to follow her around the verandah and

down the steps at the side of the house. His hand covered hers as they both reached for the pail at the same time. The heat that rose from her skin seared its way to his heart and he looked up to see her eyes just inches away.

She couldn't hide the shock she'd experienced at the touch of his hand over hers. It sent a shiver down her spine and a warmth spread from somewhere deep inside to flush her tanned cheeks.

Kiera pulled her hand from his and stepped back quickly, stammering "the tap's right there."

Laughter reached his eyes and her ears simultaneously. "Why is it that whenever we touch, I feel this charge of energy rush up my arm? You can't deny you feel it too. I can see it in your eyes. I want to know more about you, Kiera. Let me get this water for Nightsong and then we are going to talk about why this is."

"You have a vivid imagination," she stammered. Attempting to still her racing heart and mask her emotions, Kiera turned back up the stairs and allowed him to draw water for his horse, all the while thinking to herself "this can't be happening! What's going on? Am I dreaming this?"

He filled the pail with water and walked around the verandah to the front of the cabin, placing it on the ground in front of Nightsong. Before taking a drink, the horse nuzzled Joshua's shoulder and murmured his appreciation.

Kiera shook her head in astonishment. As they both sat again, she said "I've never seen anything like that. How long did it take for you to train him to do that?"

"Oh, it's more like *he* trained *me!* Animals are very intuitive. We just have to be open to listening for what they say. Didn't you spend any time on the Rez or with your family as a kid?"

"No. My father worked on the pipeline. After he died, my mother and I stayed in Calgary. She didn't think she'd be welcome among the people on the reservation after being married to a white man. Feeling lost without my father, she found the bottom of the bottle more appealing than living. She died not long afterwards. That's when my grandmother took me in. I'm grateful to her. She gave up a lot to ensure I could get an education.

"I did learn a lot from her, but I didn't really pay much heed to how she'd learned what she knew. She didn't share a lot of the stories her family handed down, what with having gone to a residential school and all. She hasn't talked much about the old ways, until just recently."

"I'm sorry to hear that Kiera. I have a similar story. There's only my sister and I left. She married and then her husband left her. Her nursing job helps her out a lot. I do the best I can with the old farm I bought after studying animal husbandry at school.

"But I am coming to believe that we've been introduced for a reason. Something bigger than both of us has something in mind for us to work on together. Do you trust your intuitions?"

"I usually have good sense enough to know when to take my umbrella with me. Beyond that, my art is pretty intuitive. Why do you ask?"

"I prefer the company of animals but I think you're someone very special and that you're being led to create art that speaks to people. This painting will incite people to question if there is more to what they see. It will make them think about Mother Earth; about the creative process and their role in the creative process. I think we are to work together on this because of what I've seen and heard in the past few days."

His manner became quite intense and it made Kiera more curious about this striking young man. It took a while to get him to open up to it but finally, Joshua shared the story of Eagle Man. He finished with the message he had received that two women would help him develop the skills he needed to fulfill his destiny as Walks Through Time.

CHAPTER 9

A GIFT FEATHER

Kiera offered to make dinner if Joshua would stay. They continued to talk long after they finished eating. "There's something about his eyes" Kiera thought to herself. "They just draw you right in. It's like sailing on a river of cool water – right into his soul. He's so sincere in his passion to fulfill the destiny that Eagle Man saw for him. He trusts in the reality of his experience, and how is his vision any different from what I've been seeing? The Temple initiation certainly felt real to me!

"His voice has a melody that is at once deep and rich, yet powerful like a strong heartbeat. Just before he pauses to take a steadying breath, his voice gets this little catch in it, as if he can barely contain his emotions. And I can *feel* the roller-coaster of emotions he's going through in the telling of it. It's the same euphoria I felt while dancing in the Temple and so full of the wonder of how this is all possible.

"I so want to jump in and tell him everything I've seen too. But I have a deep sense that it is not time for my story yet. I'm not sure how I know this, but I think I am just meant to listen and wait. My story will be told some other time.

"So here I am listening… or trying to. I can feel this energy pulsing gently back and forth between us. Its ebb and flow seem to draw him closer too… he's on the edge of his seat. And why is everything so quiet? Are even the birds listening to him? My skin is tingling with the expectant presence charging the air! I could see the torment in his eyes earlier as he relayed the message of Mother Earth and our Turtle Island home." Kiera suddenly sat further back in the chair, knocking it against the window sill, startling both of them.

Joshua suddenly became aware that Kiera was deep in thought. "What's wrong?"

"I don't know quite what to say. You have just confirmed what I've been hearing the past few days. I thought it was a series of paintings that I was being prompted so strongly to do but now I'm thinking that maybe there is more to this than I first thought."

"Eagle Man said I would know when I met the people who are to help me. I believe we were supposed to meet. I think your grandmother is the Elder who will be guiding us."

"Grandmother has been doing a lot of watching and is waiting very impatiently for something I believe she thinks is going to happen very soon. Some of the things she's said lately have made me shake my head. I just find it really weird that she can know so much about our indigenous culture, despite the fact that she was taken away to a residential school as a child. She didn't spend a lot of time living on the Rez when she came home. She feels much more comfortable with the people at Church. Her faith is her life."

"Still, Eagle Man felt very strongly that she will know how to help. Maybe she is an intuitive. You know, *connected* to Mother Earth?"

"I often wonder if someone isn't whispering in her ear to tell her what I've been up to. It wouldn't surprise me."

The two continued to talk easily about life on the edge of the Rocky Mountains, enjoying the company and getting to know one another for several hours.

As the sky deepened toward dusk, Joshua and Nightsong left Kiera standing on the verandah, the paints long ago stowed away and the dirty dinner dishes piled up in the kitchen sink.

He almost didn't want to leave, but knew in his heart that this was just the beginning. He'd wanted so badly to pull her into his embrace and kiss those sensuous lips. He wondered though, if he could risk getting shut out of her life. She had seemed so nervous when he said good-bye, almost afraid of him. So, he swung his leg over the horse's back and turned to go. As Nightsong cantered into the woods, Joshua looked back over his shoulder and waved once more.

He had been surprised by her invitation to stay for

dinner. It had been so easy to share his experience on the ridge with her. It felt *right* somehow. His heart was full and he felt hopeful – for what, he wasn't sure, but it was a feeling that spread from his heart throughout his body and seemed to envelope Nightsong as well. The mustang appeared to dance through the woods and up to the top of the ridge toward home, the distance seeming to be negligible.

It had taken a good deal of time to share his story about Eagle Man, Chief Rain Dancer, and the rest of the clan. She was the only person he had told. He wasn't really sure anyone else would even believe that he had been able to walk through a wrinkle in time. It was pretty incredible when he thought about it himself.

Having told Kiera about his experience, Joshua felt a weight lift from his heart. Sharing it felt right and she listened with such an intensity that he knew she believed him. He grew up believing that anything was possible, but even he had never expected this kind of thing to happen. But she had believed him! A warm, slow grin spread across his face and his eyes, filling him with bright hope that he had found the people he was told could help him achieve his purpose – or at least one of them.

The two returned to the farm in record time and having made a mental note of the direction and landmarks that would become a well-worn path in the days and weeks to come, Joshua directed Nightsong to the barn. He leapt down from his back, grabbed a bucket and filled it with feed, along with a fresh bale of alfalfa, on his way to

Nightsong's stall. His friend was waiting, having already slaked his thirst at the trough.

"You've earned your dinner today, for sure Nightsong! I want to thank you for your part in introducing me to Kiera. You knew before we saw her at the spring in the forest, didn't you? I am so grateful, so incredibly grateful."

Joshua proceeded to give the mustang a rub-down while the horse ate. When he was finished, a carrot appeared before the horse's muzzle. Nightsong turned to nip at Joshua's shoulder and graciously accepted the carrot.

"Time to check on the rest of the horses. Sweet dreams, my friend." Joshua really didn't need to check on them since his foreman, Tom, would have already made sure the horses were all bedded down. He made the rounds anyway. It was his habit and fulfilled his responsibility to the herd.

After closing the barn door for the night, he noticed something fluttering in the light breeze on the ground by the corner of the building that hadn't been there earlier in the day. Moving toward it, he realized that it was a feather – but not just any feather… it was an eagle feather! Joshua looked up to where the stars had begun to appear in the night sky and glimpsed the eagle soar overhead. It circled above him and then flew off toward the trees at the far side of the paddock, toward Kiera's place.

"Well, thank you! Yes, you have been instrumental in our meeting too, haven't you? I am so grateful. And thanks for the feather! I guess this means I'm on the right path and that Eagle Man is happy that I met Kiera. Thank you."

Thinking he was one of the luckiest men alive, Joshua walked to the house full of awe and wonder at the immensity of the Universe's wisdom. He tucked the feather into the frame over the door once inside, and whispered, "Thank you" once again.

CHAPTER 10

CREATION'S SEED

Kiera could barely sleep. She tossed and turned, anticipation and excitement playing havoc in her stomach. After managing to sleep fitfully, she found herself lying awake very early in the morning, her thoughts filled with her encounter with Joshua. She had been mesmerized by the way his laughter lit up his eyes and how they seemed to go so pale and thoughtful when he spoke of his experience with the Medicine Man in the valley.

She was a bit more than confused about the strange tingling she felt, as though her body received an electric surge whenever they touched. It was very disconcerting. Kiera had not planned on feeling this kind of attraction to a man – any man – at this point in time. It was important that she establish herself as an artist and pay down some of her school debts before getting involved with anyone.

"Isn't it too soon to feel such a strong attraction? How do I know it's real?" she asked herself. "This is just crazy! I am not going to get any more sleep so I may as well get up and start working on another piece for the show."

The pre-dawn light cast a rosy glow over the eastern sky as Kiera stumbled to the kitchen to brew a pot of coffee. "I might need an extra cup or two this morning," she thought wistfully to herself.

Filling her kettle at the sink, Kiera glanced out the window just in time to witness a small fox slink out from the path in the woods and enter the garden. It suddenly pounced on something she couldn't see amidst the greenery. Moments later, the fox emerged from the garden with a rodent dangling from its mouth and darted back into the woods. Kiera marvelled at the efficiency and stealth of the sly little fox, so dainty on its feet.

As she continued to watch the dawn awaken life on the edge of the forest, another image grew in her mind – a story of creation and the part we play as co-creators of our own little universe.

Kiera pulled a sweater over her tank top and tugged it down past the waist of the peasant style skirt she had chosen from her closet. Equipped with paints, brushes, and canvas, she headed to the front verandah to set up the easel.

A thermos of coffee beside her and the song of birds in the trees, broad strokes of colour were splashed across the canvas. A base of midnight blue covered the top two-thirds of the canvas where it met crystal clear mountain blue water. On one side of the canvas Kiera started to draw the profile of an old man's face. The old man's mouth was puckered up, as if he were exhaling a very deep breath. In the water was a very large turtle, built up with wadding to add texture and dimension. Standing on the turtle was a woman tossing a stone into the water.

On the stone was a seed, fashioned from a mixture of paint, bits of grass taken from the edge of the forest, and gesso. It seemed to glow from within while fingers of a violet flame embraced it with tenderness. The seed was cracked open and rays of pure gold light shot forth carried by dandelion fluff. Two small shoots extended from the core of the seed, reaching for the heaven above. Each leaf had begun to unfurl itself from the centre of the seed, revealing a heart shape. One leaf was cadmium yellow and the other was a royal purple. Within each heart, identical flames glowed with warmth but were painted with opposing colours: the flame on the yellow leaf was violet and the flame on the purple leaf was yellow.

Kiera placed her brush in the jar of turpentine and stood back to examine the effect. The impact of the image and its three-dimensional effect was simple and yet stunning. It wasn't anything like what she'd had in mind when she began to paint so early this morning. Not dissatisfied with the results at all, she headed into the house in search of food.

A tuna sandwich in hand, Kiera emerged to look again at the painting on the easel. Puzzling over the significance of the flames on the twin heart-shaped leaves, Sasha's reference to the duality of life sprang forward in her mind. "There are so many dualities in life though," she thought. "Does he mean the duality of the sexes, night and day, right and wrong, or what? And why does it seem that there are two possible stories here, one being the original indigenous creation story and the other being the creation of life from a seed? The two leaves seem the same and yet, one is painted a different colour than the other – the opposite colour on the colour wheel!"

The old man and the woman on the turtle were parts of the creation story told by the Siksika, a branch of the Blackfoot tribe of Alberta. She'd read a book that said the Blackfoot people envisioned the Sun as the creator of the Earth. There were many variations on the story, though they all had a similar theme. They gave the Sun the personification of an old man, though he really was genderless, and called him Napi. The way the story went, Old Man lay on a log in the water with four animals – an otter, a beaver, a muskrat and a turtle. Each took their turn going down to the bottom of the water in search of dirt or signs of land. The otter, beaver and the muskrat all died, having found nothing. The turtle died also, but not before returning to the floating log with mud in his mouth. Old Man took the mud, dried it in the sun and then tossed it on the back of the turtle. Sky woman looked down from the heavens and rained upon the mud causing the land to grow from it.

"Is there a deeper meaning here? Is the seed, the seed of man, his offspring, a creation born of love in concert with the Creator? They say that a part of Old Man lives in everything he created, including people, plants, and animals. If so, then is the flame a representation of the spark of Creator within the newly created form? Are these two leaves twins?"

So many questions rose in Kiera's mind.

A brilliant flash of light brightened the sky and Kiera stepped off the verandah to look up at the sun overhead. It shimmered and seemed to vibrate so much closer to earth than she'd ever noticed before. Usually it was the moon that seem to loom close enough to touch, but not the sun. It was now a brilliant fiery ball in the sky that seemed to have flaming fingers reaching out from all sides at once. The sky was brighter than it normally was, even for a sunny July day.

It was hard to look at its brilliance, so Kiera tried not to look directly at the sun, for fear of injury to her eyes. It was so beautiful and hard not to want to watch such a unique solar display.

In a week when so many exciting and meaningful things were happening, she had to wonder what this meant. It felt as if these solar flares were holding some great import for her specifically, but what?

***

The morning was half gone, and the day was warm and bright by the time Joshua finished the barn chores. He'd finished the plans for the shelter in the back pasture and supplies had been delivered earlier that morning. His lead hand, Tom, had helped transfer the load of wood to his pickup and then they headed out to where they would erect the structure. Tom and another of the ranch hands had levelled the ground the previous day, setting out stakes to mark the base.

When they pulled in alongside the cleared ground, Tom jumped out of the passenger's seat and headed for the back of the truck bed. Joshua reached for his work gloves, tucked down behind the driver's seat, and joined him. Tom was handing down the wheelbarrow when the sky brightened with an unusual intensity. They both looked up to see the sun shimmering and undulating above them. Joshua was still wearing his sunglasses and noticed what seemed like bright flares of light extending from the edges of the sun.

"Must be some powerful solar flares" remarked Tom. "You can't usually see them this easily."

"No, I don't think I've ever noticed them, though I've heard they happen with some regularity," Joshua replied.

"There are some old legends that would have us believe that Old Man Sun was responsible for creating the earth. Maybe he is trying to create something new or repair some of the damage we've done to the earth by sending flares of solar energy."

Joshua stopped pulling the 4x4 wood posts from the truck bed and thought for a moment before replying. "Anything is possible. I suppose that the earth needs all the help she can get and if the sun wants to send more energy to her, maybe we should be grateful." Tom went back to work unloading and moved the shovel and several posts over to the cleared base.

Joshua's eyes watered as he leaned back to gaze at the sun and its radiant brilliance. He took a deep breath into his lungs and held it for a moment before letting it go slowly into the air again. There was no wind to carry it away and the heat of the sun's intensity grew. Joshua closed his eyes and sent off a silent greeting to the sun to say, "Thank you for the warmth, the energy and the light by which we work." It just felt like the right thing to do.

He felt the eagle's shadow fall across his face. Looking up, he smiled. The eagle called to him and then, lifting wings as broad as a barn door, disappeared.

"I guess this shelter won't build itself. Tom, I'll dig the holes for the posts if you'll start mixing that Sakrete to fill them. I put a hose down behind the water crate in the truck bed." Joshua then picked up the shovel and turned all his attention to digging.

CHAPTER 11

DANCING LIGHT

Building the horse shelter in the back paddock over the past couple of days had proved to be a very hot, gruelling job. Once the concrete had set around the post holes, Joshua and Tom had measured and cut the braces for the side walls, built a flat shed roof structure and fitted it onto the top of the posts. Filling in the three wall panels went quickly enough and it was only mid-afternoon when they finished the job.

His muscles already ached and there were still the house chores to do before he could get something to eat. He wanted nothing more than a nap right now. Joshua turned on the tap over the all but empty water trough next to the pasture gate. The small shade tree next to it wasn't enough to stop it from evaporating quickly in the day's heat.

Nightsong sidled over and went into his shoulder for

a long nuzzle, knowing that Joshua had been working hard to provide a summer shelter for him and the rest of the small herd on the farm. A carrot was the only reward he would get though. It was too hot for even a short trip into the hills at this time of day.

After the chores were finished, Joshua finally sat down in his favourite chair. He leaned his head back, closed his eyes, and was out like a light. Exhausted, Joshua fell into a deep sleep.

***

"The view from above our Turtle Island is nothing short of breathtaking! The way the rocky peaks reach for the Heavens and the Sky People, kissed by the icy breath of the high winds, with a permanent dusting of snow, even in the midst of summer. I love the way the trees struggle for purchase on crevasses, tilting dangerously over abysses.

"From way up here, I can hear our Mother sigh – her song on the wind carries me so high above to dizzying heights. My sharp vision allows me to see the tiny mole or mouse moving quickly through the fine gorse and brush on the mountainside far below.

"I feel her gently caress the feathers of my wings while I float suspended on her breath. She lifts me up and I soar. On her inhale, I dive down so fast I barely miss tearing my wings on the branches of majestic firs. The freedom I feel is exhilarating!

"I see things differently than you do, Walks Through

Time. I see every living thing as energy undulating up, down and sideways, depending on where it is in the earth's grid. In this form, my vision is so acute that I can identify the different plant species used as medicine by the original people. There are many that have been forgotten, even by our people. You must learn to identify them and remember them again. Their medicine is needed by the people.

"There is a nice patch of sweetgrass down there and see that bush by the knoll of that foothill? It bears white berries in the fall. You call it witch hazel and the whole plant has healing properties. That butterfly weed over there in the ditch has flowers that support a healthy body to fight the spring and early summer colds. And that vine growing up that tree trunk chokes out pain; it's good for the Elders.

"In time, you will learn more, but for now, enjoy the feeling of the wind in your face and listen to the Mother. Learn the sound of her voice so you will know it and be able to listen to her message. She speaks to us in many languages, but you will understand them all if you can recognize her voice.

"Right now she is weary. She has difficulty processing what the people are doing to her water and the way they are stripping the land bare. It hurts her to see her children causing one another so much pain. She is afraid that she will not be able to continue to provide for us much longer. See how she weeps when the monster machines plunder her – the holes they dig fill up with water and mud as she tries to protect her hidden treasures.

"And still she gives the harvest of the field and the fruit of the trees… and the beauty we see all around us. I revel in her embrace upon the wind and pray that our people will answer her call for help.

"If we remember to connect with the Great Creator and draw that energy down into our being, she will lift her energies from the core of Turtle Island to marry the two, providing us with balance. It is this balance of the two, the Father and Mother energies that can help heal us all. The Elders can help you to remember how to achieve this."

***

Joshua woke with a start, his body vibrating like a small drum playing a continuous note repeatedly.

Intuitively aware that something or someone was infusing energy into his being, Joshua took several deep breaths; and held it in his lungs before exhaling or inhaling once again. Lifting his hands to rub the sleep from his eyes, he noticed a soft glow shimmering around his fingers. He watched, entranced as the energy glimmered and danced. The colours seemed to melt together but then a finger of light would burst forth from the tip of a finger that was brighter and clearer than the rest. Mostly they were soft golds, greens, and violet seemingly layered one on top of the other. The outer silhouette exuded its own vibrant layer of colours.

Enthralled with the discovery, he wondered if Kiera had seen anything like it and was surprised when the colour shifted to a brighter golden-green and extended another inch or so from his hands. Its transformation to a brilliant white golden glow extended into his heart and filled his chest as he thought of Kiera.

He had to know what this light was all about – that and the tom-tom drum in his belly. Although, that could have something to do with the fact that he had only eaten a peanut butter sandwich before passing out in the chair. More likely, it had everything to do with riding the wind with the eagle.

Resolved to find some answers, Joshua remembered the words of Eagle Man about the wise Elder who would be a part of his journey. He was determined to call Kiera later on to ask about her grandmother.

Glancing at his watch, he realized it was still early enough to go for a short ride to help settle his mind.

***

Kiera had been reading for some time. The day had become very hot, unusual for the mountain region. The bees had stopped buzzing lazily around the flowers in the garden and even the birds were resting this afternoon.

She had started to read the library book called *Spirit Talk* when she got home from town but hadn't picked it up since then. She had only read a couple of chapters, the first being a synopsis of spirit animals and how they came to be identified. The book had jumped from the table, much as it had done in the library, clattering on the floor several times since then. After lunch, Kiera settled in a chair to read beside the open window. She wondered how much of the heat was due to the solar flares she'd seen the previous day.

The book was a collection of stories about indigenous totem animals, spirit guides, and insights for divining the meaning of their appearances in daily life. An unusual book, Kiera found it interesting because she'd not had a great deal of exposure to her own Blackfoot culture. She knew what her grandmother had taught her about the migration of the Blackfoot tribe from Montana into Alberta sometime before the early 1600s.

This book explained a great deal about walking the spiritual path, from the perspective of being in deep communion with Mother Earth. It demystified the nature of taking a spiritual journey, or vision quest, and explained how to be open to the images and messages that come to us as we seek our truth. Messages come in many forms and may be as simple as a common phrase or as a complicated puzzle to be reasoned.

> *"If we are truly open to receiving the knowledge that we subconsciously seek, our truths can be discerned through spirit animals. The appearance of a specific animal is significant. Each animal portrays aspects of ourselves that may 'ring true' of our own personal characteristics. When certain aspects of the spirit animal are examined, direction may be provided for the seeker. For instance, a fox is thought to be a sly creature, but is*

actually a rather shy creature. Because the fox takes action that appears to be cunning to us humans, it has come to represent how to figure out the best way to get what we need with the least confrontation.

There is a saying that goes, 'When the student is ready, the teacher will appear'. Such is the way with spirit animals and guides. All of a sudden, a certain animal will appear to you. It may take physical or etheric form (meaning that it may not take physical form but rather one of light or spirit energy in the shape of your spirit animal.) When it appears with frequency in your everyday thoughts, your environment or in dreams, its pertinence is increased for the meaning it brings to you."

Intrigued by what she was reading, Kiera decided to read the chapter on snake as a spirit animal.

"The snake has many meanings. The presence of a snake in your dream indicates that it is important to harness your energies."

She then noticed that the snake could represent different things based on its colour. She went straight to the part about white snakes.

"A white snake is the symbol of purity, good feelings, good intentions, and a clean heart.

Dreaming of a white snake may also herald a new beginning in your life. White snakes have a positive meaning in a dream and could refer to the purest side of your soul. Snakes often have been thought to be symbolic of demons, or monsters with magical powers. A symbol of the polarity of Being, the snake is the opposite of Love (the human.) Through spiritual transformation, personal awareness of the connection of all things/ species is heightened. The White Snake's transformation from demon to human in order to experience that most human of all emotions – love – is a meditation on what it means to be human, a meditation that is an inspiration to us all. This spirit animal often appears when a sacred relationship is about to begin.

Another aspect of the white snake spirit animal is the indomitable spirit of the feminine principle, the Goddess of creation, who when invoked, leads the dance of soul ascension. The energy of the white snake rises up from the bowels of the earth to greet the Deity of Creation, as Co-creator. It brings with it the knowledge and understanding of the mysteries of creation and manifestation of spirit into being.

The power of being can only be achieved by marrying both the feminine and masculine aspects of nature in one form of creation. We come to great power by invoking those aspects from nature into our human form through the aid of knowledge gained by listening to the medicine of the white snake."

Stunned at what she was reading, Kiera wondered at the validity of this information and pulled her laptop from the bookshelf beside her chair. She wanted to know if this could be confirmed by any other sources. She typed into the search engine '*how* do spirit animals convey their messages?' A long list of references was displayed on the screen almost immediately. It seemed she was not the first person to have *heard* an animal speak!

Clicking on one of the links, she read:

"In the beginning, Wisdom and knowledge was with the animals, for Tirawa The One Above, did not speak directly to man.

He sent certain animals to tell men that he showed himself through the beasts, and that from them, and from the Stars and the Sun and Moon should man learn ... all things tell of Tirawa...

All things in the world are two. In our minds we are two, good and evil. With our eyes we see two things that are fair and things that are ugly... We have the right hand that strikes and makes for evil, and we have the left hand full of kindness, Bear the heart[10]*. One foot may lead us to an evil way, the other foot may lead us to a good.*

So all things are two, all two."[11]

Kiera marvelled at the synchronicity of this information and her most recent painting coming to life at the same time. Recognizing the deep importance of these words, she returned to read more of the book.

As the heat of the day grew more intense, dark clouds formed above the mountain peaks. A wind was picking at the branches high in the trees. The silence was broken by thunder. The winds raced across the mountain scrub and down into the valleys between, howling as they gained intensity.

The clouds obscured the late day sun as the storm breached the mountain top behind the cabin. The darkness deepened. Thunder rebounded and echoed through the valley as the heavens opened to rain on the parched land below. Lightening flares illuminated the interior of the room.

After a particularly loud boom, Kiera dropped the book from her hands when she jumped, startled by the

---

[10] In indigenous cultures, the Bear signifies courage. In this case, the heart needs courage to make the right choice between evil and kindness.

[11] Letakos Lesa-Eagle, Chief Pawnee, *Native Americans – Legends & Mythology*, Facebook post

crack and tingle of energy that filled the room."That was so close! I wonder if it hit the house."

Peering out the window, she spotted a smouldering trunk across the road from her lane way. Lightning had severed the trunk of a pine, but not dropped it, searing it black from tip to half-way down. The nearest trees were fifteen feet behind it. A bit of scrub grew in the ditch in front of the tree, though not near enough to the burn mark to catch.

"No flame – Good! Though the smoulder may be cause for concern if the rain isn't heavy or long enough."

After gathering matches and candles to set on the table beside her, Kiera settled back into the chair to continue reading. If the hydro went out, she would wait it out for a couple of hours rather than try to get the generator going while the rain was coming down. The storm raged outside the window, as Kiera delved deeper into the discovery of the duality of life for indigenous people.

> *"As our people learned from the beasts of the earth, we discovered that the duality of nature extended to man and all of the world. What we see with our eyes is a direct reflection of our inner soul.*
>
> *If we see beauty and feel joy, the feeling is reflected from within us, or it can help to make us more joyful within our souls. We must give*

thanks for the happiness the beauty brings to us, so that it will continue to live in our hearts.

What we feel inside our hearts and think with our minds will also be reflected in the world around us. Our emotions and our thoughts are very powerful. This is because we were made Co-creators with the Great Creator.

If we allow ourselves to focus on feelings of anger and aggression, we can be sure that destruction of our relationships, our homes, or our land will soon follow. In all things we must give thanks, for the dawn of the day, for waking and sharing in the greatness of this land. It is best to start the day this way. It sets the tone for the rest of the day.

Your feelings of gratitude will bring more gifts throughout the day, for which to be grateful – abundant gifts. If you pay attention and have eyes to see and ears to hear what our home and the animals will say to you.

The animals around us will reflect what we think and how we feel and be drawn to us. They are like the image reflected back to us from the water's surface under a bright sky."

***

Nightsong turned frightened eyes to Joshua, wanting a safe haven from the storm. Through the forest they raced, branches scraping Joshua's arms and thighs. Scanning the area, he realized that the nearest safe place he knew of, was the little cabin belonging to Kiera. Though there was no barn, she had a small lean-to out at the back, where Nightsong would be able to wait out the storm.

How he ended here again, only the spirits knew. Perhaps it was they who guided he and the mustang. For certain, she wouldn't have expected to see him again so soon.

"Thank God! There's a light shining in the window." he told Nightsong. Kiera's little jeep parked in the lane way assured him that she was, in fact, home.

Joshua urged Nightsong to the lean-to where he found a piece of rope hanging on the wall. He fastened it to the post and an eye hook on the opposite wall, providing the illusion of security for the stallion. Joshua removed the bandana from around his neck and shook it open. Then he folded it diagonally and tied the opposite corners to the horse's harness, covering Nightsong's eyes with the fabric. Joshua spoke softly and calmly as he did so. The pail still remained under the outside tap beside the porch steps. He quickly filled it and returned with it to the lean-to. Nightsong nuzzled his neck as the rain fell harder under the darkening sky.

"You'll be safe here. I'll just be inside with Kiera."

Kiera, hearing the tap outside, opened the side door

and peered through the torrential rain. Turning on the outdoor light, she spied Joshua coming from the lean-to.

"What are you doing here? And in this weather? Will Nightsong be okay out there by himself?"

"I tied a piece of rope across the front of the lean-to and covered his eyes. That should make him feel a bit more secure. He'll be fine. He knows I'm not far."

"Come in. I'll get you a towel to dry off," offered Kiera.

No sooner had she returned to hand Joshua the towel, when the lights flickered off and back on again."Maybe I'd better light at least one of these candles. Would you like a coffee or rather something cold?"

He nodded his thanks and mumbled "coffee please" from underneath the towel, now draped over his head.

She lit two pillar candles before moving to the stove and the kettle. "I've been doing some reading about spirit animals today. You know, I wonder whether Nightsong is your spirit animal. What do you think?"

"There may be some truth to that. It's like he reads my mind most days. We have this connection that seems to go much deeper than what most people experience with their animal companions. I know I have learned so much from him in the few years since his birth! It seems like the history of the mountains is in his blood. He is so sensitive to the energy of this area. Quite frankly, I'm amazed that he wanted to go for a run this afternoon. He would have known the storm would come, even though it seemed to come out of nowhere. It came over the ridge so fast, it's almost as if it were conjured for some reason."

"I didn't know it was supposed to rain today, but I

don't really pay attention to the weather reports. They aren't really that accurate. I was so startled by the thunder and then the lightening hit the tree across the road and I must have jumped three feet off my chair."

Laughing, he replied "No doubt! I think I saw the lightening that hit it, but didn't realize how close I was to your place. We really didn't plan to drop in like this. I would have called first had I known. I really appreciate you letting us wait it out." Pausing, Joshua said thoughtfully "It's almost as if we were guided to come here... again. I wasn't paying attention to where we were going. I was just trying to work through some things that have happened that I wanted to talk over with you. You seemed very open the last time we talked; opened to things that are of an 'otherworldly' nature."

"I have had some experiences of my own lately, and have shared only a small part of them with my grandmother. She seems to believe that I am experiencing an awakening to my heritage and beyond, to my personal destiny."

He reached to accept the fresh coffee from Kiera. When Joshua's hand brushed against hers, sparks flew up their arms. "Did you see that? That's what I'm talking about! I had this weird dream and then when I woke up, my hands were radiating this light that moved just like this. It's as if our energies were supposed to 'sync' to ignite a greater power or something."

"If you hadn't had such a good grip on the cup, I would have dropped it."

"Do you suppose it has something to do with the storm?"

"That is really freaky and it's not the first time it's happened, so it can't be the storm. I've read that the animals are aware of energy that flows around everything. I've been seeing something like an aura around plants lately. Maybe it has something to do with that."

Joshua described the light he had seen around his hands earlier in the afternoon in greater detail, as they sat at the small kitchen table. The candle flickered excitedly between them.

"I have this sense that we need to see if we can produce it at will. You know, practice to see if it can be manipulated. Hold your hand up. If I hold mine back here and then we slowly move toward one another's hands, will we see it again? Maybe we can learn to control it somehow."

The storm continued to rage outside, the thunder punctuating the charges of light and energy as their two hands moved in unison. As if charged by the energy of the storm itself, light danced from one hand to the other and back again. A blue aura appeared to form around the two, even when they were separated by several inches, and enveloped them in a haze of energy.

Entranced, their eyes met above blue fingers of light and a deep sense of wonder and appreciation grew between them.

"What is happening? This is so cool but so frightening at the same time. I think we really need to talk with my grandmother. She might be able to explain it."

Thunder rolled off into the eastern distance while Kiera and Joshua kept playing with the energy between them and shared the discoveries they'd both made that day.

CHAPTER 12

SMOKE

Drums sounded out the heartbeat of the Great Mother while a single flute rose upon the air to greet the sun, call to the birds and celebrate freedom in the air. Voices joined the drum, singing songs of gratitude to Apistotoke and Ko'Komiki'somma, rising in unison into the early morning light.

Such a display would not normally have been witness to the dawn, since praise and worship were generally thought to be very personal in nature. A man would rise from his tent and going to the water, wash his face and give thanks to the Creator Apistotoke in absolute silence. His mate would wait until he was finished or stand behind him at some distance to offer her own thanksgivings for the life that the dawn provided.

The clan danced as one, led by a man wrapped in the skin of the elk, face painted brightly with orange and yellow plant stains. Another carried the staff of the eagle, elaborately dressed with feathers and the clan colours. The dance called on the power of the Sun, the Creator and his mate, the Moon, to nourish their children, keep them mindful of the need to honour their Turtle Island home and be respectful of the seven Grandfather teachings.[12]

Drawn to the beadwork worn by an old woman sitting on a log near the outer circle, Mavis felt a gentle pull toward the Elder. Now seated beside her, the mantle of a ceremonial blanket was placed around her shoulders by a younger woman with soft, dark eyes and a single braid that hung to her waist.

Drawing the blanket closer around her, Mavis was fascinated by the ornate beading on the corners of the woollen cloth. On a circular background of deep red seed beads was superimposed a spiral of five rounds of white beads. What looked like a feather was coming out of the spiral, fabricated of long porcupine quills with red beads at each tip of the feather and a grouping of three white beads forming the feather's stem.

The elder woman picked up a large flat dish containing a smouldering ember of cedar. With a single eagle feather she offered smudge to the sky, murmured prayers and turned to fan the smoke over Mavis' hands, face, head, and shoulders.

Though she spoke in the hushed tones of her native

---

[12] The Seven Grandfather Teachings, also called Grandmother Teachings, can be found in many cultures. The basic reference used here is this one: www.southernnetwork.org/site/seven-teachings

Blackfoot tongue, the elder woman's intent was clear to Mavis.

"You must teach the young people our ways and help them remember our Creation story and that of the Sacred Pairing. Former worlds have been destroyed because people had forgotten the Creator. The Great One only asks that the survivors always love their Creator, by whatever name is known to them. They must love themselves, love the Earth, and "sing in harmony from the top of sacred hills" to keep the planet in balance.

"Each clan conducts its sacred ceremonies and demonstrates the capability they possess to bring power of snow, control underground streams, prevent cutting winds and flash floods, ensure germination and reproduction of all forms of life. Every year, the Sky People come to help our people, bringing blessings from the stars, planets, and the realms that lie beyond – including the spirit and dream worlds.

"Through the ages, each clan has identified its own sacred shrines and centers it is responsible for, placed at intervals on the boundary lines of their territories. These connect the energy lines of Turtle Island, like a grid. In some clans, the elders walk the perimeter of their territory or a symbol of it drawn on the earth, a spiral maze made up of seven to nine loops, dedicated to the Earth Mother Goddess. The walk quickens their step, alters their senses, gives them a surge of physical strength, and regenerates their spirit."

Mavis thought to herself that this sounded very

similar to the modern rite of the labyrinth, used by people seeking to go inward in prayer.

"These rituals, along with the seven Grandfather/ Grandmother teachings, ensured that while harmony existed between all who inhabit Turtle Island, the First Nations would enjoy perfect health and long life; communicate with each other and all of creation through telepathy and over long distances; know no shortage of food or energy; keep the weather and seismic forces of the Earth in balance; travel about the world using its magnetic force; know the secrets of nature, and communicate with realms of other worlds.

"An essential ingredient for our ways to function was the willing, positive participation of all of our people everywhere working together as one harmonious consciousness in energizing and being energized by the Mother's web of power on a planetary scale. It is the sensitivity of all creation *to* all creation which is the only path to true progress."

Mavis listened carefully as the Elder continued saying "It all comes down to one simple way of being: We are Co-Creators with Apistotoke, our Father, and the Earth Mother. That being so, we are the creators of our own experience."

***

Mavis realized that she had fallen asleep in the chair reading her Bible, and gave thanks to God for allowing her to waken. She offered thanks for the experience of what seemed a dream and for giving her the directive to share her better understanding of the ways of her people.

The intensity of the morning's heat was only slightly lessened by the shadow of the tall trees on the south side of the yard. A low growl from her belly told her that it was not so hot that she couldn't eat some lunch.

Mavis was washing up her lunch dishes when she heard a car pull up the lane. Looking out the window over the sink, she recognized the driver, dried her hands on a towel, and headed for the door.

"Angela! What a nice surprise! Come on in and I'll make some iced tea."

"Oh Mavis, you know I won't turn down anything cold, especially in this heat! That was quite a storm we had yesterday, wasn't it? It doesn't look like you suffered any damage though, which is good. I heard there was a tree hit by lightening near your granddaughter's place. The power was out in a few places. I hope she's okay."

"I haven't heard anything, so I'm assuming she's fine. I would have heard if she wasn't. What have you got there?"

"I brought some of your favourite lemon squares."

As the two friends settled at the kitchen table with their tea and treats, conversation filled the airy room.

"Mavis, you know that Labyrinth over at Cache Creek? The Church Wardens thought it would be fun to take a day trip over there to walk the Labyrinth and take in some of the area's Native Arts at the Interpretive Centre. Father Steve thought that we could do a brief prayer as a group and walk the Labyrinth. He thinks we may get some insights to help us figure out how we will manage to keep the Church open a few more weeks through the winter, when so few people are here. I wondered if you'd be interested in going with us?

Grinning, she replied "That sounds like a fine idea! I'll get Kiera to come too. She might find some inspiration for the paintings she's doing for the art gallery show. When are we leaving?"

CHAPTER 13

BONES OF COMMUNITY

The morning after the storm, Kiera's concentration was broken by the ringing of the telephone. Startled, she dropped the paintbrush she was holding and was immediately thankful that it wasn't touching the canvas at the time. Looking at the call display, Kiera didn't recognize the number.

"Hello?"

"Hi Kiera. It's Janet Daniels calling. How are you?"

"Fine, thanks Janet. How are you?"

"I hope it's okay that I got your phone number from Tracy, over at the museum. I didn't get it when we met at the Church. Are you free to chat for a few minutes? I can call back later if you aren't."

"Did Tracy ask you to call and tell me it was play time? I was just working on another piece for the show when you called."

Laughing, Janet explained that some of the girls were going out to meet at a local bar for pizza and wings that evening. "Please say you'll come!"

Kiera smiled to herself as she hung up the phone. She had to eat anyway and was grateful that a night out meant she didn't have to cook.

***

Kiera was almost finished painting for the day when the phone rang again. It was her grandmother. "Hi! How are you?"

"Well, I'm grateful that I suffered no damage yesterday afternoon! That was quite an intense storm. But I called because I have some things to tell you, that you'll need to know. It may help you understand a few things about our people. And I have the perfect opportunity for us!"

Mavis Deerfoot could barely contain her delight as she told Kiera of the visit from her Church friend.

"So, you see, you can come and maybe get some inspirations from the Native Art Centre there and we can walk the Labyrinth. Will you come with me? I don't know how many other people will be going, but Angela did say that we could car pool if we wanted to do that."

"Gran, of course I'll go. Um, do you mind if I invite a friend? We could go together in my car."

"You don't think your friend will mind spending time in a car with an old woman for company?"

"Oh, I don't think that will be a problem." Kiera replied, grinning to herself. This was just the opportunity that she and Joshua were after – a chance to talk with her grandmother. If they were lucky, no one else would ride with them and they could ask her about all the things they were both experiencing. They talked for a bit longer about the storm, the damage caused by the lightening, and the art show pieces that Kiera had finished.

***

When she hung up, Mavis Deerfoot suspected that a special friend had entered her granddaughter's life. She also knew, felt compelled, to make the opportunity to speak with her about this morning's vision. It was time to pass on what she knew of her clan, their culture and how it connected with the Christian faith instilled in her as a child. It was time to tell the stories of her people.

"Well, I guess I need to go outside and gather the things I might need to help tell all these stories," Mavis decided.

The heat was not quite as oppressive as it had been before the storm. For that Mavis was grateful. Taking a gathering basket from the steps of the small verandah, she moved toward a small herb bed at the edge of the trees where a stand of sweetgrass poked a bit higher than the native paintbrush flowers in front.

Mavis offered a prayer of thanks for the medicine of the herbs and told the Creator and Mother Earth the purpose of today's harvest. Mavis chose 22 long, slender leaves of the sweetgrass; 21 to weave together and one with which to tie the bundle at top and bottom. Next, she trimmed some fresh growth of the cedar and a handful of the fragrant white sage branches.

She gave thanks for the abundance of gifts from her small garden as she wandered to a chair on the verandah, where she intended to make smudge sticks and weave the grasses together into a braid. She had to remember to explain the need for the specific number of blades to use for each braid.

***

As Keira parked the car, she could hear the music blasting from outdoor speakers. Tables were already full at the patio next to the curb. Lights twinkled on strings hung above the wrought-iron gate of the establishment. She heard a shout above the din as a hand waved her over to the farthest table.

"Hey, it's so great to see you! I'm glad you decided to come out with us!" exclaimed Janet. "We thought it would be nice to eat outside tonight."

"Kiera! I'm glad you decided to take some time to be social," Tracy said as she brushed past Janet to envelop Kiera in a big hug.

"It's so nice to get out! I'm grateful for the invite. I can't remember when I last got out with friends! All I can say is that it's more than overdue. I was beginning to forget that there is a whole world out there beyond my easel," Kiera replied laughing. Waving down the table she greeted the other women, "Hi ladies."

Kiera was offered a seat in the middle of the long table, Janet to her right, Sonja on her left, with Tracy and Meadoe across the table. Several other familiar faces filled the table, all offered greetings making Kiera feel welcomed and at ease.

A waitress appeared with menus and a list of drink specials for the night. Chatter settled for a few minutes while consultations over the food selections took precedence. Murmurs of approval were heard around the table as their orders were taken by the waitress.

"How's the painting coming along?" asked Tracy. "I heard you've been busy."

"It's coming. I have eight done now, another started, and an idea for the tenth one percolating. I only hope they are what you're looking for to display in the show." replied Kiera.

"I have faith enough that what you bring for the show will more than exceed what people expect to see."

Sonja piped in, "I have another shipment of paints coming on Monday. I know you were just in last week, but with all the painting you're planning to do, you may need bulk supplies!"

"What kind of images do you paint?" asked someone from down the table.

Meadoe beamed as Tracy explained that Kiera was one the best artists in the area. "Her images come alive when you look at them. I think you'd have to call it 'intuitive' art. They elicit an emotional response from the viewer that's never the same twice when you see one of her paintings. Her style is really something you have to experience because it's beyond words."

"Oh, I wouldn't go that far, Tracy," replied Kiera meekly. "It's really just paintings of nature or whatever's on my mind. I like a lot of colour and use some cultural imagery to tell a story."

Meadoe added that, "the art exhibit showing Kiera's work will be held at the end of the summer and you can check out the exact exhibit dates on the Gallery's website and on the Village WebBoard."

Kiera was more than a bit relieved when the table conversation shifted to the community gossip and took her off the hot seat. Janet leaned toward her saying, "You don't look like you're too sure about this show. I thought you studied for this at college."

"I did but I still don't know if what I'm painting is what people want to buy to display on the walls of their homes. I mean, it would be nice to sell a couple of pieces but I don't know. My work is different somehow and it's almost like they become my children. I pour so much of myself into them. It's like they represent my journey."

"That makes sense to me! Why wouldn't you be attached to something that has monopolized your time and into which you poured your sweat and labour? When I make a bead necklace or a pair of particularly stunning new earrings, it's all I can do to part with them when I take them to the shops to sell. But I get the feeling that there's more joy in looking at your art than you realize. Maybe people just need to experience your perspective.

I've heard your grandmother tell someone that we all have a responsibility to tell our stories."

"She's right, I know. It's just that it seems so personal, what I put on the canvas. I've been sensing a kind of quickening of my work lately and it seems like everything I do, read, or think gets into a painting in some way." Laughing, she added "it's likely because I needed to get out some more and away from myself!"

A conversation from further down the table caught Kiera's attention just then.

"I got here early and when I came in, there was a group of guys over in the other corner that were talking really loudly. I think they'd had a few too many. One of them was bragging about something he found while they were hiking up on the east ridge. One of the guys told a couple of the others that they had taken some bones into the Police Station late this afternoon! He thought they were human."

"Oh, they're likely just animal bones being used to get a permit to set up another dig site. I swear, if they don't stop taking the fossils out of the ground, there won't be any ground left to hold up the mountain!"

Loud guffaws and laughter took over the atmosphere until the woman who started this line of conversation said, "It sounds like they were at a spot somewhere out near Joshua's farm, in a valley over the ridge. They've discovered some really old pottery bits as well."

"This whole area is rich with artifacts, if anyone cares to look for them. It was all Indigenous territory a hundred years ago. There are bound to be pottery pieces and remains from any number of settlements all through these mountains," remarked Sheryl from the far end of the table.

Susan added that "Long before the settlers came out here, it's said there were several tribes that travelled throughout the province at different times of the year to hunt, fish and harvest specific foods that only grew in certain areas. My great-grandmother's ancestors journeyed great distances every year – on foot. They didn't ride horses until many years later when some of the other tribes introduced the concept to them. There's a lot of indigenous history online now. I even found some websites that share their language online so that they can keep their cultures alive."

"That will be kind of dangerous, having people crawling around in the hills behind Joshua's place, wouldn't it? The horses would get so upset. They can sense things before we know somebody's there," Maureen asked Janet. "Can they be stopped? Is it on his property?"

"I don't know, this is the first I've heard of it. I'll have to ask Joshua about it."

"Ask me about what?" Joshua sidled up to the girls' table and stood behind Janet and Kiera.

"What are you doing here? It's girls' night big brother!" Janet declared.

Joshua's eyes skimmed over the low-cut, beaded top and skinny jeans Kiera was wearing and winked at her. She filled him in on the bone discovery as a warm blush rose from her chest to her cheeks.

Janet watched thoughtfully, assessing the sparkle that appeared in her brother's eyes as he hung on Kiera's every word.

"Do you mean along the riverbed that I told you about last week? I wasn't aware that anyone was hiking through there lately. That's where my ancestors used to set up their autumn camp. They harvested wild berries and other plants that grow in that area and fished the river to feed themselves in the winter. I'll have to check with the Forestry and Land Authorities to see if anyone has filed a claim. It backs onto my farm, you're right."

"Maybe we should go on Monday and check it out together, Joshua," Janet remarked. "And if anyone's up there digging around, maybe you shouldn't be out riding without taking Tom with you, just in case."

What shocked Janet even more than news of a possible dig site behind his property was Joshua's apparent new found knowledge of their family history.

CHAPTER 14

VALLEY CAMP

The weekend passed in a blur of colour and canvas. After church and a quick lunch with her grandmother, Kiera promised to make time later in the week for a proper visit. Returning home to create another painting for the gallery show was her priority.

Joshua texted late Sunday evening to confirm he would pick her up at 9:30 on Monday morning, after completing his morning chores. He was right on time.

"Morning! Are you ready to go?"

"I thought Janet wanted to do this with you?"

"She got called in to work – somebody's out sick. I'll have to take her up there another day."

Kiera had been reading on the verandah while she waited. Moving quickly, she dropped the book on a small table just inside the door. As she slung a hobo bag over her shoulder, Kiera asked "Do you mind if we stop at the library when we're done?"

***

Forty minutes later, standing in the Land Registry Office, Kiera and Joshua faced a deeply disturbed agent, who was unable to disclose a great deal of information.

"Yes, the land is actually part of the National Parks Agency. However, being a National Park property and under the auspices of the *National Parks Acts* since 1930, our office is unable to grant nor deny any applications for exhumations or archaeological digging.

"I appreciate your concerns Mr. Marshall. You'll have to go to the Municipal Office to find out how these things are managed. I can't help you, I'm sorry."

At the Municipal Office, the Town's Clerk was only slightly more encouraging. She was at least able to direct them to the Provincial Government offices in Edmonton and provided a telephone number with which to contact them.

She did say, "I can tell you that, yes, bones were discovered in a valley in the vicinity of your property and that I have directed them to the same Authority."

Disappointed and a bit more than frustrated, Joshua and Kiera left the Municipal Office. "We can get coffee at the ranch and call Edmonton from there. Then I'll introduce you to Nightsong's herd."

"Great! I will only be a minute at the library. I have

to return these CDs I borrowed and I want to pick up a guided meditation I saw there the other day."

***

They arrived just as Tom had finished brewing a fresh pot of coffee for himself.

"I was just going to fill my thermos and head on up to the ridge to mend the fence that was damaged in the storm the other day, Joshua. I didn't expect you back quite this early. I figured it might take some time to get the answers you were looking for."

"Well, we ran into a few roadblocks. Tom Stoneman, this is Kiera Clark. Kiera, Tom's the best foreman around, bar none."

"Nice to meet you, Mr. Stoneman."

"Tom, just Tom. Mr. Stoneman is my father and I ain't ready to replace him yet," Tom said with a chuckle.

Joshua poured two cups and brought milk and sugar to the table saying, "We've got to call Edmonton to find out if someone has filed for a permit to conduct a dig in the valley. Seems there's a bit of a pecking order to getting permits."

"Well, I'll leave you to it. Oh, by the way, Nightsong was real stirred up about something this morning. He was angrier than a hornet's nest in the noon sun! I thought you might want to check on him soon as you can. See you later." Clipping the walkie-talkie to his belt, Tom grabbed the thermos and left out the door.

"Nightsong is probably aware that someone was in

that valley this morning. Maybe after we make this call, we should take a ride up there and see who's there and what they're up to."

It was no easy task to reach a real live person with whom to speak at the Provincial Legislature office. As with all government offices, there were many, "Press 1 for English; 2 for French; wait for the next prompt," and go through a list of provincial offices to get to the Clerk who knew whom to contact next.

Finally, they reached Nadine in the Provincial Clerk's office. According to her, research permits are issued pursuant to various pieces of legislation, regulations and policies.

"Archaeological investigations, surveys, or excavations in Alberta must be carried out by a professional archaeologist under a valid permit that has been approved by the Director of the Archaeological Survey. They must have specific qualifications and experience that make them eligible to hold a permit in the first place.

"The Archaeological and Palaeontological Research Permit Regulation sets out the requirements and expectations for individuals applying for a Permit to Excavate Palaeontological Resources.

"Provided the permits comply with SARA, the *Species at Risk Act* requirements, they need to submit written applications and obtain approval from the Archaeological Survey on 112th Street in Edmonton before any site plan can be identified and research conducted."

"Well," said Joshua, "at least the red tape could take them a while before they actually have the rights to begin a formal archaeological dig. I'm grateful for that. Thanks for all your help Nadine."

Kiera nudged his arm and suggested, "You better get a phone number for the Survey place."

"Oh, right, Nadine, do you have a contact number for the Archaeological Survey office please?"

After thanking her profusely for all her help, Joshua breathed a sigh of relief and looked out the kitchen window toward the ridge beyond the paddock. "I hope we can stop them from desecrating what should be sacred ground."

"I wonder if Grandmother knows something about that? I mean, if the land could be termed 'sacred', could a band stop anyone from digging and removing the findings?" wondered Kiera.

"That's a good question. It seems like all you hear in environmental news these days is about First Nations rising against the government and developers against stripping the land they never ceded in the first place. You may be on to something. Your grandmother still has her Band Status?"

"She does. What are you thinking?"

"I'm thinking that maybe if she called the Band Office, she could ask if there were any indigenous claims made to that stretch along the river. Either way, we should probably take a ride up there to see what's happening. You ride?"

"Does a turtle have a shell?"

***

An hour later, Nightsong and Sundance, a young quarter-horse with a golden coat, stopped at the top of the ridge. Overlooking the valley frequented by Eagle Man, Chief Rain Dancer, and their clan, Kiera and Joshua could see that someone had been there very recently and left tell-tale signs.

"Doesn't look like anyone's here now, but perhaps they were here today. Let's take a closer look. There is a path down to the valley floor here that takes us down beside the waterfall."

From beside the riverbed, it was painfully obvious that several people had been wandering over the ancient harvesting site used by the Nakota people. Small red and yellow marker flags were planted all over the ground, staking out where bones or other artifacts had been found.

Disheartened and angry, Kiera and Joshua dismounted, leaving the horses free to drink from the river's clear water.

"Well, now what do we do?" Kiera looked around at all the markers and wondered who would be so bold as to place markers before obtaining permits.

"I brought the camera this time, so we take pictures. Once we have documented the evidence, we gather up all the markers and take them to the Survey Office ourselves. Maybe we should get a few people talking about the dedication of this as sacred Indigenous land. After all, if my ancestors camped here, they also worshipped here. I don't believe bodies were usually buried within a camp's perimeter, but a burial ground won't be far."

Joshua pulled the camera from his backpack and systematically moved across the valley clearing, compiling photographic documentation of the markers left by the intruders. Kiera, meanwhile, pulled a pad and pencil from her hobo bag and drew a detailed diagram of the survey markings, indicating the placement and colour of each marker. Each place where the ground had been physically disturbed by trowels and brushes was also recorded in great detail. Joshua also took photos of the damage caused to plants used for healing that had been identified to him by Eagle Man when he visited Joshua's dream.

Three and a half hours later, Joshua pulled into the driveway at Kiera's little cabin.

Heartbroken by the thought that sacred ground had been disturbed by some glory-seeker, Kiera said, "Thank you for inviting me along today. I will speak with Grandmother about this in the morning. Hopefully she will be able to help."

CHAPTER 15

GRANDMOTHER'S WISDOM

Kiera slept fitfully that night, worried about the implications of the archaeological markings in the valley. After coffee and an energy bar, she grabbed her bag with the drawings made the day before, and headed to her grandmother's house.

"Hi Gran!" Kiera called through the screen door as she reached to open it. "Are you busy?"

"Never too busy for you, Kiera. Come on in. I was reading the Daily Bread – God's Word for today. It's the passage that reads, "Ask and you shall receive."

"Well, that's fitting! I have something to show you and then I need to ask for your help."

As she walked to the table by the window, Kiera pulled the drawings from her bag. She relayed the details of Friday's discovery that someone had surrendered what was believed to be human bones to the Municipal Office.

Kiera then added the details of the previous day's fact-finding mission, phone conversations, and the ride over the ridge behind Joshua's ranch.

"Do you think this might be sacred ground?"

"Anything is possible. You said that this young man knows that his ancestors used this area for a fall harvesting camp? I remember when I was young, the Elders used to say 'When your feet touch the earth it mixes with the souls of our ancestors.'

"Do you know which band they were? I mean, I can call the AFNA[13] office. They'd be the most likely, being the closest, to know anything."

"I think Joshua said his ancestors were Nakota, so that's a great place to start, I guess."

The Grand Cache Native Arts Centre might be a good place to make some inquiries too. I had a feeling that our church road trip would be very important for you."

Kiera smiled broadly as she asked when they'd be going.

"It's this Saturday, remember? I told you last week when we talked about it on the phone and I thought I was the one with memory problems. Huh! Is your young man coming with us or not?"

"Gran! He's not 'my young man!' He's just a friend. And you've already met him – at church a couple of weeks ago."

"That nice young man that was with Janet Daniel's? Oh, I like him. Honey, I'm so glad you took my advice

[13] AFNA: Assembly of First Nations Alberta Association: www.afnab.ca

and have started to spend some time with other young people. I don't like that you're cooped up by yourself over there, smelling all those paint fumes!"

Kiera let out a shocked gasp and rolled her eyes.

"Don't you roll your eyes at me, young lady! You know it's true. Now let's go and make some tea. I harvested from fresh raspberry leaves early this morning. We'll take our tea and sit on the porch. I have something I want to share with you."

Mavis shared her vision of the Shaman's prayers and the importance of the smudge, and when and how to use it.

"Beginning with a prayer to the ancestors is very important. It is because they came from the Sky People, who shared their wisdom through the art of storytelling, that we have this knowledge. So, we must honour them with our thanks. Then we give thanks to the four directions of our world, as each has blessings they bestow upon us. Then we give our most humble thanks to the Creator, God, who loves us enough to provide for all our needs. Then setting our intention is next. This is what sets the energy of Mother Earth and the Universal energy to work for our highest good – harm to none.

The sweetgrass braid is said to be the hair of Mother Earth and the three sections of the braid represent mind, body, and spirit. Once braided, it is stronger than any one strand on its own, which symbolizes community and unity[14]. Some say it represents love, kindness and honesty."

---

[14] More details about this practice can be found at: hwww.wrha.mb.ca/healthinfo/news/2011/111006-sacred-medicine.php

Standing together in the shade, Kiera repeated the prayers Mavis spoke with intention. Carefully, they chose sweetgrass strands, with conscious attention to the number required for each braid, and placed them in a basket. Then they moved to stand in front of the largest cedar tree at the edge of the forest behind the house.

Mavis explained that the *Grandfather* or *Grandmother Cedar* was the largest of the cedars in the immediate area of the house. For this reason, it was necessary to give thanks to this particular tree before choosing the branches of smaller, more compact cedars to use in the smudge sticks.

"Did you know that the reason people decorate their homes with cedar in the winter is because it has medicinal qualities? It clears the air and removes the germs that create disharmony and disease.

"I add some white sage to weave into the cedar as well. There are both female and male sages. We need a balance of these to make the smudge effective for its intended purpose. It gets woven in with the cedar so that they can work together, the way we humans should work together for a common purpose. The Sky People told the Elders that it is the Creator's Will that desires specific elements and species to work together for the good of All."

They moved to two chairs positioned in the shade of a large oak tree, with a small table between them, to work together. On the table were arranged several things: scissors, twine, several narrow strips of leather, a jug of sweetened iced tea, and two tall glasses.

"Do you remember hearing about the seven Grandfather/ Grandmother teachings? We talked about it when you were quite young."

"Vaguely, but I don't remember exactly what they were. Could you refresh my memory please?"

"When we follow the seven sacred teachings of our culture, we honour spiritual law and strengthen our connection to the land. They are represented by seven animals who each offer a special gift and understanding of how our people should live together.

"The Buffalo brings the first lesson – Respect for All Life. The second comes from the Eagle and is Love."

Kiera's eyes opened wide at this revelation, though she turned her head to the sage and cedar on the table to avoid Grandmother reading anything into her response.

"The Bear brings the third lesson which is Courage. Sabe (Bigfoot) brings us Honesty. The Beaver teaches us Wisdom. Humility is taught to us by the Wolf, and the Turtle, of course, brings us the seventh lesson – Truth."

The next hour and a half flew by as several sweetgrass braids and cedar smudge sticks were prepared. Love and intent for the highest good of all was infused into each. Kiera confided that she would place the braids in prominent places around her house and begin to offer thanks more regularly to the Creator, Mother Earth, and all the blessings present in her life.

"May the Great Creator of All, I Am, bless us all," said Mavis as she saw Kiera to her car.

"Amen. I love you Grandmother," said Kiera, as she backed her little car out of the lane.

CHAPTER 16

INVOKING THE ANCESTORS

Thursday morning had begun with a light shower before the sun burned through the clouds, leaving the ground damp and the foliage fresh and green.

Kiera and Joshua dismounted just below the ridge and walked the horses down toward the valley. The ground was just slippery enough to warrant additional care on behalf of the animals.

Watching cautiously for signs of other people in the valley, they made their way alongside the waterfall and onto the valley floor. Releasing simultaneous sighs, they realized that no one had visited the camp since they had removed the survey flags on Monday afternoon.

"We can tether the horses over here, where Nightsong stayed while I visited my ancestors. I don't want them to wander off if they get spooked," said Joshua.

Strong saplings grew close to a patch of green grasses

near the water's edge. Kiera and Joshua surveyed the camp again and tied the horses loosely to one of the saplings. Joshua pointed out where the tents and campfires had been and he decided to take Keira to where Eagle Man revealed his story.

While moving to the area where the campfire had been, Joshua gathered some large stones along the way. With these, he recreated the campfire setting.

"This is pretty much where it was, in a circle of smooth rocks. I think there must be something important about the circle, since they all sat in a circle to share their stories and the tents where in a loose circle, as much as possible around the center of the camp. The women's cook fire was a bit further back, towards that large rock over there."

"Okay" said Kiera. "I've read that the circle is sacred. Life is a circle. It makes sense that people who connect with the energy of life so closely would revere the symbology of the circle."

"So, how do we do this?" asked Joshua.

"Well, I told you that Grandmother and I made sweetgrass braids and smudge sticks the other day. Apparently, there are both male and female sage and we need a balance of both to be most effective for what we want to do. I have a large smudge stick with me, just for this purpose. She told me that we need to say a prayer of thanks to the ancestors, Mother Earth, and to God. Then we smudge to all the directions and ask them to provide protection for this area in the name of your ancestors. I have some sweetgrass that we can leave for the Ancestors too. Maybe we should just set it in the circle?"

"Eagle Man smudged me before he told me the story of my people. But I don't remember what he said while he was doing it. I agree with leaving the sweetgrass here. Why don't we put it in the centre of the stone ring, sort of in honour of the camp fire?"

"That's great! I *googled* smudging yesterday and printed out some directions. They're here in my bag."

"Okay, so let's get this started! I've got a lighter right here. Do you want me to hold the smudge while you read?"

"Actually, it's better to use wooden matches rather than a lighter. I have some here. It would be a good idea for you to hold it while I read though."

A hush fell upon the valley as the birds settled, and even the breeze took a break from rustling the trees.

Joshua wrapped his hand firmly over the leather strip that Mavis Deerfoot had so reverently tied around the base of the cedar and sage bundle. Holding his breath, he carefully held the flaming match under the tip. It sparked, caught, then smouldered as smoke started to curl skyward.

"You'll have to wave the smoke over yourself first and when you're done, then you can repeat the actions to smudge over me, while I read the directions please."

As the sacred smoke spiralled higher, the aroma of cedar and sage enveloped them. Kiera began to read the directions aloud.

"I wash my hands in the sweet smoke so that they may be constructive and reach out to others in a good way."

Holding the smudge stick in one hand, Joshua

gathered the smoke to himself and pulled it over both his hands, repeating Kiera's words.

"I bring the smoke over my head and down my back to lighten my troubles and bring clarity of purpose. I smudge my eyes so that I will see good things in people and learn from them. I smudge my mouth so that I will speak good things to people and learn to choose my words carefully. I smudge my ears so that I will listen carefully to others, learn from what they say and become someone they want to talk to. I bring the smoke towards me to surround my heart so that what has been damaged can heal and what pain is to come will help me to be strong and grow in a good way. I wash my feet in the smoke so that I may walk a path full of purpose, compassion, balance, and kindness. May the smoke wash over me, collect my messages of gratitude and gather my worries. Let them rise up to the Sky World. May my ancestors see that I live with good intentions.[15]"

After having followed the smudge instructions carefully, Joshua stood reverently for a moment and said, "This is exactly the way Eagle Man smudged the first time I was here at the camp. That's crazy that you were able to find almost the same words!"

"I'm glad then, because it means we'll be able to do this the right way. But we're not done yet, because there is more to do after you smudge me too. I feel like it's really important that we both do this in preparation to smudging the camp itself."

---

[15] This ceremony is inspired from information on this website: passthefeather.org/

"Okay, would you like to read it again and I'll do your smudge? Maybe we could eventually learn to do this by memory."

Joshua began to direct the smoke over Kiera as she read through the instructions once more.

Upon completing this step, she said, "Now, keep holding the smudge in your hand and turn your body to the East. Do you know which way that is? I'm all turned around and don't have a compass with me."

"Yes. The sun is to the south and east of us."

"Alright, now we need to say some prayers, giving thanks to the Great Creator for the camp and also to each of the directions. I think we need to ask for their guidance and support to protect this camp as Sacred Ground."

"I think I can do that."

***

He watched. From the cover of thick trees on the other side of the camp, Roger Smythe fumed. His name should be among the famous archaeologists who had made the great discoveries about the history of humanity. And he stood to make a bundle here, if the artifacts he unearthed a week ago were anything to go by. He only had to figure out a way to circumvent the miles of red tape the government had wrapped around his request to begin a dig.

Roger only got angrier as he watched the pair begin some sort of indigenous ceremony. Judging by their hesitation and the fact that the woman was reading from a piece of paper, they had never done this before. It was possible that they would fumble it up. He hoped so.

Smythe realized that these two were probably connected to whomever had removed all the survey flags he and the team had so carefully placed to mark the location of their finds, evidence left behind by one of the many bands of Indians who had lived in this small valley. Hopefully, these two were not representing a larger First Nations band.

"They couldn't be! There would be more of them here right now and they'd be putting up a barricade and calling a lot of attention to this area to keep it 'safe' from us," he thought to himself.

"If they think they are going to keep me from gathering and selling the ancient pieces of pottery and arrowheads that I know are here, they have another thought coming!"

Turning away, he stormed back into the woods, having no regard for being quiet. He didn't really care if they discovered him. He would have to get what he came for another day. He would be prepared.

***

"Do you hear that?"

"Yeah, it sounds like a deer running through the trees a way over there." Joshua stood in the centre of the camp fire circle. "I feel really awkward. I hope that Eagle Man can hear our prayer. I don't like the feeling that we're being watched."

"It may be time to be seen for who we really are, Joshua," replied Kiera.

Joshua took a deep breath as he nodded and then closed his eyes to concentrate. "I give thanks to the ancestors who have guided us here and shared their story with me. I honour their wisdom and ask they continue to guide us to protect this land as they would have us do."

Joshua felt the spirit of Eagle Man beside him, as he repeated the words that rose to his consciousness. "I give thanks to the East[16], where Creator breathed life into my spirit, allowing me to enter the physical world here on Turtle Island. I am so grateful for this gift! Thank you for the world, for the life-giving Earth. I seek your help in guarding these gifts so that they may continue to feed my story here.

"Turning to the South, I give thanks for the thriving energy of Nature and the nurturing I receive that continues to feed my spirit. I am so grateful for the ancestors who have come to direct me in my soul's search for a path that will serve me well. I give thanks for clarity and the vitality of life which allows me to grow and serve a higher purpose."

Making another quarter turn in the centre of the rock circle, Joshua lifted the smoke again, giving thanks to the Western direction. "I give thanks to the West for the end of cycles – the end of the day, of tasks and challenges, and of life. In the light of death, I can accept that constant change

[16] This ceremony was inspired on information from the following websites: www.passthefeather.org; www.stjo.org/native-american-culture/native-american-beliefs/; www.fourdirectionsteachings.com

is here with me. I give thanks for this autumn harvest camp because it means that my people sought the West at the end of summer, to reflect on life and give thanks for the harvest that would feed them in winter months.

"I come to face the restful North, to contemplate the value of this space to our people and to the teachings of the Mother Earth and Father Sky. I recognize the Wisdom of our Elders and appreciate my life and ancestors. I give thanks for the rest I find in the North, for the winds that bring the Wisdom necessary to hear the stories of my people and to see meaning in them for what I need to do." Lifting the smudge stick again, he said "I seek to share the ancestors' wisdom to protect this space as sacred. I am so grateful that they have shared it with me. Thank you. I am so grateful. Thank you."

Closing his eyes and turning toward the sun again, Joshua lowered the smudge; crossing his arms over his chest, he bowed his head in reverence. Drawing in a deep breath, he lifted his head and expelled the air from his lungs toward the sky.

Opening his eyes, Joshua was met with Kiera's tear-filled gaze. Admiration and wonderment were written all over her face.

"That was beautiful! I have goosebumps! This can't fail to be successful!"

The creatures of the forest had been notably silent throughout the ceremony of smudging. Suddenly, the eagle's shadow fell over Joshua and held still for several seconds, then began a long slow spiral over the camp, stirring the air with his majestic wings.

Squirrels, rabbits and a deer crept closer to the edges of the woods, ever watchful. A single songbird began to trill, softly, gradually strengthening its song as the eagle's spiral dance grew wider.

A soft glow appeared at Kiera's left side. "Sasha, somehow your appearance doesn't surprise me. Thank you for your support!"

"It isss my honour, Kiera."

"I think we need to follow the flight of the eagle!" said Joshua. "Walk with me, but on the other side of the circle. Maybe you need to walk in the opposite direction. Don't ask me why, but I feel like this is what we have to do to 'set' the energy."

"No problem. Mine is not to ask why."

They moved in concentric circles around one another, each circle growing wider. Joshua walked clockwise around the camp fire as Sasha slithered counter-clockwise about four feet away from him. Eagle Man soared overhead clockwise at a distance wider than Sasha. Kiera stepped out around the shadow cast by Eagle Man, moving counter-clockwise, thus forming a multidimensional energy spiral.

Energy, palpable and indisputable, vibrated around their bodies, surging upward from the earth's core, through their feet, to fountain from the crowns of their heads. As the energy cascaded around them and back to earth, the sun brightened in the south and the moon's craggy face appeared in the northern sky. The spirals of energy hovered just above the treetops, lending the power of their presence to the sacred spiral.

Three times they walked the circle. Then the whole cycle twice more. Three times three. All the while revelling in the brilliant light and freshness of the earth and forest.

Coming to rest where they began, Kiera glanced toward the trees on the opposite side of the camp, to Joshua's right. The tall grasses and low shrubs were swaying gently, though there was no breeze. The colours grew in intensity. An orb of vibrant red appeared to float across the tips of the grass. It was followed by an orange orb, then yellow, green, aquamarine, indigo and violet orbs.

"Joshua, look!" Kiera pointed to the orbs and was filled with such love and gratitude, overflowing with joy. "I'll bet these are the Sky People that Grandmother mentioned! They've come to add their energy and wisdom. This will strengthen the energy we have created to protect this camp."

"Then, this must really be sacred ground," whispered Joshua, respectfully bowing to the orbs of the Sky People until they could no longer be seen. Stepping carefully over the circle of stones, Joshua moved to stand in front of Kiera. Reverently, he bowed is head to her and grasping her hands said, "Thank you. I feel like we have a chance to protect this camp because of you."

Sasha's wink didn't register with Kiera's brain. He disappeared into thin air when Joshua's arms slid around her back, drawing her into a tender embrace. His lips tenderly brushed over her own, igniting a thousand emotions before he drew away.

"I think we've finished what we came to do here. We'd better head back to the house before we start something else."

CHAPTER 17

LAND CLAIMS

The next week passed quickly, filled with everyday life and tasks. Thoughts of the kiss as soft as a feather's touch kept coming back to Kiera's mind and she found it difficult to focus on her painting. She still managed to produce an image in the likeness of the energy that flowed around the Harvest Camp, full of vibrant forest life, rain water, and the orbs of the Sky People.

On Thursday, Kiera and her grand-mother made the trip over to the Band Office to inquire about anyone laying claim to the land behind Joshua's farm.

In the car, along the way, Kiera told Mavis about the Autumn Harvest Camp experience.

"I am so proud of you Kiera. This experience will serve to build and strengthen your ties with Mother Earth and with our Creator. What did your young man think about this experience?"

"Gran, he's not 'my young man'!" exclaimed Kiera, as a warm blush rose from her chest to brighten her cheeks. Thoughts of his kiss rose quickly to mind and her heart raced.

"Time will tell." Grandmother grinned to herself.

Kiera heaved a huge sigh as she made the turn into the parking lot of the Band Office. "Well, we're here. Maybe we can get some answers to our questions this morning."

"Good morning Susan, how is your mother?" inquired Mavis as she approached the reception desk.

"She's doing as well as can be expected Mrs. Deerfoot. She hasn't quite got her strength back after her fall a couple of months ago. But I'll tell her you were asking about her. What can I do for you today?"

"Well, my granddaughter, Kiera, has a couple of questions about some land out our way. It sounds like someone is poking around on grounds that might have been used by another band a few hundred years ago. She's wondering how we could find out if there is an active Indigenous land claim which might be used to protect it from poachers of the archaeological type."

"Unless it's one of your own ancestors, I can't really help much. Do you know which band it might have been?"

Kiera answered, "The Nakota people were said to have used this stretch of land as their autumn harvest camp, according to a friend of mine. Apparently, someone found some bones that might be human out there last week. We recently learned that there is a lot of red tape around getting the permits for a professional dig site, so we hope we can find some more information about any land claims before they can begin to dig it all up."

"It would be real nice if it could be protected," added Mavis.

The encounter took an hour and a half as they asked their questions and waded through handwritten volumes of land claims – those that had been recorded, anyway.

Susan suggested that their next step would be to contact the AFNA office in Edmonton to see if they had more knowledge of the Nakota Land Claims.

When they left, the only other lead Kiera and Mavis had to go on was another telephone number to call and they were a bit disheartened.

"Well, we've done all we can here," exclaimed Mavis. "I'm sure though, that if this is a sacred site, or intended to be recognized as a sacred ancestral space, the Creator will find a way to make it happen. God can see things far ahead of us, of which we can have no knowledge until it comes to pass."

***

Roger sorted through the reams of paper and forms, issued by the government, that were required for obtaining a permit to dig at any site. His biggest hurdle would be that he didn't hold the necessary qualifications as a properly certified archaeologist in the first place. One of his professors had made sure he would never get that recognition! All because he got sloppy and was caught cheating on more than one exam. Then there was that arrowhead that had fallen into his hand from a display unit. They couldn't really prove that it was him who tried to sell it online. He still wasn't sure how they found out about it. Someone close to him back then must have ratted him out, but he wasn't going to worry about that right now.

Coming up with the name of an accredited archaeologist would be easy. There were enough of them around. He just needed to ensure that they wouldn't be available for contacting in the next month or so.

Completing the forms for the dig permits took some time. Double checking who else in the business was where and what their plans entailed for the next month would take a few days, but Roger was resolved to find out what he needed to know.

In the meantime, he would need to gather the team and get back out there to mark the survey again. The surveyor's assistant, Cheryl, had it all on paper, so it shouldn't be too difficult to recreate the grid.

CHAPTER 18

THE DRIVE

Saturday morning came lazily to life with a fine layer of thin cloud rolling in over the mountains to the west. The sun was warm and would burn through the cloud cover within the hour. It promised to be a glorious day for the drive.

A big, black pickup pulled into the lane and up to the side of Mavis's porch. She already had her purse in hand and a sweater over her shoulders as Kiera and Joshua reached the door.

"Good morning Gran!" As she stepped inside, Joshua's shoulders all but filled the doorway behind her.

"Hello Sweetheart. Good morning Joshua. It's so nice of you to offer to drive us today. I hope you have a stepladder with you. I don't know how on earth I'll ever get into that big truck of yours!"

"Morning Ma'am. I don't think it'll be a problem. I

anticipated such a thing and have a step stool in the back."

"Well then, I guess we'd better get to church to meet the others. They thought we should travel together, though I don't know how anyone would get lost. There's only one road I know of to get there" she stated emphatically.

***

A small caravan headed north-west along Hwy 40, comprised of several church ladies, dutiful husbands, and Rev. Steve. Mavis, Kiera and Joshua ended up with no extra passengers, despite the extra seating available in the extended cab.

Conversation flowed around the weather, the amount of rainfall, the number of tourists visiting this month and special activities that the community planned to sustain the industry each year.

Joshua was a bit more than grateful that they were alone in his truck, since he wasn't really comfortable with the whole "church scene". He hadn't been raised in a family that attended any more regularly than Christmas, weddings, and funerals. His sister though... well, she gained strength from the ladies from this particular congregation after she ended up on her own again and had attended church services frequently for the past year or so. He secretly wondered if there was more to this than he had experienced so far.

"Penny for your thoughts, young man. You've been quiet for the past few miles," whispered Mavis.

"Me? Oh, I've just been listening to you and Kiera."

"Are you sure there isn't something you've been wanting to ask me?"

With another hour or so to pass, Joshua sighed and resigned himself to sharing the story of Walks Through Time, with Mavis Deerfoot.

"Well" he began hesitantly, "I don't know how much Kiera has told you about what's been happening lately, but yes, I do have some questions. I know that Kiera mentioned the property that borders the back of my farm which I was told was used by my ancestors. I appreciate that you asked questions about that at your Band Office. I don't have any connections there, and the calls I made have been to government offices about permits. But beyond the land claim issue, there's been some things happening the past few weeks that have me a bit confused.

"I've been wondering if you are the elder that I have been told would help guide me in learning the ways of our ancestors. I know we may have come from different tribal clans, but I don't think our indigenous cultures are that different."

"Well," replied Mavis. "I don't know how much help I'll be. But I feel it's pretty important to share some information that's been shared with me recently. It's time to tell the stories." She reflected to herself for a few minutes and then said, "I'd be honoured to do what I can."

"I've been told I need to strengthen my blood in the

way of my people – the Nakota clan – and I'm not sure what is meant by that… I've also started to have some pretty fantastic experiences."

As he drove, Joshua's story unfolded. With a bit of trepidation, he told of Eagle Man, of being a descendant of Chief Rain Dancer, about meeting the Chief's son Red Feather, and being named Walks Through Time. He described the valley that was his ancestral autumn harvest camp and what it would mean to have the land designated as sacred ground.

After sharing his experience with Eagle Man, Joshua wondered aloud. "What I don't know is *how* I'm supposed to strengthen my blood in the way of my people. And then there's the fact that Kiera and I have started to see what I think is the Earth's energy. It must all sound just a bit like a 'tall tale'."

"I don't think so," said Mavis, very simply.

Joshua concluded by describing the energy he saw and felt around his hands. "Kiera and I were able to recreate the energy and manipulate it a bit the other day, during the storm. Then we both saw different coloured orbs in the long grass at the camp. Kiera called them the Star People. I'm curious if you've ever seen anything like it?" asked Joshua. "I want to thank you, by the way – for providing the smudge and sweetgrass braid for us."

"Well, now, I don't know about seeing anything that clearly with these old eyes," replied Mavis, grinning. "I have heard stories from some of my friends over the last little while. I do know that there's always more energy in the hills and valleys after a good storm like we had. It's like you can taste it in the air. It makes my whole body tingle with anticipation."

Deciding that it was time to admit that she had been experiencing some "quickening" herself, Kiera added, "The energy around our hands was a very bright blue colour that had sparks of yellow-gold in it. It reminded me of the energy I saw in the hot springs after the visions I told you about, Grandmother. And remember, I told you about Sasha, the white serpent? Well, there is a silver cord that connects our hearts when he speaks to me – almost as if it allows him to speak directly into my mind – but I can see the energy of the connection."

Mavis listened intently and nodded when they finished speaking. "I too, have been visited by an elder. It seems I have been tasked with sharing our culture so that it doesn't die with me."

"I have learned so much from you already," replied Kiera. "But I get the feeling that there is so much more. I'm sure that the three of us have been connected with some purpose. There's something we have to do together, something that will make a difference.

"The sadness of Mother Earth is so overwhelming right now that it breaks my heart. I can't help wondering if it has to do with your ancestors' camp, Joshua."

The drive was long and wound around through the mountains to the north and west. As they began to see the road signs approaching Grande Cache, Mavis announced that the group would stop at the Tourism and Interpretive Centre, then get lunch at the Big Horn Dining

Lounge on the main corner coming into town, before going to the Labyrinth.

"I told Angela Pratt and Rev. Steve that we had some questions to ask at the Centre, so they said we could all go there first, since it's on the way into town and on the right side of the road."

Joshua was awestruck as Kiera exclaimed, "Thank you, Grandmother!"

In the Tourism and Interpretive Centre, Joshua and Kiera went directly to the information desk while the rest of the members of their caravan spread out to explore the airy facility. Under a vaulted ceiling were a large tourist information desk, numerous three-dimensional displays of mining techniques and historical documentation, and a large eclectic souvenir shop. The second-floor gallery was suspended above three walls, overlooking the store and displays below.

"May I help you?" asked the desk clerk, looking up from a computer screen.

"Thank you, I hope so. We are wondering how to contact someone in the area between here and Jasper who might know about the migrating history of some the indigenous tribes who lived in Alberta about 300 – 400 years ago" Joshua answered.

"Well, that many years ago is a timeline that only very few would know about. Even then, the history has only been preserved orally. Have you spoken with any of the elders around here?"

Kiera spoke up to add, "My Grandmother, Mavis Deerfoot was separated from her Blackfoot clan when she was sent to a residential school. She lost the connection to her clan elders, so she suggested we come here and ask if there was someone who might have heard some of the stories."

"We are specifically looking for someone who might know about the autumn camp location of the Nakota. There is evidence of them having been in the area and now someone is trying to stake a claim to excavate the site. I think if I can prove that the ground is sacred, then we may be able to prevent the dig. I only want to honour my ancestors and don't think they'd appreciate anyone digging around if this is sacred ground." continued Joshua.

"I can appreciate your sentiments Mr. …?"

"Marshall. I'm Joshua Marshall and this is my friend Kiera Clark. I have a piece of property that backs onto the land in question, a few miles east of the town of Jasper. Is there someone you can think of who might have some history of the area?"

"There may be but I'll have to get some more details and relay your contact information so that you can connect with them. If you'll write your name and phone number down for me, I'll call you tomorrow with what information I find. Since you're from Jasper, I presume you're not staying around here?"

"That's right, we're just going over to the Labyrinth on a church outing today, returning home this afternoon. We really appreciate any help you can provide."

Leaving his cell phone and landline numbers with the

woman, Joshua turned to Kiera. "We should get back to the others."

"Grandmother said they'd be in the Gallery. I'd like to take a quick look myself. I almost think I should come back when I can spend more time here, to examine the different culturally significant pieces. There's probably some techniques that I could pick up to incorporate into my own work."

"Do artists not have a guild or something that they belong to, where they can share these sorts of things?" he asked.

"Many do belong to different guilds. There's one for just about every aspect of artistic expression that you can think of. As for indigenous cultural art or intuitive art, I've not come across any groups yet. Maybe if I knew more local indigenous talent, I might be able to form something." Examining a particularly colourful display of textile art and small paintings, Kiera mused "I should talk to the girls at the Gallery. They may have some more connections I could access."

Mrs. Pratt and Mavis walked around the corner of a partition wall and moved toward Kiera and Joshua.

"Are you ready to go?" inquired Mavis. "Father Steve is gathering the rest of the group back in the parking lot."

"We're all set" replied Kiera.

On the way out to the parking area, Mrs. Pratt admitted that she just loved visiting galleries. "There are so many different forms of artwork on display! I just love the colours and the unique way that some people are able to make their images seem to take on a life of their own, with movement and energy." Turning to Kiera she said "I have yet to see some of your work Kiera. I was so pleased when I heard that you are going to be having an exhibition of your work at our own little gallery in town!"

"Word gets around, doesn't it? Yes, I've got some pieces done for the show but there is lots more to do yet. I do hope you will be able to come and see it."

CHAPTER 19

THE INWARD WAY

The Labyrinth was in a wide-open flat space, marked intentionally with large rocks and stones to guide seekers on an inward journey.

Two other vehicles were already parked in the lot across from the sacred space. A sign read: *Please turn off cell phones and devices in respect of others using this space.*

Assembled as a group a bit apart from the entrance to the Labyrinth, Reverend Steve spoke in hushed tones to explain how to use the sacred geometry to centre the soul and find the voice of God within yourself.

"It's been used as a way of discerning God's Will for us for many, many centuries. Some say that the use of the Labyrinth goes back to even before the time of Christ and was used as a form of divination by seers. The one we see here is based on the same format and style as the one in the Chartres Cathedral in France.

"I have a little bit of information here that I printed out from the internet, to explain the Labyrinth and why we use it. A Dutch fellow by the name of Jelle Spijker Sr. wrote a paper called *The Labyrinth* and his son, who lives in Edmonton, translated it into English. This is briefly what it says:

> *'The meaning of the Labyrinth is symbolic. ... The labyrinth is an ancient symbol. It is unknown when it was drawn for the first time, but in Memphis, Egypt, a 4700-year-old seal was found picturing a labyrinth. The myth of Theseus and Ariadne is the oldest known tale of the labyrinth, but the meaning of the symbol has most likely transformed over the ages. The fascinating aspect is that the symbol appears through different parts of the world in different civilizations ...*
>
> *Jan Amos Comenius wrote* Labyrinth of the World and Paradise of the Heart *in the 17th Century. In it, he uses the labyrinth as a metaphor of the path that needs to be travelled in order to overcome the sins of the world, which in turn will lead to the achievement of divine inspiration."*
>
> *You can see that there are eleven concentric circles which are then divided into four*

quadrants. The centre consists of 6 lobes around a circular heart. The entrance starts in the west and leads to the east.'

"Spijker went on to explain:

'The rosette at the centre of the labyrinth has the appearance of a flower. Its base is formed by a hexagram within a circle. By drawing a circle within the hexagram and drawing 2 bisectors within the 6 triangles, the centres of the 6 circles forming the lobes are found. Together the 6 lobes and circle within the hexagram form the flower-shaped rosette. ...

The Labyrinth consists of 11 concentric circles. The number 11 is the symbol of the inner struggles and sin of humanity.

The 4 quadrants that are connected to each other point to the four seasons, the circle of life or time, in other words.

... The arrival at the centre formed by the rosette brings a series of new symbols and numbers. The rosette is based on Solomon's seal formed by two intersecting equilateral triangles. One pointing up while the other is pointing down. The six sides represent the 6 base metals in alchemy (silver, iron, copper, tin, mercury, and lead) and the circle in the

inner triangle represents the sun, which refers to gold. The downward pointing triangle represents the female principle while the upward pointing triangle represents the male principle. The square and compasses also form a perfect overlay. ...

The hexagram or Solomon's seal creates harmony by forming one symbol out of two interlocking triangles. In the labyrinth, it means that the initiate has found the perfect balance by conjoining the duality of the male and female powers. Mention of this marriage is made by Jesus in the Gospel of Thomas, Legion 22:

"When ye make the two one, and when ye make the inside like unto the outside and outside like unto the inside, and that which is above like unto that which is below, and when ye make the male and the female one and the same, so that the male no longer be male and nor the female, female; [...] then will ye enter into the kingdom." In Legion 11 it becomes clear that life's purpose is to reunite two into one: "When ye come to dwell in the light, what will ye do? On the day when ye were one ye became two. But when ye become two, what will ye do?" The conclusion can be drawn from these two passages that both concepts

were originally one: an ideal concept. The two were fatally torn apart and Jesus directs his apostles to eliminate the polarity between the feminine and the masculine.

The flower-shaped rosette … leads to the place where the initiate's best-kept secret lays, the hidden meaning of life."

"Lastly, he said:

"The labyrinth symbolizes the path we follow during our lives, creating the opportunity to learn more about our hidden struggles and ourselves. This awareness process provides the ability to develop our self into a balanced human being. With every step towards spiritual wholeness, the centre located in the east, a person can return, be reborn to the physical world in the west."[17]

"So, with that information, let us say a prayer together before we go one at a time, into the Labyrinth.

"Father God, we come here today in an effort to come closer to you and discern your Will for us. We welcome the energy of the Divine Trinity incarnate, the Father, the Son, and the Holy Spirit that breathes new life into each of us. We embrace the creativity of the Divine Creator

---

[17] Copied with permission of Jelle Spijker Jr. For more information about labyrinths: sites.ualberta.ca/~cbidwell/SITES/Labyrinth.pdf

and the Mother Earth, the womb of our creation. We embrace the energy of the Christed Way, modelling the new humanity in all its Glory with Grace. We embrace the Holy Spirit, the fire of life which motivates us into action. We ask that you guide each one of us to trust our knowledge of your work within us, around us and through us. Amen.

"Now, if you each want to take turns walking into the labyrinth and wait a minute or two after the person in front of you has begun. There are some benches on the outside where we can sit when you are done. I recommend walking it more than once while we are here."

A reverent quiet settled on the little Church group as one by one, they began their journeys inward.

Kiera took a step to the back of the line behind Mavis. When her grandmother had begun to walk the twisting pathway to the left of the entrance, Kiera stood at the 'doorway' and said a silent prayer of her own.

"I release all energies that do not serve my highest honour nor serve me in any way to be a better person. I Am the Divine Trinity, fulfilling my destiny at this time of spiritual quickening for all humanity."

A distinct tingling crept from the top of her head, over her shoulders and through her body as Kiera walked the path of the labyrinth. The deep sense of awe and awareness set in to still her mind - the kind that only a magnificent mountain view or deep valley canyon can create. A sense of being only a small drop in an ocean grew to behold the sense of at-one-ness with the ocean.

But for her Grandmother in front and Joshua behind her, Kiera's mind was oblivious to the other people sharing the walk, her feet moving of their own volition. It seemed they had walked this path before – together. Through twists and turns they separated and were brought back together again. "To do exactly what though?" asked Kiera.

As the path snaked back and forth through the four quadrants of the labyrinth, Kiera wondered if this was how the great white snake felt as it bellied across the earth. No sooner had this thought left her mind, did Kiera sensed Sasha's energy. It enveloped her as if she was seeing the pathway through a pair of heavily lidded, golden eyes.

"The Creator has given usss each a gift. We are co-creatorsss with the Great Cosssmic Creator, God. Asss sssuch, we each create our exssperiencssesss in this incarnation; what we are here to do and with whom we share thessse exssperiencssesss. It isss a concssept that few can acssept without great difficulty. It comesss with great ressponsssibility and isss therefore shunned by thossse who refussse to take ressponsssibility for themssselvesss.

With the gift, we are able to manifessst with the eassse of intentional thought, taking caution to be cssertain of our desssiresss and that they do not have the capacssity to harm another. Thisss isss intentional living – from the heart – and isss reflective of your Twin Flame – that Divine God ssspark if you wish to call it ssso.

"The Twin Flowers and Twin Flame petals in my paintings!" exclaimed Kiera.

"Yessss" Sasha responded.

***

Having reached the centre of the labyrinth and returned half way to the beginning again, Mavis continued to silently mouth the prayers she learned first at the residential school as a child and continued to recite as an adult and active member of her little mountain Church.

Feeling full with a love of her Creator and a deep inexplicable connection to the land around her, she continued to walk the path of the labyrinth.

Upon completing the maze, Mavis stepped over to be seated on a bench beneath a tree and began to hum very quietly at first, to herself. She heard a voice from deep within her soul. "The tiny flame of love within their souls is growing and will very soon come forth to reflect my love for them in all they do and create. They will birth forth a new humanity. You are to guide them in the ways I set upon my Son and teach them to call upon the Holy Spirit to fill their words and deeds."

Mavis's heart burst open with a great sense of joy. Tentatively she replaced humming the tune to singing the words to that age-old prayer, passed for centuries from one human to another, the prayer that Jesus taught his disciples. By this time, more of her friends had returned and in hushed tones, added their voices to hers, lifting the Lord's Prayer to heaven on wings of song.

Looking out over the members of her small church

group to her grand-daughter and Joshua, Mavis smiled and gave thanks.

***

Joshua didn't quite know what to think about the whole prayer-fullness part of the labyrinth walk, but he understood the need to go within and seek answers to the questions on his mind. As he walked the pathways a few steps behind Kiera, he thought to himself that it felt like being out riding with Nightsong – soothing. He allowed his mind to wander as he gazed lazily at her and her grandmother.

The deliberate pace of her steps in front of him was mesmerizing and so, it wasn't long before he felt, rather than heard, a deep resonance reverberating throughout his bones as he heard the words of the Great Creator. "I hid something from the humans until they were ready for it. It is the realization that they create their own reality. The eagle wanted to take it to the moon but I knew they would go there and find it. The salmon offered to bury it in the bottom of the ocean, but I knew they would go there too. The buffalo said "I will bury it on the Great Plains" but I told him that man would cut into the skin of the earth and find it even there. And then Grandmother, who lives in the breast of Mother Earth and has no physical eyes but sees with spiritual eyes, advised me to put it inside of them. So I hid this gift in their hearts. Your brothers in the south-western plains have known of this gift for a great many generations. The time was not right to share the gift among others until a time when souls became able to recognize their connection to all of creation."

Awestruck, Joshua found himself on the outer rim of the labyrinth facing Kiera, who sat cross-legged on the opposite side of the Labyrinth from him. Her eyes were closed and she seemed to be listening intently to someone he could not see. Joshua realized that just as he was hearing the Creator speak to himself, Kiera would be hearing also.

"What if we do create our own experiences?"

He marvelled at what they could create together, should they choose to work side by side, as his ancestor had predicted. A deep warmth spread throughout him and his heart quickened. Kiera opened her eyes just then and smiled. His heart beat hard and quick, then settled, full in his chest.

CHAPTER 20

JOURNEY OF DISCOVERY

The telephone shrilled through Joshua's farmhouse kitchen. "Hello!"

"Ken Strongbow calling. I hear you're looking to get some information on the Nakota around these parts."

"Mr. Strongbow, thank you for calling. Yes, my property backs onto the eastern ridge of the town of Jasper. I've got reason to believe that the Nakota used this particular area for an autumn camp and last week, I discovered marker flags that indicate that someone is intending to establish a dig on the grounds. Is there any way we can have this land identified and protected from excavation?"

"I wouldn't know for certain without being able to see the site. When are you available? I'd like to see it before I can say for sure. Then we'd have to go through the right channels to make sure it is registered as an historic area."

"I can go with you as soon as you can get here!" Joshua answered.

After providing detailed directions to the farm, Joshua replaced the receiver and uttered a short prayer of thanks.

***

Ken Strongbow was a man of some years, yet limber on his feet as was apparent by the way he stepped down from his pickup truck when he arrived at Joshua's place on Tuesday morning. His jet-black hair was pulled back into a long tail and showed more than a few white streaks.

Joshua emerged from the barn and jogged over to the truck extending his hand in greetings.

"It's good to meet you, Mr. Strongbow."

"Likewise, and it's just Ken. Mr. Strongbow is my father. I got here as quickly as I could. You said this place backs onto your property?"

"Up over that ridge there's a valley on the other side. It's about a twenty-minute ride by horse," Joshua said as he pointed to the west.

"I thought to bring Wind Dancer along because I had a feeling he'd be useful." Ken strode to the back of the horse trailer and opened the ramp to allow a handsome chestnut stallion out into the lane. "I trust his instincts about these things."

A loud snort came from behind Joshua's shoulder. "This is Nightsong. I found him not far from here after his mother died when she foaled him in a meadow up in the hills." Nightsong moved forward to take stock of the newcomer and bobbed his head. Wind Dancer responded with a similar series of snorts and head bobs.

"Okay, well, I guess that means these two are ready to go to work," declared Ken.

As they climbed up the trail toward the ridge, Ken expressed concern that the sites of many of the old camps were not clearly identified until after an excavation had been completed by private groups who sought to profit from the sale of original native artifacts. The camps that were not already registered reservations were often only revealed in stories recited by the elders. Historically, the entire continent had been home to many different native cultures. Evidence was not always easily found, unless you knew where and for what to look. Being almost old enough to be a Nakota elder, Ken knew a few of these stories.

Joshua was naturally curious about the Nakota histories but was a bit reluctant to explain how he had come to identify this particular area as Nakota when Ken said, "My grandfather was the keeper of the pipe in his time. He told me many stories of the clan that roamed this area. Apparently, they told of an old medicine man who spoke of meeting a young tribesman from the future. It is said that he was descended from Chief Rain Dancer. If there hadn't been others who witnessed the visit, no one would have believed him. It sounds a bit far fetched, but I have a feeling about this. I have been dreaming lately that our ancestors have more to tell us. But what do I know?"

The horses seemed to instinctively know the way and travelled quickly up the ridge. They had almost completed the descent beside the waterfall to the valley floor when Joshua was compelled to say, "They called him *Walks Through Time.*"

Ken was thoughtful for a moment before saying "I wondered if the old man was crazy. I guess he wasn't, was he?"

***

Reaching the valley floor, the two men dismounted and tied the horses loosely to a couple of saplings – close enough to the water for the horses to get a drink if they wanted.

"When did you say you were here and removed the survey flags?"

"Last Monday. On Thursday, we were here to smudge the camp and ask for the elders' protection. It doesn't look like anything else has been touched."

"If you called the ancestors, they will have made it very difficult for anyone to come near the camp. It's kind of uncanny how it seems like there is a barrier that surrounds it, making it invisible to people whose intentions are not in line with those of the ancestors. Makes me think that there is something here that was sacred to them. We just have to figure out what that is."

"Well, I'm not sure how we do that."

Reaching into a backpack, Ken drew out two copper L-shaped rods. "These are dowsing rods. I use them to check out the energies of an area, usually to locate water, but they can be used to sluice out a lot of information too."

"I've heard of people using them, but I've never seen them in action. Where do we start?"

"Well, first we have to ask permission from the Creator, recognize the Unseen and the Eternal. Then, we can check the energy of the land by asking the dowsing rods to locate any ley lines around here or the Hartmann grid. I brought some white river stones with me. I'll have you mark the lines when we find them please."

Holding the base of the rods loosely in his hands, Ken softly mouthed a prayer before walking a line from one end of the camp toward the other, parallel to the river. When the rods rotated in his hands to come together in a cross, he stopped and noted the location. "Could you place three stones here, to mark this spot please?" He repeated the process until they reached the far end of what was formerly the horse tethering area. Ken and Joshua covered the area of the camp, moving parallel to the first line walked, leaving a distance of eight feet between each pass over the ground.

Turning 90° from the last line walked, Ken repeated the process, thus creating a visual grid of the camp. With the stone markings in place, they were able to determine the general placement of energy lines that lay over the autumn gathering camp.

"Looks like the centre of the camp fire was where these lines cross," remarked Joshua.

"Doesn't surprise me. The Medicine Man would have used the energy produced by the dancers around the fire to draw on the energies of Turtle Island and the Creator to work his magic. I want to walk around a bit more to see if we missed anything."

Walking the perimeter of the camp, the two men felt drawn to climb above the waterfall. Getting an overview of the valley camp from beside the swiftly running water, Ken stopped just short of the point where the water erupted from between the boulders in the mountainside. Joshua turned to take a photograph of the grid markings, clearly visible from this vantage point.

As they climbed, the trees began to thin out. Approaching the waterfall's source, Ken pointed to an enormous dolomite rock, which appeared to be above and behind the falls. It was elongated and tapered to an almost perfect point, like a spire pointing to the heavens. Directly in front of it was a shelf rock, extending over the water source. He whispered, "I didn't notice this when we went down to the camp earlier. Have you seen this before?"

"No, actually, Nightsong and I usually drop down over there and come to the waterfall about half way down. We haven't come this far south on the ridge before now."

Swiftly, the dowsing rods were asked if the rocks at the top of the waterfall had some significance. The answer was a predictable and resounding "YES." Ken asked if they were part of a sacred space. Again, the answer was "YES."

"We need to get to the edge of the top shelf to see what we have here," he suggested, as he began the final ascent.

As they reached the top of the waterfall, both men were struck with a sense of awe and inspiration. Looking at the rock formation adjacent to the shelf rock, a distinct pattern became obvious. Without moving so close as to lose sight of the circle's perspective, Joshua reached for his camera and began to snap photo after photo of what appeared to be a sacred circle.

Ken spied a recently downed tree and suggested they sit down for a few moments to just, "Watch the energy to see where it moves. You can feel its power when you breathe with the heartbeat of the Mother – of Turtle Island."

Dowsing again also revealed that, indeed, a portal existed on the ridge just above the sacred circle.

Eagle made his presence known with a grand swoop and a loud "Kieerieew".

"I guess we found what the ancestors wanted us to know about. That eagle is pretty excited! How much do you know about medicine wheels?"

Joshua raised his thumb and forefinger to create a symbolic zero. Nodding, Ken began to explain that medicine wheels were only one of the uses of the sacred circle. They were granted greater respect though, since they were created and used by those appointed by the Chief of a clan who would have had a say in determining the right location for it. They were built for the purpose of "looking inward" or to communicate with the spirit world. A medicine wheel was usually located on an energy vortex where it was believed that the veil between the dimensional worlds was thinner, allowing communication with the ancestors and nature spirits. Quite often, a portal was nearby – like the one over the shelf rock – facilitating the use of energies to transmute or change things for the greatest good of the land and the people.

"They're almost a lost art! Don't get me wrong – there are still wheels being used today but usually they are only being worked by one or two people and no one else knows their whereabouts. I would imagine that this is not the only one that has been forgotten. So many of us have lost our heritage – the medicine wheels being an integral part of that heritage."

"So now what do we do? I mean, this has to be an important discovery, right?"

"How about asking your ancestors what they would have us do? It may be that the power of this wheel was awakened when you smudged the camp and asked them to protect it from poachers."

"How do we know it's 'awake'?"

"Well, I think the eagle has probably already told you, but you could start by listening with your heart, instead of your head. This is more about your intuition and your gut feeling. Nature – everything – is alive and has a spirit. The same way that the Earth, Turtle Island, has a heartbeat. When you close your eyes and listen to that pulse, you can begin to distinguish the Earth's energy generator as one frequency and the trees or rocks as another. Go and stand on the eastern side of that rock over there."

Joshua moved to stand beside the large rock Ken had indicated.

"Now close your eyes and ask the ancestors if you can be allowed to witness the energy of this medicine wheel. Raise your arms out in front of you and place the left palm facing down and the right one facing up toward the sky. We receive with our left hand and give with our right one. Close your eyes and 'listen' to the energy with your hands and your heart. Let me know what you feel."

Closing his eyes, Joshua wondered what, if anything, he was supposed to feel. He took a deep breath in and slowly released it. Almost immediately, a deep thrumming sounded in his head and heart at the same time. The hair on his arms stood on end as a tingling sensation slowly worked its way up from Joshua's down-turned palm, up through his arm to his heart and continued on a path across his body and through his upturned palm. As Joshua drew in another breath, deep into his belly, the energy grew to encompass his entire body. The sensation slowly worked its way up from the soles of Joshua's feet, through his legs, up his spine and out through the top of his head. This was nothing like the light energy that flitted between his and Kiera's fingers after the storm!

Joshua found himself standing inside a column of brilliant white-gold light. The energy seemed to swirl both upward and downward at the same time. Finding himself beginning to sway, Joshua staggered. The energy flow stopped where he bent at his waist to regain his balance. Steadying himself with another deep breath, Joshua straightened his spine again and the energy resumed shooting out the top of his head once more. He began to "see" in his mind's eye that he stood in the centre of four separate and distinct but overlapping columns of "living light".

Two of the columns of energy moved downward and inward and the other two columns moved upward and outward. Rainbows of light connected his heart to each column of energy, the colours swirling and dancing like eddies in the rocky river bed below. Brilliant blues, greens and amethyst purples were cut by flashes of blinding white-gold light bursting from a central source immediately behind his eyes. The sound of a drum reverberated loudly within his chest, his pulse quickening to match the drumbeat.

Instinctively, Joshua's hands moved to cover his eyes, though they were closed. The light shimmered before him, taking the suggestion of form.

Eagle Man's voice suddenly echoed through Joshua's mind. "You are safe here. No harm can come to you when you sit or walk in the way of our people."

The ground shifted, tilting to the right before it straightened again. Opening his eyes, Joshua felt rather than saw the life energy of every rock, tree, and creature in a dizzying dance of colours all around him. As he took a deep breath in, the energies of all living things around him were pulled into his heart space. Gently releasing his breath, his own energy blended with those of the leaves, the birds, and the rocks. It seemed to be a dance of give and take, all willing participants of a grander plan.

"This is the energy of the Mother, of Turtle Island, connecting with the Source of All That Is. This is what creates the harmony between our people and the land that provides for us. When your feet touch the Earth, your own energy mixes with the souls of our ancestors who are always singing with us.

"When we use the energy you are witnessing in this moment, with integrity and honour, we become co-creators with the Great Source. The circle acknowledges the manner in which everything in life is connected. It contains the four seasons, the four stages of life, and the four winds. It represents the continuous cycle of life, our relationship with the seen and unseen, the physical and spiritual, birth and death, and the daily sunrise and sunset. The circle is divided into four quadrants, each having its own colour and meanings. The wheel moves in a direction that follows the sun. You might call this clockwise, with the teachings beginning in the eastern yellow quadrant, where you now sit. The colours relate to the teachings of the directions, seasons, elements, animals, plants, heavenly bodies, and the stages of life.

"We have used this Sacred Circle to guide our lives in all ways for many generations. With the wisdom of our chiefs and elders, we have established many medicine wheels across the land as we travelled for food, sacred medicine, and family gatherings. They have been used for health and healing, and as a tool for teaching and learning."

"It feels so surreal – like my imagination is working overtime. How will I be able to know what is real and what isn't?" asked Joshua.

"You have within you all the knowledge you need to do what you came here to do. When you feel doubt, sit here and ask the Creator what you are to do. The answers will come to you as they came to me. This is sacred space. Our connection is made stronger here, within the Sacred Medicine Wheel."

Turning, Joshua's gaze settled on Ken, still sitting on the log. "What's so funny?

"If you could see your face – you look like a child with a new toy!"

Laughing, Joshua replied, "This is amazing!"

"Now you know what it means to be 'connected' with the Creator. It's this connection that the ancestors cultivated."

"Eagle Man is here and has just said the same thing."

"We can learn a great deal by just 'listening' to the energy around us and honouring the source of that energy."

"I guess we have a lot to remember."

"Some of the elders say it can be remembered over many lifetimes of drawing that energy into yourself. I've heard recently that we don't have the luxury of time right now. They say, we are entering a new experience – without the limitation of time and space. I'm not quite sure of what that might mean or look like."

"Maybe that's why we're here and the harvest camp has been awakened. Do you think that finding the medicine wheel is enough to persuade the powers that be to identify this as sacred ground and have it protected from those that would dig it up?"

"Perhaps. We'll have to find out."

Joshua's attention was drawn to a rustling behind

Ken. A snort erupted from Nightsong as he reached the flat area where the men had been exploring the rock shelf and the medicine wheel. Wind Dancer was right behind him.

"Well, I guess that's my cue that it's time to head back home," announced Ken.

"I guess these two got tired of waiting while we were having all the fun!"

Nightsong and Wind Dancer's heads bobbed in agreement.

Together, they turned toward the farm and moved to the top of the ridge. Having reached a point about twenty feet along the highest point of the ridge, Joshua noticed an unusual stone formation stacked in what could have been a cone shape. The large outcropping of boulders and stones of various sizes, was positioned on the side of the ridge, one hundred and fifty feet northeast, and overlooked the medicine wheel. It appeared to have caved on the lower side, revealing several bones.

"I wonder if the bones found at the camp were moved by an animal. Do you suppose they belong together?" asked Joshua. "We'd better take a closer look."

The two men dismounted, thinking it best to leave the horses at the top of the ridge, lest they stumble on the rocks nearer the cairn.

"I don't doubt for a minute that these are bones of your ancestors," replied Ken. "Only someone of great importance to the clan would have been buried so high on the ridge and overlooking the medicine wheel. See these stone beads here?"

"They look like semi-precious stones," replied Joshua.

"These were probably worn by this person as a symbol of their position in the clan. We had better smudge here, to ask for protection for these bones. Perhaps the elders at home can lead us to who may have been buried here."

"I don't have any smudge with me. I'll have to come back with Kiera to do that."

"It's okay. I have a small bunch of sage with me that we can use."

Joshua and Ken took several detailed photos of the cairn, the bones, and nearby landmarks before replacing several stones over the exposed bones. It only took a few minutes to climb the fifty or sixty feet back up to the horses on the ridge. Once at the top, they stopped to take detailed photos of the valley, the cairn, and the medicine wheel from above to facilitate clear identification of the camp area. These would be pivotal evidence in proclaiming the valley as sacred land belonging to the Nakota peoples.

As they looked once more over the valley below, their attention was caught by movement in the trees at the far end. A small group of men and two women dressed in hiking gear, with very large packs on their backs, emerged from between the trees.

Ken motioned silently to Joshua and then moved the horses quickly and carefully up a few feet to stand behind a large outcropping of rock. Joshua zoomed in with the camera's lens on the faces of the people who were now setting up what looked like a makeshift camp with a small collapsible table. They were probably here to set their survey markers again.

"This isn't good! We can't let them dig here. What can we do?" worried Joshua.

"What we can't do is confront them right now. First, we don't have authority and second, they outnumber us. Do you have any service here on your phone?"

Joshua checked, finding that he only had one bar. "The signal's not strong enough to get through to anyone at this spot. Maybe we can get back to the house and call. Looks like they intend to be here for a while."

As Joshua and Ken moved carefully along the ridge, a scream sounded from the valley below. Glancing down between the trees and rocks to the camp, Joshua pointed to the presence of a grizzly who rose to his back feet, at least seven feet tall. As the majority of the group scattered into the trees, one man stood glowering at the bear.

A deep roar vibrated over the ground and broke the stare-down. Roger Smythe had never known he could move so fast! Weaving in and out of the trees, he only hoped that his crew wouldn't leave him behind.

An eagle cried out over head. The grizzly bowed his head to his chest and closed his eyes momentarily, in deference to the great winged one. Dropping to all fours, he returned to the woods in the direction he'd come.

Ken and Joshua just looked at one another and urged the horses back along the path.

***

Tom met them in the yard. After hurried introductions and a brief explanation of their findings and the bear's encounter with what was surely the archaeological team, Tom shook his head.

"You'd better call the Park Rangers to let them know what's happening up there," he said as he led the horses to the small pasture beside the barn to see to their needs. Ken used the phone in the house to call the appropriate authorities in Jasper and in Edmonton.

It took some time to relay the information, but Ken had no difficulty reaching the individuals who could help them. They were given an email address to send the pictures Joshua had taken of the members of the dig crew. Ken was also able to reach someone he knew in Edmonton who listened carefully to the details of what they had found.

Joshua sent a quick text to Kiera to alert her that they had found something important, something that could help save the camp from archaeological poachers.

Getting off the phone, Ken relayed that the government guy suggested they try to figure out how the archaeologists were accessing the camp. They agreed that the hike would not likely be easy and may not even be close to any of the myriad trails established within the Park.

After several more calls to a couple of Band offices and local chiefs, the word would be sure to spread to all those needed to build support among the First Nations in the area. The wheels were set in motion for great change, the extent of which could not yet be known.

"Well," said Ken. "I guess that's about all we can do today. The rest is in the hands of our people and the land authorities. I guess Wind Dancer and I should be getting home."

"I don't know how to repay you, brother. It wouldn't be right if I didn't at least feed you supper before you head out. I've got some steaks in the fridge here that won't take long to cook."

"That would be nice. Thank you. I admit that being out there in the fresh air worked up my appetite. As for thanking me, you don't need to do that. It's me who should be thanking you, for bringing to light our history and for confirming the stories handed down through my family. It is an honour to know you Walks Through Time."

"I have a feeling that this is just the beginning. No doubt, we'll be spending more time together in the coming weeks. And I'm grateful to have met a relative! After our parents died, I thought my sister and I were alone in the world."

Smiling graciously, Ken replied "The elders have taught me that we are never alone. The ancestors and the Sky People are always with us."

CHAPTER 21

RAINBOW DANCER

Brilliant white orbs danced among swirls of colour in a mix of joy and ethereal beauty. Turquoise, buttercup yellow, and pale blues mixed in with mauve and magenta pigments on the canvas. Music emanated from within the movement of brushstrokes and lifted the spirit to soar with Creation into realms of unrealized bliss. Hands reached for the Heavens and hips undulated throughout the dancers' circle.

The music was strong and earthy, yet ethereal and bright. A drum beat pulsed within Kiera's heart as she swayed to and fro, keeping time with the dancers. Voices lifted out of time, praising the mighty Creator with songs of the ancestral Blackfoot peoples.

In a brilliant flash of light, a form emerged from the centre of the swirling mass of dancers, clad in dove-soft white buckskin. The ebony cascade of her hair swept the ground as she lifted her gaze to connect with Kiera's soul, while maintaining the rhythm of the dance.

"Strong young birch stands amid
fallen toothpick pines
And oaks that have lost the will to live.
Raw winds and many storms pass,
Birch bends and bows but does not break.
Roots dig deeper into the Mother
Who supports and watches through all time.
Loving All.
She will survive, though many pass and will not return.
I made a promise to our people.
When the White Buffalo Calf returned,
Great change would come.
Awakening.
The time is Now.
Remember the Mother.
Connect to Her strength through breath.
Allow Her vitality to fill you.
Feel it vibrate into every corner of being.
Drums call us to the dance, the Circle ebbs and flows.
We are the One.
One People.
One Nation.
One bridge between Sky Nation and Mother Earth.
One with the Creator of All.
Walking,
I listen to a deeper way.
Now I see, all my ancestors are behind me.

Be still, they say.
Watch and listen.
You are the result of the love of thousands."

With one graceful movement of her hand, an intricately decorated shawl, with beads of turquoise and red coral, was lifted up in the air, hiding the dancer's eyes… and the song faded back into timelessness.

Breathless, Kiera put down her paintbrush. The canvas exuded life at its fullest expression of ancestral love. And yet, there came a message: "Watch and listen. You are the result of the love of thousands."

She pondered what she was meant to watch and listen. Her heart skipped a beat and began to race as the importance of this message seeped into Kiera's bones.

"I know that I have a lot to learn and Grandmother is so supportive of all I do. I'm so busy trying to get enough paintings done for the show at the gallery, I don't know that I have time to spend on learning anything else right now. Yet, I can't help but think that this has something to do with my ancestry and maybe sharing the culture of these people."

Wondering if Sasha would have an explanation, Kiera saw movement on the plank floor at the far side of the verandah.

"You have only to asssk."

"Hello Sasha."

"Your awakening quickensss in ressponssse to the call of the Creator to fulfill your role in thisss exssperiencsse."

"It's hard to know what it is that I'm supposed to do.

Getting these paintings done seems to be about as much as I can manage in the time I've got right now."

"Yet time exsspandsss for you while you work. In fact, time warpsss, allowing you to work and learn, and to communicate with your ancssessstorsss in waysss that mossst cannot concsseive. In thisss, both you and Joshua have been gifted."

"I don't understand how to make time warp, though."

"Doesss not the clock ssslow down when you wait impatiently for time to passss?"

Chuckling, Kiera replied "of course it does – because we want it to go faster when we're eager for something to happen."

"Ssssuch isss the cassse with excssited engagement – time fliesss when you're having fun! Ssso, when you're focusssed, it can be manipulated to the sssituation sssimply by taking a deep breath and sssetting the intention to the desssired outcome. It could be asss sssimple asss sssaying sssomething like: if thisss isss meant to be, ssso will it be.

"But today you are focusssed not on the time, but rather on watching. The messsage you've recsseived doesss indeed come from one who hasss crosssed time to bring you thisss messsage. However, White Buffalo Calf Woman'sss messsage isss not about the time crosssed at thisss point, though it isss important for you to know that you have the knowledge within yourssself of all exssperiencssesss of all time, should you desssire to accssesss it.

"Her messsage isss about peacsse, love and

sssovereignty. Thessse come from being 'connected' to the Creator of All, becoming One, or At-One with All, rather than being focusssed on the 3-dimensssional exssperiencsse around you.

"Lisssten to the environment, the ssstoriesss it revealsss and recall the lesssonsss of the passst. Through thessse you can interpret what actionsss will need to be initiated to achieve the changesss that are to come. By continuing to engage the Light in your work, you will learn from the passst, the lesssonsss that can help take you into the future with gracsse and knowledge of many thingsss. Don't feel that you have to know it all now. Asss you require information and ssskillsss, they will be shown to you, rather like tapping into a hidden databassse."

"Kind of like having my own internet database in my head."

"Yesss"

"Grandmother has always said I will learn by watching what other people do and how they act. I have learned the importance of having one mouth, two eyes, and two ears!" she said earnestly.

"Mavisss Deerfoot isss one very intelligent lady who isss here now only becaussse she dessiresss to help you when you doubt your own connection to the Creator."

"I am so grateful for everything she has done to help me become who I am and supporting me throughout my life."

"She is grateful for the opportunity to sssee the changesss you will bring that create a placsse of joy and harmony on your Turtle Island. I believe she hasss told you often, that our Brother, Chrissst Jesssusss, sssaid "what I do, you will do alssso and more. For now, I will sssay Namasssté, Kiera."

A feeling of peace and joy filled Kiera's heart as she turned toward the image on the canvas. The colours brightened, lending a shimmering to the energy around the painting.

Kiera took a deep breath into her lungs, closed her eyes and opened herself to the energy of the Creator God Apistotoke. An infusion of warmth and a feeling of fullness consumed her. Kiera expanded her awareness a bit more and floated, content in the knowledge that she was meant to connect in this way with a benevolent Creator. A sense of overwhelming peace settled deep within her.

It was the call of the eagle that pulled Kiera back to focus once again on the painting in front of her.

"Well, I guess we are making progress in more ways than one," she chuckled to herself.

As she packed up her paints and set brushes to soak in a jar of brush cleaner Kiera's phone pinged with a text from Joshua.

"Found evidence – will call tonight."

CHAPTER 22

POSSIBILITIES

Mavis was puttering in her little kitchen garden, musing about the medicine of each of her plants, when she heard wings disturb the air close by her. She closed her eyes and took a deep breath, drawing the calm strength of the mountain on which she stood. Opening her eyes, she turned to the eagle perched on a branch in the fir just ten feet to her right.

In a soft voice, she said "Well, hello there. Aren't you handsome? I guess you're here with a message. What's happening on this mountain that you need the help of an old woman like me?"

The eagle blinked and lifted his head to let loose what sounded to Mavis like a war cry.

"Is that so?" she replied.

The majestic bird leapt from one branch to another, knocking pine cones to the ground with his angry steps.

Swooping to the ground, he lifted one cone and threw it as far as he could toward the house. He then threw another cone and proceeded to spit out a small stone. A second later, he tucked it beneath his wing.

Abruptly, he came to a stop and stared at Mavis, who had been standing open-mouthed watching his antics. He jumped to a spot on the ground only a few feet away and dropped his head as if bowing to her. Reaching beneath his wing, the eagle brought forward the stone and taking two strides toward her, dropped it at her feet and then retreated to a low branch at eye level.

Mavis reached for the stone saying "Well, this is an honour. I've never had a gift from an eagle before. But what have we here? This isn't just any old stone – it's an arrowhead! My, my! Seems this is pretty important to you."

The eagle made a small gravelly noise, deep in his throat.

"I'm not sure what you want me to do, especially since I don't know where this came from but I'm thinking it has something to do with protecting something important to our history."

The eagle stared into Mavis eyes. As the sense of flying swept through her mind, Mavis' stomach flipped and settled quickly. She felt the eagle soar beyond the highway and over lush trees and rocky outcrops. Seeing through his eyes, they followed a high ledge of mountain range. A beautiful valley appeared to follow a meandering river below.

In the valley was a camp of teepees at the centre of

which was a small circle of Indigenous people. A medicine man seemed to be deep in conversation with the Creator and relaying information to a young man who did not look like he was from the same time period. Judging from the appearance of his jeans and denim work shirt, the young man, through the eye of the eagle, distinctly resembled Joshua!

In the next instant, the eagle blinked and the circle of Nakota people was replaced by a small band of men armed with shovels, small knives, trowels and brushes, sifting through several areas of earth beside the same stream. One of the men held up a small item, raising the interest of the others. They rushed toward a tent a few feet away, where a table was littered with similar objects.

In the space of a heartbeat, the valley shifted to an overgrown mass of dying trees and sun-scorched plants. A lonely trickle of water was all that remained of a graceful waterfall. All traces of the autumn harvest camp had been erased.

Mavis felt the eagle's heart fill with sadness and then witnessed its transformation into overwhelming joy as the scene below shifted once more. The valley appeared to be deserted until the eagle turned and glided up the waterfall to a great shelf rock above. There, on the edge of a Sacred Medicine Wheel, stood Joshua triumphantly embracing the energies of this magnificent valley with wide-open arms. She could see what appeared to be ribbons of light and shimmering waves within the air around him. They moved and danced as One.

The eagle's cry brought her back to her body and she became aware of the solid earth beneath her feet. She looked into the face of the eagle again and said "Well, I don't quite know what to say. I guess thanks and extreme gratitude are in order."

The eagle dropped his head in a bow once again, seemingly acknowledging her gratitude.

"I feel so honoured by what we've witnessed together. It seems that you are telling me there are three very different possible outcomes to the current situation. I'll have to discuss these with Kiera and Joshua. I know they are already very concerned about the possibility of someone destroying the camp site of his ancestors.

"It is becoming more apparent that Joshua has been brought to us for a reason. Equally apparent now, is the reason for all of this spiritual awakening going on with the three of us. I know from personal experience that we cannot understand the way we have come to where we are now, if we don't look to what has come before us.

"Eagle, I can't tell you how grateful I am that you chose me to share this journey. Thank you so much!"

The sound of a jeep approaching the house from the road caused them both to look toward the road. Bowing his head to Mavis, the eagle lifted with ease onto the gentle air and disappeared over the trees as Kiera brought her jeep to a halt in the lane.

Mavis and Kiera began to speak at once. "The most amazing thing just happened!"

Laughing together, Mavis said "let's get some

lemonade and then we can share our stories together, one at a time."

"I got a text from Joshua. They've found some evidence!" blurted Kiera.

Knowingly, Mavis just grinned and opened the door for Kiera to pass through.

Comfortably settled in the kitchen with a plate of cookies and fresh lemon balm iced tea, Mavis suggested that prayers of appreciation and sincere gratitude be given in thanks for the day's revelations.

"Creator God, may we be ever mindful of Your Will and have the grace to heed it always. We ask that you would give us the gift of discernment and allow us to clearly see the best way to serve for the highest good of All. We are so grateful for your hand in today's experiences and for Joshua's discovery. We know that there is some action for us to take and trust that you will make it known very soon."

"Amen," declared Kiera.

Mavis chose her words carefully as they sat together enjoying the refreshing lemon balm tea.

"I've had an interesting visitor today. An extraordinary eagle came to see me when I was out in the garden."

"I thought I saw an eagle up over the trees when I parked in the lane!" exclaimed Kiera.

"I can't begin to describe our visit without saying that I have never, in my entire life, experienced anything quite like this! Not even when your grandfather and I used to explore the mountain before your mother was born. He took me on a journey. In my mind's eye it was like looking through the eyes of the eagle himself."

Kiera choked out "Oh my God! That's amazing!" she declared, almost swallowing whole the piece of cookie she had in her mouth.

"I would never have believed it possible. I mean, I know I talk to the trees, the plants and all God's creatures, but never have they 'spoken' in such a way to me." Mavis continued to share the message of the multiple possible outcomes concerning the future of the Autumn Harvest Camp.

"Maybe we should include the camp in our prayers until we find out what more can be done to protect it from becoming another excavation dig," Kiera suggested.

***

Night had fully cloaked the mountain when Joshua called Kiera to ask if they could meet with her grandmother the following day to share what he and Ken had found. It felt good to hear her voice and he wanted nothing more than to share it all right now. Knowing that it would be better to tell them both at the same time, he diverted the conversation to ask about her day.

Kiera shared her grandmother's vision with the eagle and wondered if it could have been a message from Eagle Man.

"Anything is possible. I don't discount it one bit at this point. He did say that the three of us would work together, so… probably."

They talked a bit more before saying goodnight. Kiera could hardly wait to hear about the discoveries that Joshua had made at the camp and perhaps to share another kiss.

CHAPTER 23

STORYTELLING

Kiera pulled into Mavis' driveway just seconds ahead of Joshua. Jumping out of her Jeep, she grinned and exclaimed, "I could hardly sleep last night for all the excitement!"

"I know that feeling really well!" he replied.

"Good morning!" greeted Mavis from the door. "I thought we might have some lunch outside while you tell us your news Joshua. Kiera, could you help me carry some dishes out to the table, please?"

Handing over a grocery bag, Joshua said "I brought some radishes, early peas, and other greens that Tom picked this morning from my garden. I gave them a quick rinse before I left home."

"Well, thank you Joshua! That's very kind of you. We'll just put these in a bowl then. I think I have some dressing there in the refrigerator door."

When everyone was seated, Mavis recited a simple prayer of grace over the food adding "thanks for the Ancestors who are guiding us all at this time. We are so blessed that they have chosen these young people and this old woman to speak for them. Please continue to guide us and show us how we can be of greater service. Thanks be to God."

"Now, will you tell us what happened yesterday?" Kiera asked, as she bounced in her seat.

"It seems kind of like a dream but I'll do my best to remember it all. Ken Strongbow came down from near Cache Creek. He was called by the Native Centre after we were there on Saturday. He brought his horse with him and we rode up to the camp. It didn't look like anything had been disturbed since we did the smudging. And thanks, by the way, Mrs. Deerfoot, for the smudge sticks and sweet grass! Wow! That was quite an experience, doing the smudge of the camp." Turning to Kiera, he said "I hope you told your Grandmother all about that."

After having been assured this was the case, Joshua described the discovery and rebuilding of the cairn of stones. He took care to provide intricate details of the elaborately coloured stone beads. Joshua took a deep breath in and sat forward on his chair as he said, "and then the most amazing thing happened! We saw a group of people come out of the trees on the far side of the camp valley and move to set up what looked like a grid that resembled the survey flags we removed last week. I don't think they even noticed the river rocks we used to mark the ley lines! We moved up higher on the ridge and hid our horses behind some large boulders. I took some photos of the people, as best I could with the zoom lens on the camera. Ken thought it would not be wise to confront them – it would be best to call the Park Ranger's Office from the house.

"I think the ancestors called in some help because before we had gone more than a few steps we saw a grizzly wander into the camp. He stood up and roared! Most of the people ran for the trees, back the way they'd come, leaving everything behind; except for this one guy. He seemed to be the one in charge – and not very smart if you ask me. You don't usually confront a grizzly and get away with it. But he succeeded after realizing the bear was a greater threat than not being able to collect his treasures!

"The eagle flew over the valley at that point and seemed to call to the bear after the last guy headed back through the trees. The bear was on the opposite side of the river, so not terribly close, but I don't doubt for a minute that he wouldn't have hesitated to barrel through the water to take the guy out!

"And then the bear did something I've never seen before. He knelt down and bowed to the eagle, got back on all fours and wandered away!"

Mavis and Kiera listened in awe while Joshua shared his amazement at the level of cooperation between the ancestors and the animal kingdom. Their attention had been so intense that Kiera, Mavis and Joshua had been transported back to the valley camp as Joshua relayed the events of the previous day.

"I hope that fella said some prayers to thank God for sparing his life yesterday afternoon!" Mavis would always see the blessings in any situation.

Mavis, Kiera and Joshua were startled by the sound of wings moving the air between the branches of the cedar trees at the edge of the small garden. The eagle chose that moment to swoop down to perch on a branch close to Joshua's chair. A sound much like an old man's mutterings came forth from the bird before it spat a large jasper bead onto the table to the right of Joshua's plate. Lifting its wings wide, the eagle then moved effortlessly to a larger branch just a bit above them. "Kierrrieeeew!"

"I thought for a moment he was going to hit my head with his wing!" exclaimed Joshua. "Thank you, Eagle Man. I guess we missed one of the beads that should have been put back in the cairn."

Kiera's mouth hung open, having been rendered speechless by the eagle's appearance.

"That's the same one I told you visited me yesterday, Kiera. I am sure of it. That is one determined ancestor!"

Joshua turned to look at the eagle above him and a deep sense of inner strength grew in his heart. "I believe this is just the beginning of some pretty amazing times."

"I don't doubt that at all," Kiera replied.

Turning to look directly at Kiera, and then Mavis, Joshua announced, "By the way, Ken has asked that we not share the actual location and our findings with anyone just yet. The Rangers will send a couple of men to retrieve the stuff left behind by the archaeologist's team. Ken has spoken to a few of the Elders and is trying to get a fix on who may have been buried up there. We don't want people climbing around disturbing the site or trampling the medicine wheel either. The energy is pretty strong but I don't really know much about it yet. I got the impression from Eagle Man that it was used for a number of reasons, but mostly to connect with the Earth Mother, Turtle Island. He did say it was used to control the weather, bringing rain in drought times and flood the valleys to ensure an abundant harvest. Ken says that the portal is wide open between the two worlds, just at the edge of the circle overlooking the falls.

"This bead is a sign that there is some great significance to the person whose bones we found. I expect to hear from Ken in the next couple of days. Apparently, we are related. He has heard stories from the Keeper of the Pipe, who is one of Ken's Elders. They thought that the old Medicine Man was crazy. It was kind of humbling to hear him tell the story he heard as a child from his own grandfather. It didn't take long for him to figure out it was me, after I told him that the young man from the future was named *Walks Through Time*.

"When we found the medicine wheel, Ken asked me to step into the sacred circle and stand beside one of the larger stones to 'sense' the energy. It was so powerful that I got dizzy quite quickly, but then Eagle Man appeared and showed me how to 'see' the energy with my inner vision – connected to the Earth. I have the feeling there is more for us to learn about this and there seems to be some urgency – more than just getting the land designated as *sacred*. It's like we are supposed to use it as a tool to do something. Mrs. Deerfoot, do you have any idea what this means or how we would do that?"

"Oh, I don't know, offhand. But I can ask some questions. There are still a couple of Elders up the road at the reservation that would not hesitate to share what they know of medicine wheels and how to use them. But I think the two of you will need to work together, as in our creation story, one man and one woman working together to do what you are here to do."

"I can't wait to see this medicine wheel, though. I wonder who would have been buried all the way up there. Wouldn't you think there might be some markings on the cairn?" asked Kiera.

"The way the stones had tumbled, if there were markings, they may be difficult to find now. I'm sure that Ken's people would know what to look for though. I will try to remember to mention that when I talk with him again. I feel like I've been introduced to a whole other part of my family. It feels kind of exciting – almost as exciting as meeting Eagle Man and finding the camp!"

"We are all just one big family under our Creator God, Joshua. I'm certain that this is His way of helping us remember that."

"I would like to figure out a way the three of us can go together to the camp to get both of your impressions of the energy and what we might need to do with it. Have you ever been horseback riding Mrs. Deerfoot?"

CHAPTER 24

LEARNING THE BLESSINGS

"Wah-na-gish Nikomanikihso Hano-o-maniquikisoha lo so mahaniiqua."

The words reverberated through Mavis' body. Though she did not understand them, they spoke to her heart with a fervent love for All That Is.

The Elder continued to gaze into the fire, though she didn't appear to see the flames. "All is not what it seems and all that is heard vibrates within the heart in ways that either harm or nurture. The one tongue that speaks with love has more power to heal than many tongues who seek to destroy. You are such a one whose Light is very strong and carries the Light of the Ancients and Spomitpiksi – the Sky People. My greeting comes directly from them in the tongue of their Light language."

Mavis didn't quite know how to respond.

The Elder continued "You need not understand with

your mind. Your heart speaks the Wisdom of those same Sky Grandmothers. Some times you allow yourself to doubt your value to the Great Creator Apistotoke and the Original Peoples. Don't! You speak what others cannot yet hear for themselves and your words will be heard by those who will take what you know and use it to make a better place – a peaceful existence with our Turtle Mother."

"You speak of my granddaughter Kiera and her young man, Joshua. I really wondered how I was to be of aid to them. Joshua believes that I hold wisdom that will help save the autumn harvest camp of his Nakota ancestors. I doubted that I could be of much help because I have lost so many opportunities to learn about my own culture when I was taken away to the church residential school.

"I know I have learned things in my life and from some of the people with whom I've kept in touch on the reservation. But I doubt that what I've learned is enough to help them. After all, I don't have the connections to people who know how to protect our land."

"It is your deepest connection to our Turtle Mother that they need. The young people of your time are evolving as direct descendants of the Sky People, with gifts of vision and fully activated energies that will allow them to speak 'heart-to-heart' with others. It is this connection that will allow subtle languages to be brought forth that transmute energy and translate for others a greater awareness of the Truth. They will lead in the ways of our collective ancestors to demonstrate a new way to connect and live in harmony with the Earth and her creatures. But they need you to teach them how to connect more fully, to be able to 'listen' to the language of the animals, to the language of Mother Earth herself, and to divine meaning from all experience.

"To begin, you must teach them to make the most valuable connection – the deep soul connection with the Elements – Earth, Air, Fire, and Water.

"Turtle Island feeds us and gives us shelter, sustenance for our life, and the First Peoples are honour bound to protect that which gives us life. We have come to live 'as One' with the Mother that nourishes us, in harmony with All That Is. Generations of our descendants have forgotten the Way to live in harmony – with our Earth Mother and with one another. They will need to be reminded of how we are to live. You shall remind them."

"I have always tried to honour the ground on which I walk. Where do I begin?"

"Their heartfelt connection to the Mother must be a conscious commitment. It begins by connecting to the Earth. Both your young people have a deep respect for the beauty of the Mother, but aren't yet fully committed to a relationship with Her. They must ask to be in constant communion with the Mother. To do this, take a walk in the forest or the field. Pick up a leaf that has been discarded by a tree or bush. Ask permission to become One with the leaf. Ask the leaf to become a part of your Being. Talk with the leaf. Breathe with it. Listen for its heartbeat. It wishes to be One with you – for you to be whole together. Think of what troubles you or gives you pain in your life. Take a deep breath and then breathe out this pain onto the leaf, breathing forcefully without blowing the leaf away. Release the pain of what isn't working in your life to the leaf. It will take your pain and compost it, turning it into something beautiful in the next growing season. Thank the leaf and place it gently upon the ground again.

"Kneel and place your forehead upon the Earth and breathe in the essence of the Mother's nurturing love. Breathe Love back into the Mother. Thank her for supporting your life. Get up and walk with a new awareness of the Mother who loves us. See the Earth through her eyes.

"Take a deep breath into your belly and hold on to it. Then expel the breath quickly. Like this – Haa! Take a few more breaths, holding each one for a bit longer than the last one. Release each breath quickly. Ask the Air if you have permission to become One with it. Ask the Air to become One with you. Take another deep breath, into your heart space. When you release the Air, let it take what no longer serves you: the feeling of being separate from others; the pain of relationships; of conditioning. Give it all to the Air to be taken away on the wind to where it will be cleaned and made new by the breath of the trees and plants. Thank the Air for allowing you to build relationship and to feel Air coursing through your body, making you feel alive.

"Fire is the third element. Ask permission from Fire to know its nature. Look deep into the centre of the flames. Envision the Fire in front of you and draw the flames toward you with your breath. Imagine the flames being drawn into you and filling up your body without burning your flesh. The Fire purifies and clears away what holds us back from being our best selves. The way silver is purified by Fire, allow Fire to burn away your regrets and your cares. Breathe out the impurities as if you had to cough. Fire makes you strong like silver once it cools. Give thanks to the Fire for cleansing you and allowing you to be strong and new.

"The last of the elements is Water. This is of the greatest importance because it is Water that feeds the Earth, the plants and the creatures who walk upon it. Without Water we would be dust!" The Elder reverently lifted a small clay vessel decorated with brightly coloured geometric designs and spoke over it... "Miigwetch". Handing it to Mavis, she explained "Ask Water to allow you to become One. Then sip slowly. Feel Water enter your body and feel it fill your mouth and move into your body. Feel it being drawn into your stomach and to every part of your body. Feel it move into each tiny drop of blood that flows in your veins. Feel it nourish you. Thank Water for giving you life.

"You must teach the young ones to ask Water to bless their bodies and the land so that the Earth may be All that Creator desires. They must learn to seek out the Creator with gratitude for each and every day; for the sunrise and the heat of the day and the way in which the plants are able to grow and become food and medicine for the body. They must thank Water for nourishing the food and thank the food for nourishing the body. Then the body must be thanked for serving the heart and the Great Creator. It is the Sacred Circle of Life for which we must be grateful. At the centre of the circle is the Water – always the Water is at the centre of Life."

Pulling her ceremonial shawl closer around her thin shoulders, bent with age, the Elder continued "It is a joyful duty to teach the young. When they are eager to learn and have the attention of the Elders it shows how much they respect the Creator – not just the Elders. As Elders we have as much to learn from them. Don't forget how to laugh and let them keep you youthful."

"I am honoured and only hope that I can serve in ways that support the best for all of us in accordance with the Will of the Great Creator," replied Mavis.

"Dear Sister, you have no need to worry. You have all you need within you. Mikii no soh no ma Kiiat-suma-kit-sima. Sstik-ah-somma li-kit-somma."

The words, still sounding strange to her ears, bore a resonance with many languages of indigenous people everywhere. Yet, Mavis knew instinctively this was the language of the Star Grandmothers – a language of Light.

Mavis watched the camp fire smoke rise high and wide, dispelling the vision and the Elder with it. When she opened her eyes, Mavis felt a settling within her heart, a strong knowing of purpose and Divine guidance. Breathing this new sense of knowing into her entire being, she allowed it to fill every cell of her body, feeling empowered and strengthened in ways she had not felt for many years. Exhaling, Mavis Deerfoot felt called to release all thoughts and energies that would prevent her from being a perfect vessel for the knowledge of the Elders and the Spomitpiksi.

CHAPTER 25

A'HO

The forest howled with the wind. Branches rubbed against one another, their squeaks and groans echoing out into the late hour of the day.

"Snow comes – and soon. We should have moved our people to the winter camp several days ago. We'll need to move quickly now that the sickness has passed," Chief Rain Dancer declared thoughtfully. Eagle Man only nodded his agreement.

Rising with the agility of a man one quarter his years, Eagle Man left the campfire, stopping only briefly at his tent before heading up the well-worn trail to the top of the waterfall. The water flowed out of the rocks at the top of the ridge before cascading down into a waterfall to form the wide river edging the valley in which they had camped for more years than Eagle Man had known. The water was both giver of life and medicine for his people the past two months. It washed away the sickness in the north where they bathed and washed their clothes. The water replenished and fed their bodies at the base of the falls on the south end of the valley.

Their stay here had been extended when several members of the clan had fallen ill with an intestinal sickness. This had befallen the clan after they had received visitors two weeks earlier – three traders with whom they had shared a meal, including beans already cooked and stored in some round, metal containers. The cans had been dented and rusty. Fortunately, not everyone had eaten heartily of the offering. The Chief and a few others had only suffered for a few hours while others had been ill for several days, and left too weak to stand for a few more days after that. Thankfully, it had passed and they were able to move to the mountain caves that would protect them from the winter's fury.

There was much to be done before breaking camp at dawn. Half-way up the mountainside he stopped and approached a great cedar at the edge of the trail.

"Grandfather Cedar, I am so grateful for the wisdom you have shared in all the times I have walked this path with you. I will never forget. I ask your permission to take from one of your descendants, five small pieces of cedar to offer up with prayers this night. Your medicine is so powerful and I know that it will carry my prayers high up to the Creator. Îsnî'yes!"

Choosing a young cedar only as tall as himself, he carefully pinched off five small leaf tips, dipped his head in gratitude and continued to make his way up, stepping over loose rocks and muddy puddles.

Eagle Man continued to climb past the waterfall to a place just a bit higher and behind a stone ledge above it. Here, there was an opening in the forest canopy. The Sacred Medicine Wheel waited expectantly and an immense eagle soared on the raw winds that carried him effortlessly amidst the dark clouds.

Reverently placing his feet upon the flat shelf that reached far out above the waterfall below, he raised one hand, holding high one of the pieces of cedar.

"A'ho! Creator of the Great Mystery, Great Spirit, I come before you tonight in gratitude and with humility to offer thanks for All That Is. I am Eagle Man of the Nakota People: son of Running Buffalo and Raven; grandson of my father's father – Red Thunder[18] and my father's mother – Misty Water; my mother's father – Three Arrows and my mother's mother – Dancing Pony. I am proud great-grandson of my father's father's father – Medicine Bear and father's father's mother Morning Song; my father's mother's father – Walks with a Limp, my father's mother's mother – Sage Brush; my mother's father's father – Red Fox, my mother's father's mother – Laughing Brook; my mother's mother's father – Finished First, and my mother's mother's mother – Moonshine.

"The seasons change and it is time to move on from this place. Before we do, I would like to offer my prayers of thanks to you for the use of this land and this camp

[18] Some common names of the Nakota tribe may be found online: www.lakotamall.com/common- names-with-the-tribe/

which has provided us with valuable food that will feed us through the time of winter resting. I offer this cedar for the land for which we are so grateful." Eagle Man gently placed a small piece of the cedar on the edge of the stone ledge, where the wind swept it up and lifted it high in the air. "I ask the wind and cedar to carry my prayers out to all the land. I am so grateful for the ways in which the land has directed us through the changing of the leaves and the medicines that appear only in the fall of the year. Îsnî'yes!"

Transferring a second piece of cedar to his right hand and raising it high above his head, he continued. "I ask this cedar to carry my prayers to the air which has thinned and grown cold. I am grateful for the breath that nourishes the bodies of my people. I am grateful for the cooling temperature and the wind which tell me that it is time to move from this place." Eagle Man released the second piece of cedar onto the winds to be carried high into the night sky.

"I offer this cedar for the Fire that has kept my people warm as the nights have grown cool and for the Fire that cleanses the Earth when it is time to feed the land. I am grateful for the Fire that feeds my soul with the knowledge of the Great Spirit and the Ancestors. I ask that Fire continue to warm my people through the cold days ahead and accept this cedar to keep pure their Spirits and those Spirits around them. I am so grateful! Îsnî'yes!" Placing the cedar on the stone at his feet, he struck a flint against it, causing it to spark and ignite. Burning brightly for a second, it faded to a smouldering pile of dust and was carried away on a strong gust of wind.

Standing tall, another piece of cedar held high, Eagle Man called out, "I offer this piece of cedar to the Waters. I ask that Water carry the Spirit of Life into every living thing, into the Earth, into the trees, into the sky where it can be returned to the earth again. I ask that the Waters continue to flow, reaching out through all the land to nourish the Mother and her children for many, many years to come. I am so grateful!" Peering over the ledge, he dropped the cedar into the foaming waters just below. "Îsnî'yes!"

"I offer this last piece of cedar for the memory of the Ancestors, the Nakota Nation and all the generations yet to come. I am grateful for the wisdom that has been passed through the Star People to the Ancestors, because it has been shared with me. I ask the Ancestors to continue to share their knowledge with our people so that they may prosper through all the ages. I am so grateful for the opportunity to have met the one we call Walks Through Time! I know that this descendant of our noble Chief Rain Dancer will come to lead our people back to respect our home. He will carry the wisdom of the Elders with honour. I ask this cedar to carry blessings for all of our people throughout time." With that, the cedar was lifted from his hand by the eagle, who had suddenly swooped low and was gone in an instant on expansive wings.

Turning to the Medicine Wheel, Eagle Man walked in a sunwise manner, softly intoning the songs of the circle he had learned as a babe in arms. As the winds rose, so did his song, until it rang throughout the valley.

Returning to his starting point after several passes around the wheel, he stepped into the centre where a huge stone stood erect, pointing skyward. He reached into an ornately beaded medicine bag that was slung across his body. The bag was made of the softest suede and decorated with beads carved from colourful gemstones of turquoise, jasper, and carnelian. Taking a smaller bundle from within, he opened a small roll of well-worn doe skin, softer than fur of a new born rabbit. Eagle Man withdrew a braid of sweet grass and lay it on a crevice in the centre stone, offering it to the Creator.

"Îsnî'yes! Îsnî'yes!! A'ho! I am grateful for the recovery of our people from the white man's sickness. We are so thankful for the wisdom of the Ancestors who taught us how to gather medicines from the trees and plants that you created which heal our bodies. We are so grateful!

"As we leave from this place, I humbly request of Great Spirit, guidance and protection for my people and all who come after them, on their journeys on this land. Keep this Harvest Camp safe from evil spirits who would seek to destroy its beauty and strip it of Creator's bounty. Allow this Sacred Circle to continue to serve the land and our people in ways we cannot imagine. I am so grateful for the experience of its magic and the ability to co-create a safe and generous place for our people to gather. I ask Great Spirit to hide it from the eyes of those who do not know the way of our people until such a day when the People return.

"I am a humble servant who asks these things. I am grateful and honoured to have served the spirit needs of the Nakota Nation in this Sacred Space. A'ho!"

Crumpling with exhaustion to a heap on the ground beside the boulder, Eagle Man rested for a while. He dreamed of speaking with Walks Through Time, in this very same sacred space, sharing the wisdom of the Sacred Circle and how to work with the energy of the land for the good of the People. Hope rose in his heart for a future where all people remembered how to live in communion with the energy of All That Is in the world. A smile wrinkled the leathery skin of his face.

He woke when Thunder Beings unleashed a torrent of rain, making his descent back to camp treacherous. Approaching the ancient cedar, Eagle Man slipped in the mud and caught his moccasin on an exposed root. Unable to reach a branch of the tree to break his fall, he knocked his head against a rock.

Day broke hours after the midnight storm. The camp was a hive of activity. Some women were making the morning meal, while other members of the tribe packed food stores, bedrolls and tepees. Eagle Man's absence was noticed when he did not appear to break his fast. Chief Rain Dancer sent three scouts up to the Sacred Circle to see if he was still invoking the Great Spirit to guide their journey.

Several minutes later, they returned, carrying the Medicine Man between them. Chief Rain Dancer mourned the loss of his dear friend and spiritual mentor. Departure from the camp would have to wait.

The ground had been dried enough by the return of the sun to make the climb easier for the clan members the following day. At the Sacred Circle, many took turns walking the way while Red Feather and three others carried the body of their Medicine Man to a place on the ridge, chosen by Chief Rain Dancer, that overlooked the medicine wheel. Stones and small rocks placed around the body formed a cairn to protect it from weather and animals. Before sealing it up, Eagle Man's intricately beaded Medicine Bag and Bundle were placed inside. His spirit would have the necessary medicine to carry him to their ancestral home among the Star People.

***

From his place on the ridge, the spirit of Eagle Man watched as his people trailed single-file out of the autumn harvest camp in the valley below. Raising his hands to the sky, he offered a blessing once more, that his people would prosper and live well.

CHAPTER 26

CLEARING FOR HARMONY

A bee droned industriously as it gathered pollen from the flowers at the edge of the verandah where Kiera sat reading. The book, propped on her lap, had "called to her" when she returned the meditation CDs the previous week. It was an older book, published in 1987, which looked to be well-read.

The fourth chapter on chakra energy activation captured her attention. As she read, the words came alive, creating colourful visuals filled with a magnetism that was surpassed only by the euphoria she felt while standing before the easel with a paintbrush in hand.

> *"Opening and clearing the Chakras of energies that do not serve the highest and best for your continued good health is both positive and safe. It is imperative for any woman aspiring to heal herself and others.*

Let's begin to explore these energetic centres together.

Begin by taking a deep breath into your belly, in through your nose and hold it while counting to four. Gently release it, as if you were blowing out a candle. Draw in another breath, holding it in your body, and gently let it go. On the next breath, breathe in deeply through your nose and feel the air being drawn all the way into your belly. Feel it expanding through your body – radiating into each and every cell of your body. Release the breath and breathe normally.

Ask the Divine Source of All That Is to bless you with guidance and protection while you learn to work in harmony with the Energies of Life. Draw a circle around you of the purest Divine White-Gold Light and breathe into it. Feel its gentle embrace around you. Express your sincere appreciation for this guidance and protection without needing to understand it or from whence it comes.

Now, bring your attention back to your physical body and the subtle layers of energy that surround it. The Root (or Base) Chakra is found at the base of your spine and connects you to the Earth. The colour of this Chakra is a true and vibrant red. Its energy is primordial, sexual, and denotes heat, strength and life force. It appears as a cone, the smaller tip beginning at the tailbone and spiralling clockwise toward the front of the body. The flower appearance resembles that of a four-petalled lotus.

Take another deep breath into your belly and imagine that you are growing a tail from the base of your spine spiralling deep into the Earth's core, connecting with the Earth's own power centre. See that energy radiating back to you, travelling back up through your tail as a scarlet red energy force. Breathe that energy up through your tail into your spine. Allow the red colour to swirl around in your Root Chakra and then squeeze the perineum (the small muscle slightly behind the vaginal muscle) to shoot the energy up through the spinal cord to your crown at the top of your head. As you exhale, see the energy pour as a fountain from your crown, down your sides, and back down to Earth again.

Notice if and where the energy stops or if the flow gets slowed at any point. You may wish to intone the sound associated with this Chakra – 'uuh' (as in 'cup') – while you repeat the process. If you sense resistance or blocks, repeat the process of bringing the red energy up into your body and pushing it through again, until it flows freely. Pay attention to how it feels to be supported, nurtured and inspired in this way and then let it go."

Kiera found herself breathing as directed and marvelled at the intensity of the red coloured energy swirling up through her body.

"The 2nd Chakra is the Sacral (or Belly) Chakra and it is orange in colour. The centre of the Chakra is located just below the navel and is fixed to the spinal cord in the same way as the Root Chakra, although it attaches at the first lumbar vertebra. This Chakra corresponds with life force and creativity. There are six petals on this Chakra's lotus flower and when it is functioning at its optimum, it resonates with peace and rejuvenation.

Take another deep breath, drawing in the colours of Autumn – deep oranges, crimson, copper, and russet – up the spine to the belly. Allow the rich warmth to swirl clockwise in the opening of this Chakra, stimulating the emotions of creativity and energetic flow. You may intone the vowel sound 'ooo' (as in 'coo') while experiencing the energy of the 2nd Chakra. Squeeze the perineum to send the *energy up your spine to fountain out your crown and down your outer body, before returning to the Earth.*

The Solar Plexus (Psychic Centre) is the 3rd Chakra and is the emotional seat of the body. Here is where you 'feel the room' when entering or 'play to the crowd'. It is the place where 'personality', balance, and power sit in the body and allows you to connect with the energies around you, giving and receiving vibratory frequencies with others. Food, physical nourishment, and maintenance are processed and distributed from this centre of the body. The colour of this Chakra is bright yellow and its flower has ten petals located at the opening of the stomach, just beneath the bottom of the rib cage.

Take another deep breath. Imagine the sunshine feeding your body, drawing this bright yellow up from the Sun at the core of the Earth. Feel the warmth and vibrancy climb up through your feet and into your upper abdomen. Feel it swirling into the Chakra while you sound its vowel 'oh' (as in 'know'), feeling more confident as you sound the Chakra awake. Again, send the energy up through your spine when you intuit the time is right. Exhale as the energy pours out your crown to envelop your body in its bright yellow light.

The Heart Chakra is the half-way point of the body's energetic field. It is either a bright green or a soft rose colour and quite often can contain both colours, flowing in opposite directions, in perfect harmony. This centre connects the higher and lower energy centres of the body and is often said to be two Chakras operating as one. This Chakra is connected to the first thoracic vertebra and extends to the midpoint between the breasts on the front of the body, below the breastbone. This is the centre for reconnecting with Source Energy (whether or not you call this God, Life Force, Creator, or any other name) and its attributes are love and compassion. Green is associated with healing, sympathy, and success and is grounded in the Earth. Rose is the colour of love, positive self-love, and the ability to care for others. Both are soothing colours, blending the energies of the lower and higher Chakras in the body's centre for intuition and 'inner knowing'. When in balance, this Chakra's energy embraces the Oneness of All, the At-one-ment – both within and without the physical form.

Cleansing and opening this Chakra to its perfect balance is a two-step process. Imagine the colour of a fresh green apple in your mind's eye. Draw this bright green energy up from the core of the Earth, through your feet and up into your body, pulling it up to swirl in a figure eight pattern over your breastbone. Breathe it deeply into your Heart Chakra. Make the sound 'ah' (as in 'mama') and notice the way it resonates within the heart chamber. Continue to breathe with this energy, holding it in your heart space.

Now, drawing your awareness to a point about nine feet above your head, imagine a six-pointed star shining brilliantly down over you. A thin silver fibre cord (or column) extends from the bottom of the star, connecting to your crown. A column of brilliant white-gold light connects the top of the star to the Great Central Sun far above. The energy pouring into your personal Soul Star is limitless and never ending. It contains the frequencies of all colours of light in one.

Mentally visualize a soft rose-coloured energy being poured down from the star above and into your crown while you take in a deep breath. Draw the energy down through your head, neck and shoulders into your heart.

Allow it to swirl in a figure eight pattern over your Heart Chakra while sounding 'ah' once more. Notice the subtle difference in the way you feel as both the grounded green and the gentle rose Divine Energies dance together, uniting within your body, yet retaining their individual colour properties. It is safe to feel and to know that all is just as it should be. Allow these two energies to co-exist for a short time with no judgment. Just experience. When you are ready to do so, exhale, sending both the green and rose energies down into your abdomen and down through your legs to the very core of the Earth."

Kiera gasped in ecstasy as her awareness was heightened by the duality of the energies drawn from the Earth and the Heavens. "It feels as if my heart is doing a happy dance! What an amazing feeling!" Kiera continued to read.

"The 5th Chakra is the Throat Chakra, governing sovereignty, joy, innocence, creative expression, and hearing. Its colour is the purest aquamarine of the sea. Connected to the 3rd cervical vertebra in the neck and opening to the small hollow at the base of your throat on the front, this Chakra's flower has sixteen petals. This is the centre of clairaudience, where intuition and spirit

guides are heard. When blocked, it becomes difficult to express oneself effectively or be 'heard' by others.

Breathe in a clear aqua-blue from the star above your head, and draw it down through your crown into your throat. Allow the aqua energy to wash over your Throat Chakra in a clockwise direction while sounding the vowel 'eye' (as in 'I'). Gently releasing your breath, rinse the energy downward, through your feet to the core of the Earth.

"The Third Eye is perhaps the most well-known of all the bodies energy centres, known for its connection to spirituality. It is centred between and slightly above the natural eyes and is associated not only with clear vision, but with the 6th aura level – that being the spiritual body. It connects to the spine at the first cervical vertebra. Its colour is the deep indigo blue of the Cosmic Heaven, purifying and electric. The centre's ninety-six petalled flower reflects the significant increase of vibratory rate from the sixteen petals of the Throat Chakra. The development of 'clairvision' or Inner Sight allows one to "know" – in the spiritual meaning of the word – and to move between the mental and

psychic energy fields, discerning both inner and outer reality.

Imagine the deepest indigo night sky, illuminated with millions of stars, high above. No sound disturbs the peace of this vista. Breathing deeply of its tranquility, draw the indigo blue energy through the silver cord extending from your own star, suspended above your head. Allow it to settle through your crown into your Third Eye Chakra, feeling it swirling clockwise, spiralling toward the spinal connection. Intone the vowel 'aye' (as in 'say') with conviction and confidence and be aware of the intensification of this indigo energy. By connecting this energy with the energy of the Heart Chakra at the same time, one may affect a healing transmission from a distance. While exhaling, allow indigo blue light to travel down throughout your body, through all of the lower Chakras, and out through your feet, back to the core of the Earth.

The final Chakra is the Crown, located at the top of your head and just slightly above it. This corresponds with the higher spiritual aura and vibrates with a rich violet colour, having no spinal connection. Its energy is so highly dimensional that it is viewed as having 960 petals and as a 'crown of glory'. Rather than being warm or cool, the violet colour of the Crown Chakra holds the highest frequency of all the chakra colours, bringing with it inner power, psychic development, influence, and transcendence. This is the place of 'pure knowing', 'pure intuition' and 'Spirit'. Developing this Chakra strengthens an individual's deep connection to the Source of All That Is, Divine Source, God, and leads to intense personal peace and profound change. It is the realization of God within.

Imagine a rich violet aura being cast around your physical body, emanating from your Soul Star. Breathing more deeply, draw the violet energy into the crown of your head and feel its light filling your Crown, swirling and ebbing, flowing as a feather dances on the breeze. The sound of this Chakra is the vowel tone 'eee' (as in 'we'). Feel the peace that radiates from within the violet aura as its sound resonates within your body, feeling the violet energy surrounding your entire being, protecting you. Ask for guidance and inner knowing. Invite whatever image suits your understanding of a Supreme Creator (by any name you choose) to come to your awareness. See the connection between this Divine essence and your own consciousness of self. Sit with this exchange of Love's guidance. Ask for peace and understanding and listen to any message you might receive. Take time to honour your own connection with this Divine entity.

When you are ready, invite this essence to more fully connect by breathing deeply and becoming One with it. Draw the Divine entity's essence in through your Crown and into your Heart centre – for the Divine is you and you are the Divine! Sit with this realization for a while and just relax into it. Notice the strength and comfort that comes from this communion. Allow the emotions to flow and fill your physical form.

Now, as you exhale, ask for all energies that no longer serve your highest good to be released. See them in your mind's eye, flowing down through your body's energy centres, washing away all that is not of value for your future self. Thank the Earth Mother for taking these energies and returning them to her core, where they can be transmuted to feed and nourish the Earth.

An eighth Chakra, called the Transpersonal Point exists several inches above the Crown, resonating with the 'Om' of Divine Oneness.

It has no real physical attachment to the body, belonging to the spiritual realm, and appears as a rainbow of all colours at once in a prismatic white light."

Kiera instinctively raised her hand to a place about eight inches above her head and felt a distinct electrical charge tingling in her hand. Awestruck she exclaimed "That's so amazing!"

"Allow yourself to experience this pure white rainbow of light by seeing it pouring forth from the Soul Star connection far above you, down into your Transpersonal Point above your head. Feel the energy flowing in a figure eight formation within this Chakra. Its blessings now bathing you with Divine liberation, love, and light. Allow the white light energy to continue down through each of your body's Chakras, weaving the sign of infinity within each individual Chakra before moving to the next. Grant yourself permission to hold this Light in all the newly emptied spaces within your body's energy centres, becoming a radiant glowing body of Light. Release any excess white light into the Earth through your feet.

There are other, smaller energy centres in the physical body. Two small roses appear at the shoulders, sometimes called severity *and* mercy, *'shouldering' the Heart Chakra. Other Chakras used in healing include the palms of the hands and the soles of the feet. The feet are our simplest and most effective connection with the Earth's energy, both for drawing energy in and for grounding out unwanted or negative energy (as in cleansing.) The hands become more sensitive with intentional use and also have smaller energy centres at the finger tips. The colours associated with these Chakras differ for each individual and according to their intent.*

It is important to remember that we are never alone. Therefore, when we meditate on the Chakras (or for any other reason) we should recognize and verbalize an appreciation for the guidance of the Divine Creator, God, Source (or whatever name you choose) and also to thank our Spirit Guides, those whom we may or may not see who have chosen to mentor us in our Awakening.

Now take several deep breaths and open the eyes, stretch the limbs and other parts of the body to gently waken them. It is highly recommended that a journal be kept to record your experiences of the energies each time they pass through your awareness. This will allow you to see progress over periods of practice.[19]*"*

Kiera set the book aside and drank deeply from the water bottle that had been sitting on the table beside her. "Hmmm. I am not quite sure but I feel like something has changed in a big way." Taking a small notebook from the bookshelf beside on the other side of the room and finding a pen on the kitchen counter, she returned to the chair. Writing the date at the top of the first page, she wrote:

"I Am Divine Energy and the Divine is the I Am that is Me."

[19] This Chakra Meditation was inspired by Diane Stein, as outlined in her book: *The Women's Book of Healing*.

CHAPTER 27

FINDING THE PATH DOESN'T HAVE TO BE DIFFICULT

"Joshua! It's Ken Strongbow calling. I've heard from one of the government offices we called, that there is indeed an archaeological claim being made to work the area of the Autumn Harvest Camp. The archaeologist has been told that we have reason to believe the ground is a sacred site. Apparently, he didn't take the news very well at all, but he'll have to stand down to allow time for an investigation into our claim."

"Already? Wow! Well, I didn't think the archaeologists would waste any time getting their permits, since they've already been there to survey the area. I'm surprised that they haven't been back, myself, but maybe the ancestors are making it hard for them to find the site again."

"We can only hope! Anyway, I'm thinking that you

should take someone else with you and ride up to the camp to see if you can follow the route that they would have taken to get into the camp. They have to be coming in on a route that travels over more level ground than the ridge access. It's the only way they'd be able to carry in the heavy equipment they would need to conduct a full dig. I'd venture to say that they may even have used ATVs, so you should be able to find a wider path with evidence of damage to the underbrush that should be easily noticed. I'd come down to go with you but I'm talking with some of the Elders to discuss a plan for how to raise awareness of the camp and an interest in protecting it."

"That's a great idea Ken. I have already talked with Kiera about going up to show her the medicine wheel. We'd love to find a way to get her grandmother up there to see if she can sense anything. Do you need me to come up and speak to the Elders about the camp? Will they need to know about how I met Eagle Man? I'm not sure anyone would be inclined to believe me and public speaking is not really my thing, but... I'll do what is necessary."

"That will need to happen, yes, but let me speak with them first. Then we'll get you, Kiera, and perhaps her grandmother, if she's able to come. I'm sure the Elders would want to meet everyone involved so that we can work together."

"Okay, just let me know when. We'll try to find the way the archaeologists have used to get into the camp."

"Fine. I'll call you tomorrow and let you know where we're at."

"Thanks Ken. I owe you one!"

"There are no checks and balances here Joshua. We all work together. Later."

***

Joshua and Kiera poured over aerial maps of Jasper Park and the adjacent area, while Mavis prepared a fresh jug of lemon balm iced tea. She added a bit honey to sweeten it "just a bit".

A plate of sliced apples and chunks of marbled cheese was pushed to one side of the table when the maps were opened flat in an effort to determine the location of the Autumn Harvest Camp.

"I wonder if we could see this better on Google Maps?" wondered Kiera aloud. "I brought my laptop in case you think we could find it that way."

"I don't know. We could try. I'm pretty familiar with the area behind the house, but that doesn't mean they couldn't have used an old miner's access from back in the day. There are some old trails that are still 'barely there'. It's likely they used one of them. If we could even find one of those on a map or something resembling a thin spot in the vegetation, we could go check it out with the truck."

"Where would you say, on this map, is the Autumn Harvest Camp?" Pointing to the map of Jasper Park, Mavis suggested that they begin at the approximate camp location and work outward from there.

It didn't take very long before Joshua located the waterfall and its resulting watershed on the map. Finding the nearest paved highway was easy; it lay several miles from the camp site according to the maps.

Mavis pulled an old magnifying glass from a drawer in one corner of the kitchen. "Here, try this. You won't have to squint so hard."

"Thank you, Gran!" said Kiera.

Cross-referencing a provincial map and the National Parks map, they found what looked like an old logging road leading off an unpaved road from the highway about twelve miles out of town. Joshua used a highlighter to identify the locations of both the camp and a possible entrance on the map and looked up at Mrs. Deerfoot.

"Have you got a small ruler please? I'd like to figure out the distance we'd need to travel from this spot and then figure how to best make the trip in."

Mavis walked to the same drawer from which she'd retrieved the magnifier and returned to the table with a 12" wooden ruler.

"Thank you! It's about three inches. If the map scale is one mile per inch, then it looks as if it might be a bit of a hike into the camp. I could do that reasonably easily myself but if we took the horses, we could ride in fairly quickly," pronounced Joshua.

"That would be great!" exclaimed Kiera.

"Mrs. Deerfoot, have you ever ridden a horse?"

"Oh my! It's been a long time Joshua, but I used to ride pretty often when I was younger. I'd love to get to see this medicine wheel that your ancestors walked. There has to be a reason why I've been brought into this project. Maybe we'll find out when we see it."

"I'll drive the truck in as far as we can so you don't have to ride too far. I have a gentle old mare, Luna, who is not as tall as some of the others. I'm certain she'd love the chance to get out on the trail, and Kiera and I can help you get on and off of her."

"When can we go?" Kiera asked excitedly.

"What's wrong with right now? I'll call Tom to get the horses ready and into the trailers. I think he should go with us, just in case we run into any problems."

***

Kiera peered around what seemed like the end of the old logging road. "It doesn't really look like much of a trail, does it?" She took a couple of steps toward a downed tree where the trail began. "But then again, I think I see a candy bar wrapper over there, peeking from under that log."

Tom and Joshua led the horses, one by one, out of two trailers, and arranged them so that one of the mares was closer to a large outcropping of boulders. Joshua thought it would be easier for Mrs. Deerfoot to mount his older mare there.

"Maybe we should ask for some guidance before we head in to the camp?" asked Kiera. "What do you think?"

"Inviting the Creator to be with us at any time is always a good idea Kiera," Mavis replied.

"May I?" asked Joshua. With nods of approval from Kiera and Mavis, he spoke from his heart, offering gratitude to the ancestors who extended an invitation into their world and for the support of those who see the Autumn Harvest Camp as sacred space, a place from which to connect more deeply with the Creative Force of God and the wonders of the Earth Mother, Turtle Island. He asked the Creator to bless their journey into the camp with the wisdom to honour what was found there; the discernment of its meaning for this small group and the awareness of Earth's inhabitants; for guidance through a forested mountain path travelled by the ancestors and a safe journey into the gifts of the past.

"Amen," said Mavis. "Chi Miigwetch, Joshua. That was just what we needed."

"Well done," added Tom.

Joshua laughed a little self-consciously. "I don't know, but I sure hope so!"

The sun glistened off the leaves of the trees as horse flesh rippled beneath them. Joshua and Nightsong led them away from the horse trailers, through a wide, natural break between the trees. Mavis followed him on Luna, the mare who had nursed Nightsong as her own. Kiera followed Mavis on Sundance while Tom brought up the rear on a chestnut roan named Dancer.

"This brings back so many memories of times spent with your grandfather, Kiera. We used to ride for hours through the mountains together, before the children came along. There was a stable not far from where we lived that was owned by friends of his. We were fortunate that they allowed to use the horses in return for the exercise we provided for them. I may have a bit more padding now, than I did then, but it might be a good thing today!" Mavis' laughter rang out through the trees. "I'm grateful that you found a way for me to witness this momentous discovery, Joshua. It means so much to me."

"Eagle Man said that you are opening us up to our indigenous heritage – even if you are not yet sure of it yourself. He said you will know what to say when we need advice. I have faith in that."

Tom took the opportunity to ask, "Tell me more about what this is all about, Joshua. You've been distracted a great deal for the past few weeks and haven't really said much more than the fact that you discovered your ancestors' harvest camp."

They took turns re-telling the events of the recent weeks, and shared their individual calling to connect with the Earth Mother and reclaim the treasure of their collective heritage. They each told of being tasked with sharing that knowledge with the world, so others would learn to extend compassion for Creation and return to the *knowing* that All are Divine and At One.

"So, what do we expect to learn today?" Tom inquired.

"We need to track the route that the archaeological team used to find the camp. This will allow us to know how to further protect the area from archaeological poaching. Ken Strongbow – you met him the other day – has filed notice directly with the government authorities who can have this area classified as 'protected' under the authority of the local First Nations. We know that Eagle Man and Chief Rain Dancer built a medicine wheel above the falls, to the south of the camp. We also know that someone with high status in the clan was buried near the site of the sacred circle. We just don't yet know who that is, but I'm sure we'll figure that out very soon."

The trail narrowed as Joshua finished explaining the goal for this foray into uncharted grounds. The overhead canopy became more dense, casting shadows over the small group.

A sharp "Keeriew!!" sounded above.

"I guess the ancestors have asked the eagle to guide us." Joshua's face beamed with the knowledge that Eagle Man would direct their path. "Hold up for a minute. Look at these branches! They've been broken – probably when the others came through here."

Nimbly dismounting from their mounts, Tom and Joshua closely examined the broken branches and trampled saplings a few feet ahead.

"I'd say we're heading in the right direction," affirmed Tom. "Listen. I think I hear water over there to the right of us."

Tom led his horse off on an angle saying "Give me a minute to see how close it is." A few minutes later, his voice rang through the trees as he called to the others to follow.

Emerging from the treeline, they discovered a river with a narrow band of pebbled soil alongside. Joshua looked to Kiera and said, "Are you thinking what I'm thinking? That this is the watershed from the camp?"

"We wouldn't have been led this way if it wasn't. We must be close."

It took only fifteen minutes more to make their way to the autumn harvest camp by following the river. The ground foliage grew thicker just before they reached the meadow that hid the camp from the rest of the world. The sky opened above, revealing the magnificence of the eagle soaring overhead. The sun glistened off the rocky ledge above the waterfall at the far end of the camp.

The space felt far more expansive than it measured. Perhaps, because they had transcended the barrier of time, the connection made with the past expanded their collective awareness, making the distance from where they entered the Camp to the base of the waterfall seem so much farther than its approximately 225 feet.

Mavis broke the group's silence saying, "The Elder who has been visiting me lately said I need to teach you to give thanks for all we receive, as well as how to build a deeper connection with Mother Earth. She gave me such a detailed description of how this is to be done. I have to wonder if perhaps you are teaching me that my own connection only scratches the surface."

"I don't think you give yourself enough credit, Grandmother. I have learned so much from you and you surprise me with more of our culture every day. I don't doubt that what you have been shown will be very important in making our gratitude more complete. Would you tell us more about your vision while we make our way up to the top of the waterfall?"

"That is a most spectacular sight," muttered Tom. "I had no idea this was back here. For sure, there's lots for which to give thanks just here along the river."

"I recognize some of the plants that Eagle Man

showed me were valuable medicine for the people," added Joshua. "More for which to be grateful."

"Yes, the Creator is a marvellous and thoughtful provider," replied Mavis. "I can imagine that your family was able to harvest much from this area, Joshua. I see some vines in those trees that are likely grapes and over there at the edge of the water, on the other side, are some plants whose roots are kind of like a potato. They are very small now, but will be much larger in the fall."

Joshua had dismounted and led Nightsong to the water for a drink. "We should probably let the horses drink now before heading up the ridge. The way is a bit tricky. I want to show Mrs. Deerfoot the way the camp was laid out." Moving toward a large flat rock, he led Mavis' horse to stand beside it so that she could dismount and walk around a bit before heading to the medicine wheel.

"Ooomph!" She said as her feet touched the ground. "This is a good idea to stretch our legs. I will feel this ride for a while, I think. But it is so worth the effort!"

Joshua pointed out where many of the tents had been placed, the central camp fire and the cook fires, along with the natural horse paddock. He noted that the majority of white stone ley line markers, placed by Ken and himself, had remained untouched. It was very easy to see the image of the camp overlaid on the grid-lines of the valley floor.

Satisfied that they had all envisioned a similar image of the ancient camp, the four walked back to where the horses grazed on the long grasses near the water's edge. The large boulders provided a step-up, making it easier for Mavis to mount Luna again. She continued telling them of her vision and the wisdom shared by the elder woman while they wound their way from the bottom of the falls. The path was not as difficult as they had anticipated it to be. It was as if the way had been made clear for their ascent, worn by others over many lifetimes.

About half way up, an ancient cedar stood to one side as a sentinel. Its girth was substantial. Clearly, it had been standing for many hundreds of years.

"Perhaps we could stop here just for a moment to offer gratitude for this Grandfather Cedar? It was likely here when your ancestors walked this path Joshua," remarked Mavis.

"I seem to remember passing it when Ken and I were here."

"Grandmother, look! There are some smaller ones just up the way. Do you think we should gather some to take with us to the Medicine Wheel?"

"I believe you are reading my mind, child." With a deep sense of purpose and reverence, Mavis spoke the age-old prayer of gratitude to the Grandfather Cedar and asked permission to share its wisdom and medicine.

It was Kiera, who carefully dismounted to ask permission of the cedar saplings to share their medicine at the Sacred Circle. Then she snipped five small pieces and placed them in her backpack.

CHAPTER 28

WALKING THE WAY

"The view is exactly as the eagle had shown me," exclaimed Mavis, breathlessly taking in the grandeur of the view from the top of the falls and the size of the Sacred Circle built by Chief Rain Dancer and Eagle Man. "It takes my breath away!"

"Even I can feel the power in this place," remarked Tom. "And I haven't had much more exposure to our Native heritage than you have, Joshua. The air feels like it's just buzzing with energy."

"From below, you wouldn't even know this was here! But it makes so much sense if you think about it. Just a quick question Joshua – are we far enough from the cairn you found? I don't want to disturb it by tethering the horses here." Kiera asked as she dismounted from Sundance.

Joshua turned and pointed to a spot about a hundred

and fifty feet further up the ridge, to where the repaired cairn was visible. "It's far enough that it is safe to say we won't disturb it. We could erect a temporary corral of sorts for the horses."

A small patch of greenery on the south side of the flat area around the medicine wheel allowed the horses to graze without wandering too far. Tom and Joshua located several long, thin tree branches that had been brought down by the wind some time ago. Carefully, they strung the branches fence-like between the upright branches of the healthy trees around the horses. This allowed the horses to move around a little, rather than being tied to one spot while they grazed.

Moving toward the generous ledge above the waterfall, Kiera produced the small pieces of cedar she had harvested on the way up from the camp below. Handing them out, she said "I picked enough that we may each offer our own prayers and one extra for the ancestors. Maybe you'd like to have that one Joshua."

Joshua accepted two of the small tips of cedar branches and took a step toward the edge of the rock ledge, above the waterfall. Holding the cedar high in the air, he proclaimed, "Ah'o! Creator of the Great Mystery, Great Spirit, I come before you today in gratitude and with humility to offer thanks for All That Is. I should introduce myself with apologies for not having recognized the place you hold for me in this life. I am Joshua Marshall – Walks Through Time; son of John Marshall and Susan James Marshall; many times great-grandson of Chief Rain Dancer of the Nakota First People and friend of a great

Medicine Man, Eagle Man – Spiritual Leader of the First People of my Nakota Clan.

"The seasons changed and they have moved on from this land, but their spirits have returned to teach us the old ways. So that we may take responsibility once more for protecting the land that feeds our Nations. I offer this cedar in memory of the ancestors who have gone before us and for all that I have yet to learn from them and others along the way. I'm so grateful for the ways in which the land has spoken and called me to my destiny.

"I also give thanks for the wisdom that has supported my journey to remember who I really am. I am so grateful for the people you have brought into my life, and I ask you to bless them with abundance, patience, and discernment. Guide them in the ways that serve us all in a good way. Îsnî'yes – Thank you!"

"That was lovely, Joshua," sighed Mavis. "I am sure that our Creator will honour your heartfelt plea." She moved a few steps closer to the ledge as Joshua stepped back to stand beside Kiera. Sighing deeply, she lifted her eyes heavenward and said, "Hello again, Lord. It's me, Mavis Deerfoot, an old woman filled with renewed joy. I have to tell you how grateful I am for the opportunity to stand here in this sacred place, and be able to look out over the majesty of your creation. It is such an honour to be called to witness the awakening of these young people to their destiny – at Your hand. Chi Miigwetch!

"I know you have a plan for my life, and that it is far from being over! I pray you grant me the wisdom to support these young people in whatever way is best for them. I am open to your Will and graciously receive what guidance you may provide. I am so grateful! Miigwetch!"

A gentle breeze lifted the cedar from her hand and carried it aloft for several seconds before allowing it to fall gently into the cascading waters below the ledge.

Tom extended his arm to Mavis, to steady her as she backed across the uneven stones. "I don't know that I have the fancy words to express my prayers, but I'll give it a go anyway.

"Father Creator, Tom Stoneman here. I come humbly as a witness to this sacred ceremony. I don't know much, but what I do know is that we must walk together to care for the world that you gifted us. Our stewardship is necessary for the survival of all. I thank you for supporting me in all that I do, by giving me a job and meeting my needs in simple ways. Thank you. I ask that you continue to bless me with your kindness and guide me according to your Will. Amen."

Kiera was the last to offer her prayers. "I'm just so grateful for all the fantastic experiences of the last couple of weeks. I'm not sure where to begin."

Offering her support, Mavis replied "Just speak from your heart – the Lord will guide you, if you ask."

"Thank you, Grandmother." Taking a deeper breath than usual, Kiera embraced the myriad emotions within her heart and began to offer her gratitude. "Divine Source of all life – God. I feel like I should introduce myself properly. I am Kiera Clark, daughter of Ruth and Donald Clark, granddaughter of Mavis and Daniel Deerfoot. I know that Mom, Dad, and Granddad are with you and watch over me. Tell them not to worry – I believe I'm finding my way, and I'm grateful for the love they freely shared while they walked this land. I cannot express how grateful I am for Grandmother! If not for her, I would surely be a lost soul, wandering aimlessly.

"I want to thank you for trusting me with my destiny, and for the people you have brought into my life, making it so much richer. I'm so grateful! I don't know what the future will bring, but I know that I am ready to do what is required of me; to listen to the prompting of the Mother and those who would guide me; to follow Your Will in protecting this land; to be a conscious leader to others who have forgotten how to live life as a Co-creator. Miigwetch! Thank you!

Prayers as old as the Earth herself, burst from all of their hearts and were lifted onto the wings of a gentle wind, taking with them the little cedar offerings. They fluttered and danced in the air before drifting into the water, connecting with the Earth again.

They gathered at an opening in the stones at the eastern side of the Sacred Circle, as it appeared to be the natural place to begin their walk. Mavis knelt to placed her hands on the Earth, as she began to share what the Elder had taught her about the importance of connecting with the Earth in meaningful ways. This sacred space would bring much more power to this lesson than they could even imagine.

Taking turns, they each knelt, thanked the Earth and then walked the Medicine Wheel four times, once for each direction. In humble reverence, they walked the path of the ancestors in the manner taught to the medicine men by the Sky People. Joshua, Kiera, Mavis, and Tom moved as One through this sacred space – each one entering into meaningful conversations with their own souls.

The four spread out around the circle, deep in thought. Simultaneously, they turned inward to the stone standing erect in the centre of the Medicine Wheel and breathed in the strength of the moment. Eagle Man dove from above and landed on top of the centre stone. With his beak, he tapped three times on the stone's surface.

"What does that mean?" asked Tom.

"I think Eagle Man is pleased that we are here." Speaking directly to the majestic bird, Joshua said, "It's you up on the hill, isn't it?"

The giant bird hopped on one foot and then beat the stone with his beak three times more.

"Well I guess you got that one right!" laughed Mavis.

As laughter rolled out over the autumn harvest camp, the eagle stayed with the four of them while Mavis completed sharing the message of her own vision with an Elder. When she had finished retelling the lesson, Eagle Man voiced his applause. He bowed to Mavis and then to Joshua, then spread his wings and was carried high into the air as a breeze suddenly arose.

Delighted with the events of the afternoon, the small group marvelled at the valley below once more before mounting their horses to leave the Sacred Circle and the Autumn Harvest Camp.

CHAPTER 29

SPIRIT GUIDES

Joshua and Kiera walked hand in hand into the trees across the road from her cabin, along the trail to the hot spring, just as the light was fading behind the ridge above them.

"Thank you for finding a way for Grandmother to come with us to the Medicine Wheel, Joshua. I don't think she'll forget this outing for a long time. She may be a bit sore for a couple of days, unless she's got some ancient remedy up her sleeve." Kiera laughed at the probability.

"I'm just grateful that she was willing to go. Her wisdom and deep connection to the Earth is something that we have to develop in order to be able to thrive as humanity, like she said. Eagle Man was adamant that your grandmother is a vital part of remembering that connection and passing it on to other people. It was obvious to me when Eagle came to speak with us at her house. That blew me away!"

"Me too! I've watched a lot of animals and birds around my place in the past, but I've never seen anything like that! She mentioned he'd visited her before too, when she told me about seeing the different possible outcomes of this situation. It's really rather humbling to think that this connection exists between all creatures."

Walking further into the forest, they considered what they hoped would happen when they met with the Elders up at Cache Creek. Joshua told Kiera, "Ken Strongbow called the house just before Tom and I finished the chores. He phoned because we have been invited to drive up there in two days, to meet with several members of the Council of Elders to share our discovery. The Elders have experience obtaining protected sacred status for other sites around this area."

"Wow! I wonder what they'll say?" replied Kiera.

The two lapsed into silent reverie for several moments while their feet found harmony moving in unison into the heart of the forest.

As the shadows lengthened and the birds began to settle, Kiera marvelled, "The forest really comes alive at night. Though sunlight is hidden by the night, the moon mirrors its energy and wakens all that is mystery within the soul. It stretches with the rise of the moon, and grows into fully awakened intuition – breathing the wisdom from ages past into each present moment."

"An artist *and* a poet!" Joshua gently squeezed her hand. A gleam of admiration shone in his eyes, as their near-grey colour shifted to indigo. Joshua turned to pull Kiera into his embrace.

A wolf's howl shattered the silence of the deep woods. Eagle replied to his call to gather, swooping down between branches of fir, aspen, balsam, and white birch to land on a branch beside Joshua's shoulder. A low rustling and golden glow alerted Kiera to Sasha's presence in front of the pair. After a brief nod in the direction of the hot spring, Sasha disappeared.

"I guess that means we're being called," Joshua surmised.

"I agree. It sounded like a summons to me, and my body is starting to feel like it wants to jump right out of my skin with excitement – not just at the thought of hearing what they have to say."

Since they were very near her favourite place in the forest, Kiera suggested they could sit on the large rocks beside the hot spring. There, they could listen to what their spirit animals had to say. With a sweep of his hand, Joshua allowed her to lead the way.

Sasha was already coiled comfortably on a smaller flat rock at one end of the steaming pool when they arrived at the spring. The eagle settled on a low branch of white birch, just above and to the left of Sasha, then hopped down to perch atop a larger rock. Light shimmered and grew around his form until it was so bright, they could no longer see him clearly. Kiera and Joshua shielded their eyes until the light receded a few seconds later.

Transforming from bird to human form, the Medicine

Man said, "I thought you may be better able to relate to me in this way, though by the looks on your faces I should have first advised you that this was indeed possible."

Expecting Sasha to have made a similar shift, Kiera was surprised to find he had not. He replied "You have become quite comfortable with thisss form and though Joshua is not accussstomed to hearing a ssserpent ssspeak, he will acssept it easssily enough."

Eagle Man continued, his image wavering slightly, "We are only able to lower our vibration to this level for very short periods of your time. In fact, all things are possible, limited only by your own mind. But this is not why we are gathered here now. We wanted to share with you our deep appreciation for your work today at the autumn camp. It is a great honour for us to be able to witness the growth within both your souls.

"This is only the beginning though. The point of this earth-walk is not where or how far we move our feet, but how far we are moved in our hearts. Our lives are both a walking and a weaving. When a two-legged child is born, it is wrapped in a blanket. The blanket symbolizes our belonging place, a place where we are loved, nourished, and welcomed. Everyone deserves a place like this. Turtle Island was intended to be that place for all creatures as sons and daughters of the Great Creator. Many civilizations have forgotten *how* to walk *the good way.*

"There was a time, long ago, when a woman brought a message from the Great Sky Nation to the people of our ancestors. She appeared to two young braves. One had a pure heart. The other did not. His soul was tortured by greed and hatred. She released him back to the Creator. She told the man of integrity to gather all the people to hear her message. The people were connected to the land and so, understood that her message was going to be important for them. They built a long house to hold the entire village under one roof for the special ceremony that she would lead with them. When she arrived, she appeared as a white buffalo calf. We called the buffalo Thunder Beings because when they roamed freely across the land, their movement sounded like thunder.

"As she came nearer to the village, her form changed from the buffalo to one of a beautiful woman in a pure white doeskin dress and beaded moccasins who appeared to walk on a soft cloud. Her long black hair was tied in two braids that hung almost to the ground and were moved by a gentle breeze. When she walked upon the earth, the land breathed an expectant sigh."

Kiera's eyes grew as wide as saucers.

Eagle Man continued. "She entered the long house and walked sun-ward around the circle of our people four times, greeting each one – child, elder, chief, and all in between. She performed a ceremony to teach the sacredness of life. She taught about creation and the harmony that must exist between a woman and a man. You see, woman is the womb of all creation and man must support her in her creativity. From her medicine bundle, she gave us the Chanunpa pipe. It demonstrated how we come together, breathing as one, to create a life in harmony with the Great Creator and All That Is. She taught us the prayers that manifest us into Being at One with the Great Creator, Wakan Tanka.

"Before leaving our people, she instilled in each heart her prophecy. She promised to return in a time of great change. We would know the time was near when the Sacred White Buffalo Calf returned to roam the land once more. When she walked away from our ancestors, she took on the form of the buffalo again."

Kiera's face lit up as she said, "I read on the internet that a new white buffalo calf was born a few weeks ago in Colorado! Apparently, there have been several births in the last few years in North America." Thoughtfully, Kiera remembered the dancer who had appeared in one of the paintings she'd produced for the upcoming art exhibit. "Sasha, do you think it's possible that White Buffalo Calf Woman is the one in the painting?"

"Yesss, child. It isss she. White Buffalo Calf Woman hasss returned and isss available to mentor with thossse who will lead people back to *the good way.*

"The imagesss you paint create a shift in the heartsss of thossse who view them. It opensss them to desssire a deeper connection and allowsss them to begin to remember who they truly are. They begin to recognizsse their intuition as a guidancsse sssyssstem for their livesss. They begin to trussst the Creator'sss Will and to know an intenssse and reverent Love for All That Isss."

"I feel so honoured that White Buffalo Calf Woman has chosen me to announce her return. I guess I have to trust that what appears on the canvas will have the effect you say it has, Sasha."

Joshua chuckled saying, "I don't think that's going to be a problem."

"You are being guided in thisss way becaussse you agreed to do ssso, long before you entered thisss experiencsse on Earth. Now that you are consciousss of developing your awarenesss and relationship with All That Isss, you will noticsse the quickening."

"It does feel a bit overwhelming right now" Joshua admitted "with everything that Kiera, her grandmother and I are learning lately. I feel like it's all coming together though, like pieces of a puzzle. We each bring a piece that is completed by what someone else learns."

"Like the way you said the prayers over the waterfall at the medicine wheel today, which made me appreciate so much more the way Grandmother taught us to connect with the various elements of Mother Earth – Turtle Island" added Kiera.

Eagle Man beamed with pride, though the First People took measures to guard against having too much pride.

A great light filled the space they shared, causing Kiera and Joshua to shield their eyes once more. It lasted only a split second and then faded as quickly as it came – the darkness of the forest surrounded them again.

Opening their eyes, the pair found themselves alone at the edge of the steaming hot spring.

"Wow!" Joshua's one word may not have been elegant but it captured the depth and level of influence of the encounter they shared with Sasha and Eagle Man. "My heart feels as full as the first time I saw you – here at the spring."

Kiera turned to Joshua. "What do mean – here???"

Sheepishly, Joshua took both of Kiera's hands in his own, gently rubbing the backs of them with his thumbs. Lifting his eyes to meet her stunned gaze, he told her of the night when he and Nightsong came upon the vision of a dark-haired maiden bathing by the light of a full Buck Super Moon.

CHAPTER 30

SETTING INTENTION

Kiera woke to sunlight streaming across her pillow. Blinking, she executed a distinctly cat-like pandiculation[20]. Feeling groggy yet totally relaxed, her body hummed with satisfaction as she fully woke from her sleep. When the memory of the previous night came flooding in, she recalled the shock and amazement she had felt at knowing that Joshua had shared the same full moon at her hot spring! Emboldened by their shared experiences, his tender embrace brought their lips together in an explosion of emotional energy, which took them both by surprise.

"His kisses – Oooh, every time I think about being in his embrace, I get this warm flush like I've never felt

---

[20] Pandiculation is generally defined as the act of stretching and yawning, especially upon waking. Some good examples may be found here: www.rmtedu.com/blog/pandiculation

before. I get tingly all over! His lips are so soft and full. They are a direct contradiction to the firm angles of his cheeks and jaw." Thoughts of being in his embrace continued to distract Kiera while she dressed and ate breakfast. Shaking her head, she decided to focus on the plethora of tasks to complete for the art exhibit. Kiera had no time to waste on frivolous thoughts of a man.

Having moved to the verandah with her paint and supplies, Kiera stared at the blank canvas, paint brush in hand. There were so many moments that had implanted themselves indelibly in her mind from their trip to the medicine wheel on the previous day. How to choose which one to start first was the question.

Swirling Divine energy had ebbed and flowed around and through the four of them at the top of the waterfall. Grandmother's lessons of creating a deeper connection with Mother Earth – Turtle Island – and the elements had touched Kiera's heart and soul so deeply that she'd felt tears of ecstasy when she felt the Earth Mother recognize her own soul.

"How do I even begin to capture than in an image?" she wondered. "Then there was the expansive wonder of the beauty of the camp from the view above the falls; the feeling of flying on the wind when our cedar fronds were lifted in prayer; and I'm certain that Eagle Man was there, speaking through Joshua – especially in the way Joshua prayed his gratitude for the guidance he's received! The fact that Grandmother was able to ride horseback and walk through the Medicine Wheel was so amazing in itself, and I'm so grateful that she was compelled to come with us – without questioning whether she would be able to or not. It's kind of humbling to witness the strength and conviction she bears."

"She isss a willing Ssservant, revered for her dedication to the One you call God." Sasha had languorously spread himself in the sun, and lay zig-zagged across the verandah steps. Lifting his head in a nod toward the canvas, he asked, "What isss the messsage you intend to convey in thisss particular image?"

"That's a good question Sasha. I'm not in the habit of thinking that way before I begin a painting. Usually, I get an image in my mind and translate it to canvas, focusing only on the techniques required to create a desired feature or texture.

"I have so many images in my mind right now. I started to sketch some ideas last night after Joshua left, but I'm not sure which one to begin with now. They all seem to have different themes."

"Which themesss ssseem to be of priority to you?"

"Well, there's the connection with the Mother, Turtle Island. Also, the importance of prayer and gratitude for all things in our lives. The environment is pretty big for me – especially now that we are focused on having the Autumn Harvest Camp dedicated and protected as Sacred Ground. There's a 'family' theme that seems to be growing in my belly," laughed Kiera. "It's like we're all connected – One Being – with each other and have shared knowledge and experience. It's hard to describe, but it's almost as expansive as the air around the camp was yesterday. It seems to be continuously growing."

"It growsss with your own growth. If you could be more ssspecssific, what would be your primary focusss today?"

"It would have to be the way in which we are all connected – not just to the Earth and the Elements, but to one another."

"And how would you dessscribe that connection?"

"As deep and as old as the Earth herself! But there's a part of me that feels a 'disconnect' too. And maybe it's not me, but the general disconnect society has for the Earth. That's why she needs to be remembered; the reason that we need to raise awareness of the way we are destroying our habitat. It's like two sides of a coin."

"It isss the duality of humankind. The posssitive and the negative. A balancsse mussst be ssstruck between thessse two. You will need to be very ssspecssific in the messsage you portray in order to provoke an emotional reaction from your viewer." Sasha closed his eyes and allowed this thought to ferment within Kiera's mind. "What outcome would you like to sssee for the people who view your art?"

"I'm not sure I've ever given much thought to that. I just want them to enjoy my paintings – and maybe make a purchase!" Sobering, Kiera thought more deeply. "I would want them to be encouraged to share my vision of a world of peace and harmony, where Turtle Island is granted respect and care."

"Okay. Ssso, how doesss that world look to you? Be very ssspecssific about what detailsss you envision. Thisss isss important. The clearer the outcome in your mind, without engaging in limited thinking, the more it will allow the end resssult to be even more excsseptional than your desssire."

"Hmmm. I can see a world where everyone works together for the highest good for everyone. It's not that far a stretch. I think it is very much like the feeling of expansiveness we experienced yesterday saying our prayers of gratitude over the waterfall."

"It will become more imperative that you learn to ssset your 'intentionsss' before you begin your work – in what ever it isss you do. Your objectivesss must be clear, sssimple in their dessscription and limitlesss in their posssible outcome, desssiring only the highessst and the bessst for All. You mussst alssso remember that we do not have the *right* to limit the experiencsse of another individual. By thisss I mean, that we cannot impossse our own desssire on another. They have the Free Will to choossse their own realization of an experiencsse.

"When your intention isss in harmony with Divine Will and the highessst and bessst for all Creation, there isss no limit to what can be achieved or created. It isss all in alignment for the bessst outcome.

"When the mind putsss limitsss on the desssired outcome, it redussces sssignificantly what can be created and may not meet what is bessst for all. The problem comesss when holding tightly to what you want endsss up making you unavailable to ressceivee giftsss that may enhanssce other areasss of your life."

"It's kind of like the simplicity of following the Grandfather/Grandmother Teachings: Humility, Honesty,

Courage, Love, Wisdom, Respect and Trust. It doesn't get any easier than that," replied Kiera.

Taking several deep breaths, she closed her eyes. On the next breath, Kiera experienced a flow of energy moving from within the Earth's core, rising up through her feet. Simultaneously, a brilliant white light pierced through the top of her head and moved down to blend with the energy of the Earth Mother, in the centre chakra of her body – her heart.

Breathing deeply once more, she became aware that she was standing inside of an energy bubble that moved continuously through her body, like a torus. A fountain of energy flowed from the top of her head, pouring over and around her down into the ground, and back up through her feet.

A vision emerged in her heart space of energy swirling into the shape of a sphere. Rich blues and greens, wrapped in white-gold translucence, morphed into a beautiful globe, alive and brimming with hope.

Blinding white light exploded above her as the image faded. The intense sensation of light stayed with her, as Kiera took another breath deep into her belly and exhaled slowly through pursed lips.

An otherworldly energy began to stir the air around the canvas and easel. Opening her eyes, she saw how the image would begin to appear on the canvas before her. As it called paint to the brush, Kiera lifted her voice heavenward with offerings of immense gratitude. Kiera asked that her hands be guided to present this message in ways that would open the hearts of all who have eyes to see.

"May this gifted vision bring Hope to the ancestors who guide us. May all who receive its message feel compelled to become co-creators of Heaven on Earth."

CHAPTER 31

FAMILY OF ONE

Mavis, Kiera, Janet, and Joshua headed out early in Joshua's big pickup truck toward Cache Creek. They planned to meet with the Council of Elders of the Stoney Nakota Nation at the Community Centre. The Council often made use of a small gathering room there, and today, they intended to discuss how to proceed with protecting the Autumn Harvest Camp.

"When Ken called me the other day, I honestly didn't expect a meeting so soon! I guess the elders feel a strong need to move quickly on this issue, before anyone has a chance to desecrate the grounds of the camp and the Medicine Wheel. It would be a real crime to lose that connection to our family's heritage."

Janet was honest in saying, "I had no idea you were even remotely interested in our family history, Joshua. This came as quite a surprise!"

"It surprises me too, Janet. I had no interest until that day when Nightsong and I headed up the mountain ridge and came upon the camp."

Up until the previous night, Joshua really hadn't shared much with his sister about meeting Eagle Man and Chief Rain Dancer, their many times great-grandfather. She was not convinced that he didn't really need some psych evaluation, in her opinion. After learning that Ken Strongbow had driven all the way down from Cache Creek to check it out, she had to agree that there must be some thread of truth to the story.

"I'm grateful you invited me to come along with you today. It will be interesting to see how we are all related," Janet mused.

"Are you sure they really want Grandmother and me to sit in on this discussion?" Kiera asked, feeling a bit shy about meeting the Elders. The respect which they were granted by the Nakota clan was a bit daunting and unfamiliar for someone not raised in the indigenous culture. Mavis had certainly taught her to respect her elders, but this was a far different level of regard than what she had experienced from the fringe of the white community where she was raised.

"Ken specifically asked for the two of you to come with me. I think it has to do with Eagle Man's prophesy of the two women who would help me connect with my culture. He is very sure that the Elders want you to be included in today's discussion."

Mavis added, "I hope we don't keep them waiting too long. Are we almost there?"

They all laughed at her childlike inquiry as the sign for the Cache Creek Welcome Centre appeared ahead of them.

***

A small table was set to the right of the entrance in the gathering room. As they approached, a young woman stood up to greet them. Simultaneously, Ken Strongbow shouldered his way through that same door into the lobby saying, "I'll be right back."

In his haste to check on the arrival of his guests, Ken almost plowed right into Joshua. "You're here! That's great. Welcome!" Ken extended one hand to Joshua while clapping his shoulder with the other.

"Ken Strongbow, I'd like to introduce my sister, Janet Daniels. And this is Mavis Deerfoot and her granddaughter, Kiera Clark. I couldn't have begun this adventure without their help."

"It's an honour to meet you all. Most everyone is here. We're just waiting for a couple more people to arrive who are coming from a bit further away. I'll get you all to sign in with Jeannie please, so we have a complete list of who is here today. When you're done, come on in and we'll get you settled. I've saved seats for you at the other end of the room."

Mavis asked discreetly, "Mr. Strongbow, is there a powder room where I can freshen up after our long drive?"

Kiera, Janet, and Joshua signed the meeting register

while Ken showed Mavis the way to the women's washroom. A few more people arrived in the following ten minutes. When Mavis rejoined their small group, Ken led them to their designated seats.

"The Elders have already smudged. I love the fragrance of sage," commented Mavis.

Once they were comfortable, Ken stood up and announced that the meeting would begin. Thirty-five people were present, the majority being the Council of Elders and some of their adult children. The chairs had been arranged in a circular fashion, allowing everyone to see and be seen. Ken nodded to one of the older men who was seated half way around the east side of the room. He stood slowly and gathered a half shell and a braid of sweetgrass[21] from the floor in front of his chair.

Moving to the centre of the circle of Elders, he said "A'ho! In honour of our Ancestors, we call this gathering to witness the wisdom and guidance that they continue to provide for us as we offer gratitude for ourselves and for the seven generations to come." That said, he lit the braid and began to smudge the hall. He asked for clarity and direction on how to proceed and asked for protection from those forces who would dishonour the ancestors and bring harm to the Autumn Harvest Camp of the Nakota people. He offered gratitude for the youth who would lead the way in designating a Sacred Site.

---

[21] Sweetgrass is used in prayer, smudging and purifying ceremonies. It is usually braided, dried, and burned. It is usually burned at the beginning of a prayer or ceremony to attract positive energies. www.northernc.on.ca/indigenous/four-sacred-medicines/

Then smudging himself, he passed the braid and shell to each member of the circle for them to do the same.

"The Elders and Ancestors have been waiting for this time. I am grateful to stand among the members of this Council of Elders and be able to see what was prophesied come to pass. We have a duty to our Earth Mother, Turtle Island, to honour, respect and protect her. We will do what we can to help."

A reverent peace grew in the room while the sweetgrass was passed from one person to the next. No one broke the silence – rather, they allowed it to breathe through them, adding their own prayers for the greater good of all. Even as the sweetgrass required rekindling, an aura of solidarity swelled throughout the band of people brought together by the Ancestors.

Pausing to allow the last person to complete their smudge, Ken said, "Îsnî'yes – Thank you, Ray." Then he began the meeting by asking everyone to introduce themselves. Turning to Joshua, Janet, Kiera and Mavis, he smiled and added, "this may take some time, for people who are not accustomed to our introductions. Our Nation believes that we cannot know who we are unless we know from where we come. We are fortunate to have among us, much of the knowledge that has come from the Star People through our Elders. As a world that has forgotten how to be this deeply connected with our heritage, we have much to learn from the oral teaching our Elders."

A handful of the Council members chose to share their indigenous names as well as their common names and their deepest wisdom with respect to our connections with one another and the blessings of the Union of Nations under the leadership of the Earth Mother. Two men had driven from a greater distance – one from a government office in Edmonton and one from the Wabamun Creek area where the Nelson House trading post[22] was kept by the Nakota people. The last to introduce themselves, Joshua, Janet, Mavis and Kiera gave their names and stated from where they had come. Mavis added timidly that she was a descendant of the Siksika Nation and made a reference to the reservation where her parents had lived.

Ray stood again to begin the meeting by saying, "I am grateful that you have all come today. It is important that we share our stories, so that we can know our history and be guided to a future that supports all that is good about our lives here on Turtle Island. I say Îsnî'yes – Thank you!

"I spoke with only three of the Elders before calling this meeting, as Ray mentioned. There have been signs that the Ancestors are talking to us about the preservation of the lands – particularly lands used by the Nakota people many hundreds of years ago. I have invited guests here who have heard the Ancestors speak to them. They have called on us and asked for our help.

"We've all heard the stories of a time when our people used to camp high up on the mountain ridges in the autumn months, where the Ancestors met a young man

[22] A short historical article includes information about the formation of Nelson House by the Hudson Bay Company: www.mhs.mb.ca/docs/mb history/15/hbc.shtml

they claimed was from the future. Many of our own people have laughed at, and scorned the story, yet the story continues to be told to this day. The actual location of the Autumn Harvest Camp has been hidden from us for more than a hundred years now. Recently, it was located by Joshua Daniels, whose property is just on the other side of that same ridge. I was invited to go to look at the site a few days ago. What I found was proof that Eagle Man was not crazy! The story is true. I'll let this young fella explain the rest of it. Allow me to introduce to you, our brother, Walks Through Time."

As Joshua stood, shocked whispers passed through the assembled group, while five white-haired Elders simply nodded and grinned.

"I don't know if I'll ever get used to my new name. I can only hope that I continue to deserve it. Much has happened in a very short time. I came upon the Autumn Harvest Camp of Chief Rain Dancer one day while riding along the ridge behind my horse farm. As I looked down on the valley below the falls, I saw tepees and people around a camp fire. They wore clothing that the First People would have worn about three hundred and fifty years ago. A young man waved me down from the ridge and said that they had been waiting for me. I was introduced to the Chief, who is my many times great-grandfather; his son Red Feather, the man who had waved me in; and Eagle Man, their Medicine Man. It was Eagle Man who told me that I was descended from the Chief, and that the eagle had told them when I would arrive. Theirs was a small party that had come to the camp two months ahead of the remainder of the band, who were at Lake Wakamne for the summer." Chuckling, he added, "It was quite an experience and I wondered if I hadn't suffered sun stroke and dreamed the whole experience!

"A couple of weeks later, someone in town mentioned that human bones had been found somewhere near my place. They thought that an archaeologist was planning to conduct a dig to exhume what indigenous artifacts they could find.

"My friend, Kiera Clark, and I rode up to the camp and found survey flags that had been placed all over the valley and there was evidence of shallow digging in some areas. We took a whole lot of pictures and removed the flags. I have no experience in dealing with these kinds of things, so I asked Kiera to see if her grandmother knew what to do. We knew, in our hearts, that there was something special about this valley. A few days later, thanks to Mrs. Deerfoot, we were able to return to smudge, and ask the Ancestors to protect the camp while we sought help to see if any land claims had been filed.

"I am still kind of amazed at the fact that we found ourselves up here in Cache Creek so soon after that. We then asked at the Information Centre if there was someone who would have knowledge of the area's history – that's how I connected with Ken Strongbow. He came down to my place almost immediately.

"When Ken and I returned to the site of the camp, we found evidence we think will make this piece of land worthy of Sacred Site designation. We discovered a Medicine Wheel on a ledge above the falls. It would appear that when Kiera and I smudged to invoke the protection of the Ancestors, the Medicine Wheel was awakened. I don't know anything about them – or didn't until Ken came along. The circle seems to exude power and it's really incredible to feel that energy when you're standing in the centre of it.

"We also found what appeared to be a cairn when we were heading back up to the top of the ridge and the east side of the valley. It had been set into the side of the mountain, facing the Medicine Wheel. The cairn had been damaged by time and possibly animals. There were still many bones left inside and some very intricate beads – jasper, carnelian and turquoise. We thought it must have been someone very important to the clan, so we replaced as many stones as we could, to protect the Ancestor's Spirit.

"As we moved along the ridge above the camp, a group of people came into the valley from the north end. They very quickly began to map out the valley with survey markers again. We figured them to be archaeologists. Then Ken and I witnessed a bear lumber out of the forest. Someone screamed. The grizzly stood up on its hind legs, frightening the group. He was still on the opposite side of the narrow river that feeds the valley, but they recognized the threat. That bear effectively protected the site of the camp area from the intruders! When he bowed to the eagle, who had appeared overhead, I knew that this was an intervention of the Ancestors. We called the Provincial Park Rangers to report the illegal dig when we returned to my place.

"At Ken's suggestion, Mrs. Deerfoot, Kiera, and I returned to the camp with my lead hand the other day. We found the path by which the intruders had travelled into the valley. It appeared that the Park Rangers had retrieved all the equipment the archaeologists had left behind in their haste to leave.

"We climbed up to the top of the waterfall, to where the stone circle, or Medicine Wheel, is located. The power of this circle is so tangible! With guidance from Mrs. Deerfoot, we offered prayers to the Ancestors with cedar, releasing them over the falls before walking the Sacred Circle. I've never seen anything quite like it, but then I really didn't know much about my heritage until I met Eagle Man, Chief Rain Dancer, and Red Feather. I've come to learn so much in the past few weeks, and I'm both humbled and grateful."

Joshua took a deep breath before saying, "To be honest, I didn't think I had any family left except my sister. Now, I come to find out that we have a whole village! I can't begin to tell you what that means to me." Joshua took a moment to blink back tears and choked on the lump that had formed in his throat.

Looking to each of the Elders around the room, Joshua said, "I'm not sure where we go from here. I know that we need to stop the archaeologists from disturbing the Ancestors and the camp. I believe that I was brought to the camp for a reason. I am certain that we are to learn how to use the Medicine Wheel again – to walk the circle for our future. I'm sure that we can find a way… together. Thank you."

"Îsnî'yes, Joshua. I know, for myself, I was blown away by the sheer intensity of the power at the harvest camp and the Medicine Wheel. I believe that the connection to the Ancestors is very strong there and that it was awakened by you and Kiera. Your intentions must have been very clear and honourable. Even the horses seemed to respect the energy there!" Ken laughed, remembering the way the two horses sensed when it was time to leave and directed the men toward the cairn. "I think we won't have to wonder long about who is actually buried in the cairn. Just so the rest of you are aware, we did cover all the bones and beads that we found, in as much the way of the Ancestors as possible to preserve its integrity."

Joshua stood again and said "Excuse me, Ken. I forgot to mention that we did confirm the other day that the cairn protects the body of Eagle Man himself. This may sound even more far fetched – but an eagle brought a single bead to Mrs. Deerfoot's house while Kiera and I were having lunch with her. When he dropped it on the table, I realized that the beads we found resemble those I saw on Eagle Man's medicine bundle."

"I thought it might be," exclaimed Ken. "Now, I'm sure there may be some questions."

The room filled with murmurs of surprise, knowing nods of approval, and sheer excitement.

One of the younger men raised his hand and asked, "The threat of archaeological digs is very real, as we well know. Do we know if the folks who found the first bones have filed for permits?"

"We don't know that yet. I would imagine that permits won't be forthcoming immediately, given the amount of red tape this kind of endeavour generates. However, we do know that they were ambitious enough to survey the area and take some relics. Although, we don't know who these people are or what organization they represent, we did see them return to the camp as we were leaving it. I don't think they'll be returning terribly soon though – especially after the grizzly showed them the way out of the valley," he chuckled.

The man who had come from Edmonton, stood up. He had said his name was Roger Long. He was here to represent the office of the Heritage Division of Alberta Culture, Multiculturalism and Status of Women. He respected the grave nature of the situation and admitted to being one quarter Sioux.

Turning his attention to Joshua, he continued. "I heard you say that you have detailed photographs of the site. I presume you can also provide latitude and longitudinal coordinates, so it can be found again?"

Joshua informed him that they had been able to identify the location of the camp on a map of the Provincial Park.

Mr. Long nodded and continued. "Good. Under the *Alberta Heritage Resources Act*[23], Part 3 – Historic Resource Management, Section 16; the Autumn Harvest Camp, the

---

[23] Alberta Heritage Resources Act: Queen's Printer www.qp.alberta.ca/1266.cfm?page=H09.cfm&leg_type=Acts&isbncln=9780779822591

grave, and the medicine stone circle all qualify as historic resources. I can get our team out there to assess the site pretty quickly. Once our experts take a look at it, we will be able to tell you what we can do to protect it."

CHAPTER 32

SACRED SPACE

The path of advocacy was both exciting and intense, carrying Kiera and Joshua along on a journey neither of them had anticipated for themselves. The two had led the government authentication team to the Autumn Harvest Camp and the Medicine Wheel. While there, they had staked out a temporary fence around the cairn to provide further protection for it. Extensive documentation of the discovery's historical nature was filed in triplicate with the appropriate authorities.

Usually, the gears of any governmental process were found to move extremely slowly. In this instance, the complete opposite transpired. The Provincial Park officials, once notified of the impending protection status, developed a security protocol until such time as the official status could be posted at the site.

Joshua liaised with the Council of Elders, the office of

the Heritage Division of Alberta Culture, Multiculturalism and Status of Women, and the Jasper Provincial Park Rangers. The additional activity and the energy of the stone circle provided Kiera with endless inspiration for her art. She was easily able to fulfill her obligation to provide fifteen paintings for the gallery exhibit, though doing so made it challenging for her and Joshua to find time to be alone together.

As the days began to shorten and temperatures cooled in the mountains, Kiera and Joshua learned what it meant to *go within.* Each discovered new ways to learn, absorbed information quickly, and integrated their newfound knowledge into their daily routines until practice made recognizing and using the ambient energies automatic. Together, they stepped more fully into an intuitive life – embodying what they learned from their spirit guides and from one another. They found they worked well together, even while crafting simple, yet elegant frames for Kiera's art.

Autumn whispered the summer away in the blink of an eye. So much had been accomplished. Excitement grew among residents and tourists alike, as news spread about the historical relevance of the area. Those closest to Kiera were thrilled with the impending opportunity to view her work.

***

Kiera parked her Jeep in the lot adjacent to the gallery. It was early still, and yet the lot was half-filled with vehicles. She noted Ken Strongbow's big truck and several friends' cars. A few spots from the end of the lot was a big panel van equipped with a small satellite dish on top of it. Stencilled in large red print on the side of the van were the call letters of a major tv broadcast station from Edmonton.

Drawing in a ragged breath, Kiera shuddered. Mavis reached for her hand to offer her support and strength. From the corner of her eye she saw Joshua walking toward the passenger's side of her car to open the door for Mavis. Janet squealed with delight as she ran around the vehicle's front end to hug Kiera as she exited the vehicle.

"I'm so excited for you! I can't wait to see all the work you've done for this exhibit. I've told everyone I know that they have to come out to see it. Meadoe said they are anticipating a full house tonight. Are you ready? Oooh! I love your dress."

Kiera had taken great care in choosing what to wear. The simple black cocktail dress, fashioned from dupioni silk cut along princess lines accentuated her sleek figure. Her grandmother had gifted her a single strand of pearls in honour of completing such a large work of art for this exhibition. Black patent leather kitten heels completed the look of understated elegance that belied the lack of confidence Kiera felt. "My stomach feels like it's full of butterflies! I don't think I was this nervous for the final art show at school last year," remarked Kiera.

Stopping before the entrance, Mavis said "I am so proud of you Kiera. I know that at times this summer you wondered if you were up to the tasks that the Creator

God had set before you. Both you and Joshua have accomplished amazing things and I couldn't be more excited for both of you. Now, let's go see how much your work will impact this community due to your efforts!"

"Thank you, Grandmother!" Kiera said, gently squeezing Mavis' arm.

Joshua opened the door for the women to walk through. The strains of soft drum music matched the beat of Kiera's heart when Joshua stepped between her and her grandmother. Placing one hand on Kiera's back and taking Mavis gently by the elbow, Joshua escorted them into the first of the gallery's display areas. People milled around and down the hall, spilling into several other areas. An older couple eagerly examined the framed paintings on one side of the room while a small group of people sat on a bench discussing another of Kiera's paintings.

The gallery was housed in a very large, chalet style building sectioned off into several small viewing rooms, set off from the central space of the main floor. Three of Kiera's paintings were displayed on easels directly ahead, two thirds of the way into the centre of the main room. Beside each one was a wrought iron stand holding a sign. These three pieces were designated as a fundraising donation toward the preservation and maintenance of the Autumn Harvest Camp and the Medicine Circle of Chief Rain Dancer and Eagle Man of the Nakota Nation. On a fourth easel was a 20" x 16" full colour aerial view of the valley, the sacred stone circle and placement of the burial cairn. The paintings would be auctioned at the end of the two-week long exhibit. The resulting proceeds would be used to contribute to the production of signage designating the entire camp area as sacred ground, and possibly a couple of benches for visitors. A government grant had been approved to provide maintenance of a hiking trail from the nearest access road into the valley.

The local branch of the Historical Society had offered to partner in producing two large, permanent signs depicting the life of Indigenous First Nations to be placed strategically within the valley and at the entrance to the Medicine Wheel. The cairn was to be preserved with protective fencing and a small memorial plaque in memory of Eagle Man, Medicine Man of the Nakota First Nation.

Joshua, Kiera, Mavis, and the Council of Elders had agreed that it was important that the Wisdom of the Ancestors be shared with as many people as possible. In this way, they hoped that humanity would gain a deeper respect for our connection with All That Is and recognize the intrinsic and interdependent relationship of humanity and our environment.

"Here's our guest of honour!" Tracy exclaimed, as she approached Kiera from one side of the viewing area. Kiera walked into Tracy's outstretched arms and received a warm and generous hug. "There are so many people here that I want you to meet. First, I want to do some general introductions to start the evening and then our press connection wants to get a couple of photos of you with the collection you have donated for the auction. Let's get you some champagne before we start."

Leading Kiera and the small entourage toward a corner to their left, Tracy commandeered a tray of crystal champagne flutes from the bar. Satisfied that everyone was suitably prepared to toast the success of Kiera's first local art exhibit, Tracy handed the tray back to the bartender and moved to a microphone set up near the bar. Taking Kiera by the hand, Tracy tapped the mic to get everyone's attention.

"Good evening everyone! I'd like to have your attention please. I know there are visitors throughout the building and I would like for everyone to join us here, in the Carlyle Room, in five minutes.

A tall, distinguished man strode toward them as Tracy pulled Kiera a few steps away from the microphone. "I need to introduce you to this gentleman. Mr. Demelio, may I present Miss Kiera Clark, our feature artist. And this is her grandmother, Mrs. Mavis Deerfoot; Mr. Joshua Daniels, and his sister, Ms. Janet Daniels. Kiera, Mr. Demelio is the owner of an eclectic collection of Indigenous art in Ottawa. He has generously loaned them to a small gallery there for the next three months, so that the public can enjoy them as much as he does."

"Miss Clark," he said, taking her hand, "it is a pleasure to meet you. Your work is so exhilarating! I understand that a great deal of the inspiration came from the discovery of an old Medicine Wheel in a valley near here. I can only imagine the effort it took to do what the group of you have accomplished in a few short weeks."

"Thank you" replied Kiera. "I still have to pinch myself to see if I'm not dreaming all of this!"

"I realize that there are a lot of people who would like to congratulate you tonight, so I won't take much more of your time." Drawing a business card from his pocket he added, "I wonder if you would call me in a day or two please? I'd like to arrange for your work to be exhibited in my friend's gallery in Ottawa. I believe that the world needs to experience your perspective in order to wake them up to the plight of our planet. Your creations can't help but activate the awareness necessary to make a difference."

"Oh my! Thank you! Are you sure? I don't know how to thank you," stammered Kiera.

"I am certain. When I arrived here this evening, I was absolutely entranced by the energy of each of your paintings. I know that they hold great importance." Leaning in, he whispered "I have placed a sizable bid on each of the paintings you have offered for auction."

"Wow! I am so honoured. Of course, I'll call you on Monday if that's okay."

"Certainly. Thank you. Enjoy your evening and congratulations on a very successful showing!"

Mavis, Joshua, and Janet beamed at Kiera as she stood registering the compliment made by Mr. Demelio. Meadoe joined them just as Tracy took hold of her arm to lead her back to the microphone. The room quickly filled with guests who had all come to see her work and support a great cause.

Tracy began, "Welcome everyone, to our first gallery showing of the intuitive work of artist Kiera Clark! We are honoured to have her here with us tonight to launch a very important fundraiser for the Sacred Land Dedication of the Nakota First Nation's Autumn Harvest Camp, the Medicine Wheel, and the prestigious burial ground of one of the Nation's most influential Medicine Men.

"When I asked Kiera at the beginning of the summer to produce a few pieces for a showing, aside from knowing that it would touch the souls of people who experienced her work, I had no idea what to expect. Her unique painting style is described as 'intuitive' because it expresses the emotion of an image, rather than a realistic visual rendition, and incorporates textures and media that increase the visceral experience of the viewer. In addition to the fifteen paintings that were contracted for the show, Kiera has donated three exceptional productions for the auction being held at the end of the exhibition. So, you have lots of time to enter your bid on all three of these paintings. We won't mind if you check back several times throughout the next couple of weeks to be sure yours is the highest bid! Kiera, would you like to say a few words?"

Stepping up to the microphone, Kiera cleared her throat. "I'm so honoured that you've all taken the time to come out to the gallery in support of our fundraiser and the work I've done. We're so grateful. I'd like to thank my grandmother for believing in me. Without her insight and love, I don't know if we'd be standing here. I'd also like to thank my friends, Joshua Daniels, Ken Strongbow, the Council of Elders, and the whole host of Ancestors, Spirit Guides and our Turtle Island home."

Joshua stepped forward at that moment, to whisper

in Kiera's ear that Mr. Long had arrived and asked to say a few words.

Nodding her head in approval and noting his appearance behind Joshua, Kiera spoke, "I'd like to introduce someone else, without whom the dedication of the camp would not be happening. Mr. Roger Long is here from Edmonton. I'm really sorry," she added, "You'd think by now I'd remember the proper name of your office!" Laughing she stepped back to hand over the microphone.

"Thank you. Good evening Ladies and Gentlemen. I am here representing the Office of the Heritage Division of Alberta Culture, Multiculturalism and Status of Women. I've had the distinct honour of working with both Mr. Daniels and Miss Clark over the past several weeks in identifying, mapping, and recording the details of what we are calling the Nakota Autumn Harvest Camp.

"The designation of the camp came about as a result of someone finding human remains while hiking up in the valley. The individual who made the report also filed a claim to conduct an archaeological dig under an assumed name. He has since been arrested for attempting to sell artifacts found at the site on a subsequent visit he made." The audience gasped and murmurs of indignation moved as a wave through the gathered guests.

"The artifacts have been recovered and have been sent out to a specialized lab for carbon dating and authentication, after which they will be displayed at a local heritage museum. I'm pleased to say that the Nakota Autumn Harvest Camp more than exceeded the requirements for designation as a Heritage Site and will, therefore, be protected from any future opportunists.

"What these two don't yet know is that the waterfall in the camp valley is being officially recognized as Eagle's Falls, being named after the clan's Medicine Man."

Shock and amazement registered on the faces of Kiera, Mavis, Ken, and Janet as tears of joy filled Joshua's eyes. He reached out to clasp Roger's hand in his.

"I don't know how to thank you, man."

"Nothing to thank me for. You did the work and it's an honour to have been a part of preserving the memory of your ancestors into perpetuity. By the way, Kiera, I don't know if I'm too late to place the starting bid, but I'd like to put a bid of $1,000 on one of the paintings being auctioned." The roar of many hands clapping filled the space of the gallery.

Roger shook hands and chatted briefly with the small group that had gathered near the microphone before moving away to explore the exhibition of Kiera's work.

Joshua leaned in toward Kiera and whispered in her ear, "Well, I guess there's only one more thing left to do."

Kiera looked into his eyes questioning "What do you mean? We can't do anything more until the exhibit ends and we close the bidding on the fundraiser."

With that, Joshua pulled his hand from his pocket to reveal a small velvet box as he knelt on one knee before her. Mavis gasped and held her hand over her mouth, daring not to breathe.

"Kiera, together we've learned how much we need to grow in order to walk *the good way*. There is so much more to learn. I can't begin to imagine doing that without you by my side. Life will be filled with so much more wonder and grace as we continue to share what we learn together. Will you marry me?"

Flipping open the top of the box, Joshua revealed a stunning ring of small diamonds that framed a central turquoise stone. "Eagle Man told me to keep the bead that he gave us when we were at your grandmother's that day. I had it mounted for you." He gulped and begged, "Please say yes – don't keep me in suspense!"

Kiera, eyes brimming with joy, extended her hand for him to place the ring upon her finger.

CHAPTER 33

KUNDALINI RISING

The sun was just about to breech the treetops as Joshua loosely draped Nightsong's reins over the arm of a sapling. Kiera followed, gently leaping off Sundance and tying her to one of the branches, lodged between two trees, that had been used to corral the horses almost a month ago.

Joshua realized that walking the Labyrinth at Cache Creek had settled his soul in the same way as the Medicine Wheel of his Ancestors. The energy was like a magnet and had drawn him to spend every spare moment at the Medicine Wheel.

The sky was clear, brilliant and full of the sounds of a mountain waking to greet the day. Birds fluttered about the trees feeding on small bugs on the leaves and trunks. Flying squirrels dove from tree to tree, chattering to one another in animated voices. The scent of pines and moss filled the air with a fresh woodsy aroma that enticed the mind to store it as memory. These perceptions combined and tugged at both their hearts. The mountain was home.

The few short weeks of summer had passed in a flurry of activity. They had come to the Medicine Wheel to give thanks, offer smudge and reflect on their recent accomplishments.

Joshua took Kiera's hand, gently rubbing his thumb across the turquoise stone of the engagement ring she'd accepted the previous evening. He escorted her to the edge of the Sacred Circle, and gazed at the standing stone that was at its heart. It stood shoulder high to an average six-foot man and had one crevice at the top that sank three feet into the centre of the rock. Many profound grooves scarred its surface, appearing to have been carved by nature.

Joshua led the way as they walked in the footsteps of the Ancestors, walking the circle from the east southward, adding their energies to the evolutionary spiral of life force connecting all of Creation to the Great Mystery of All That Is. Allowing herself to be directed, Kiera became more acutely aware of the abundance all around her. Colours intensified before her eyes and the sun's warmth radiated through her body. Her awareness became one with her surroundings. The sound of birds rustling through dense tree foliage and small animals foraging in the undergrowth enveloped her, and seemed amplified to the point that she salivated, anticipating the small morsel of food just in front of them.

Returning to the east, Joshua continued to walk in a

circular pattern, moving ever closer to the great central stone. As he reached the centre of the spiral path, he examined the small grooves on the edges of three flat horizontal surfaces on the Standing Stone. It appeared as if they had been chipped out by hand with a rudimentary chisel. They each measured between six and ten inches in length and were five to six inches wide. It was hard to tell if the dark staining on them was natural or from something that had burnt itself into the stone.

"I wonder if Eagle Man burned sage or sweetgrass here," he mused.

"Wouldn't it be likely that many years of sage, cedar, and sweetgrass have blessed this rock? I'll bet their smoke walked the Sacred Circle with him and many others," replied Kiera.

"Then we'll do as Eagle Man did and offer smudge on all three ledges – together – the first one to honour the Earth and all the Elements that feed and nourish life, the second for the Ancestors who paved our way and continue to guide us, and the third for the Creator of All That Is." Joshua lit a smudge stick and called the smoke to wash over himself, repeating the words they had learned together. Kiera did the same and then moved to stand opposite Joshua, on the other side of the large central stone.

Three small bundles of cedar, white sage, and sweetgrass had been carefully woven with prayers of love and gratitude under the watchful eye of Mavis earlier in the week. One burning bundle was placed on each of the three ledges. Joshua offered their prayers of gratitude and fell silent. Kiera's heart was filled with appreciation.

They had followed the sun's path from the east, which led to the Great Central Stone and the *innerstanding* that all answers lie within the soul's connection to Mother Earth and to Father Creator. Once again, they gave thanks for greater awareness of the energies all around them. Then, the two turned as one to retrace the steps of their inward route.

Grounded in the joy of the moment, Kiera sighed. "I love the feeling of peace and being centred I get when we are here walking the Circle."

"I know. It takes my breath away every time!" The water called to him as it poured forth from beneath the shelf rock to Joshua's right. Its song was a never-ending flow of playful splashes on the smaller rocks below. The water's source wasn't visible from above the shelf. Curious, he walked down the path a few feet, to explore the underside of the shelf rock. Stepping carefully onto wet stones beneath the shelf, he discovered another ledge.

"Kiera, come see this!" he called.

Not far behind him, she slipped her hand into his to see what he'd found. Together, they walked behind the curtain of water onto a shelf that spanned the width of the water's fall. The ledge was narrow and smelled of algae growing on the rock face behind the falls. The water seemed to roar in their ears as soon as they stepped into the hidden space. A fine mist filled the air in front of them, at once cool and refreshing.

Their joined hands, raised up together, parted the wall of water before them. An image wavered before their eyes. A group of clouds were tiered, like a staircase, ascending high into the sky. One of the uppermost clouds was shaped like a buffalo. In an instant, it transformed into the shape of a woman. As she descended the cloud stairway, her image came into sharp contrast with the surroundings. Drawing nearer, her image shimmered in the midst of the water, directly in front of Kiera and Joshua. White Buffalo Calf Woman greeted them with a warm smile. Stretching her hands toward them, she touched their brows – anointing both of them.

"One drop of water connects you with All That Is."

At her words, one drop of water fell from each of her outstretched hands. As the droplets landed, one on each of them, and permeated the skin of their brows, a perfect sphere became visible to their inner eyes. It was translucent with a sheen that seemed to float, and then shifted into an explosion of colour reflecting all the shades of the rainbow. Limitless energy expanded in the next instant, into a brilliant display of light radiating in all directions from the sphere.

She continued. "Just as a river flows upon the Earth, feeds the ground, and nourishes the trees and plants, so too does it strengthen the medicine each one offers for the good of all. The water passes into the creatures of the land as they quench their thirst, becoming part of them also."

White Buffalo Calf Woman stepped to one side and pointed to a vision which had appeared in the valley below the falls. An ancestral grandmother scooped water from the river into a small clay cup and lifted it to the sky. As she took a sip of the water, Kiera and Joshua felt the water trickle down their own throats, and became aware of its energy as it travelled through their bodies. The water coursed into their blood and nourished their souls. They felt the grandmother's song of thanks and praise for the gift of water, as it echoed in their hearts.

"When water returns to the Earth as fertilizer, the Great Mother filters the pure element of water and carries it to the lakes and oceans. There, each drop is combined with others who share their connections with the Earth and its creatures. While each droplet retains its individuality, it is also part of the wholeness of the streams, the rivers, the lakes, and ultimately, the sea. When the Sun shines its radiance upon the lakes and oceans, the water rises into the sky and the Thunder Beings gather it to be dispersed upon the land once more as individual droplets that carry the knowledge of All That Is. Water remembers the essence of the Great Mother. The Great Mystery of the divine nature of all life was imprinted upon the water by Father Sky so that we would always hold that knowledge within us. In the same way, Spirit memories of all time (past, present, and future) and space are recorded in water.

"You are a vital part of All That Is. By asking the blessing of water's medicine for your body, it will activate your ability to access the knowledge of the ancestors and allow you to preserve the lessons you learn for the children of the future. In the way that each snowflake is unique, each one is a part of the One Great Ocean of Life. Integrate this knowing into your awareness of the oneness of all life and you will unleash a continuous stream of abundant, unconditional love and support. Remembering this connection will assist you to live *the good way.*"

Kiera replied, overcome with emotion, "I will never look at water the same way again. Thank you so much for sharing this lesson with us." She hesitated, then asked, "How can we continue to grow and support what is best for All of Life?"

Smiling benevolently, White Buffalo Calf Woman placed a hand over both Joshua and Kiera's hearts and spoke into their minds – without audible words. "With attentive engagement, you have embarked upon the development of your Light-bodies – the energetic life force that flows through and around your physical form. There are some specific practices that will enhance your awareness of that subtle force. They begin with conscious breath."

Joshua's and Kiera's eyes closed gently as they were drawn toward inward sight. "Breathe into the Oneness within. Still your mind by releasing your thoughts with your next exhalation. Notice the tug and pull in the energy centres within your physical form. Notice how each one flows in multiple directions. Now become aware of how they continuously flow into one energetic harmonization of energy – together. Breathe once more, into that one force that is your Light essence, and feel your awareness of it expand.

"Now, draw your attention to the space slightly behind and above your eyes, to your third eye energy centre. See within its core, the geometric form of a Merkaba[24] – two interlocking tetrahedrons, one pointed up and the other, pointing down. Allow the Merkaba to spin in a clockwise direction. With your next in-breath, witness this energy moving toward your throat centre, then through the heart centre, and continue this way down through each of your energy centres. Releasing your breath, allow this Merkaba to gravitate to the central core of our Turtle Island home. Witness it resting there to gather and draw into itself, the platinum white-gold crystalline energy of Gaia. With each rotation of the Merkaba, feel it gather more power.

"Begin to draw the Merkaba back up through the layers of Mother Earth with your next inhalation. Let it stop at a place just below your feet, where it spins – transforming its energy into a platinum disc. Now allow it to move upward once again, raising a column of light around your physical being.

"Feel it radiate, as it climbs up around your feet, your ankles, your knees and up your legs. Allow it to rest briefly, circulating around the base of your spine, igniting new frequencies within the root chakra. Notice the sensations in your body as this energy continues to ascend, creating a cylinder of light encompassing your physical form, continuing its upward journey. It pauses at

[24] To gain greater understanding of the Merkaba, check out these weblinks: https://www.ancient-symbols.com/symbols-directory/merkaba.html and https://en.wikipedia.org/wiki/Merkabah_mysticism

each of your chakra centres, fully illuminating them with the brilliance of the platinum white-gold light. Once it has reached the top of your head, feel the light ascend to a place just above it, where it spins once more – filling in the space above you with a second disc – thereby sealing your body into a 12th dimensional shield.

"Turn to face one another and playfully and lovingly, allow the energies of each chakra to connect with your partner's corresponding chakra. Respect the love you share with one another in this way. Then, focus on the energy of the root chakra and allow that energy to build between you. Breathing in with intention, allow your joined energies to rise up to your belly centres. Embrace the creative force that grows between you. Allow this energy to flow through each of your body's chakra centres, building intensity as your focus point travels upward to the crown of your heads. Here, the energy rushes out of the crown to envelop your bodies together, in one continuous spiral of energy – with no beginning and no end – cycling upward and over you, simultaneously combining your energies into one larger field around you. In this way, you give yourselves completely – to one another and to the Divine Union of Two made One. Through this exercise, your Life Force – which many call Kundalini – awakens your spirit to knowing and to the development of self."

Following the instruction of White Buffalo Calf Woman, Kiera and Joshua stood in euphoric delight, joined in a spectacular union of tangible rainbow energies. A brilliant white flash illuminated the space around them as Kiera recalled the blended energies of the twin flame flowers she had painted almost six weeks ago, the image imprinted upon both their minds.

"Breathe deeply and *innerstand* that you have grown so much in a short space of your time. Creator is so proud of all you have achieved." White Buffalo Calf Woman then turned to ascend the staircase of clouds with graceful fluidity. Once at the top, she was joined by the Buffalo Thunder Nation. Bowing their heads as one, they disappeared.

Awestruck, Joshua turned to Kiera and pulled her into his embrace. Gently brushing her forehead with a kiss, he said, "I can't imagine having this experience with anyone but you. I'm so grateful that Eagle Man brought you to me. Îsnî'yes – Miigwetch – Thank you! There are no words to adequately describe my gratitude."

"The past few weeks have been surreal for me. I'm so grateful to Eagle Man too and that Grandmother asked me to take her to Church that Sunday! Having these experiences with you; working with Sasha and Eagle Man to learn how to do what was necessary to protect this beautiful camp and the Medicine Wheel; I've found such an intense purpose for my life's work – my art. I don't think it would have happened if it weren't for meeting you."

Not able to wait any longer, Joshua drew her into an urgent and passionate kiss. As emotion swelled between them, their kiss deepened. Time stood still as their bodies wove more tightly together and merged into one. Rapture stole their breath as they swayed, and losing their balance, became one also with the wall of water.

"Aach!" Kiera screeched as the full realization of the water's glacial temperature registered in her mind.

Joshua broke into a fit of laughter, pulling her back from the edge of the shelf upon which they stood. "Let's get out of this wet spot!"

Stepping out from behind the waterfall, the valley seemed to ripple and flourish before them, green, lush, and full of the promise of a lifetime of blessings to experience together.

ABOUT THE AUTHOR

Laureen Guilian lives in a small community on the shores of Lake Huron in Southwestern Ontario with her husband, fur and feather kids. Occasionally some grandchildren are enticed to come play in the sand for a while. Words are her life – whether spoken with love and intention, written with wit and a laugh or chanted to the wind and the willows.

When not writing her next book or penning a journal entry, you'll find Laureen in a magical garden entertaining the faeries and dragons. They get a kick out of what she considers a well developed garden! She also loves to host tea parties with old friends and new or advocate for an urgent passion.

Laureen Giulian will lead you into a world of wonder and power, allowing you to discover aspects of yourself that you didn't know existed!

This book produced in
Myriad Pro – 13 pt font
for easy reading.

CPSIA information can be obtained
at www.ICGtesting.com
Printed in the USA
BVHW030448170322
631198BV00001B/2

9 781982 275754